PENGUIN BOOKS
A WRITER'S NIGHTMARE

R.K. Narayan was born in Madras, South India, and educated there and at Maharaja's College in Mysore. His first novel *Swami and Friends* (1935) and its successor *The Bachelor of Arts* (1937) are both set in the enchanting fictional territory of Malgudi. Other 'Malgudi' novels are *The Dark Room* (1938), *The English Teacher* (1945), *Mr. Sampath* (1949), *The Financial Expert* (1952), *The Man-Eater of Malgudi* (1961), *The Vendor of Sweets* (1967), *The Painter of Signs* (1977), *A Tiger for Malgudi* (1983), and *Talkative Man* (1986). His novel *The Guide* (1958) won him the National Prize of the Indian Literary Academy, his country's highest literary honour. He was awarded in 1980 the A.C. Benson Medal by the Royal Society of Literature and in 1981 he was made an Honorary Member of the American Academy and Institute of Arts and Letters. As well as four collections of short stories, *A Horse and Two Goats*, *An Astrologer's Day and Other Stories*, *Lawley Road* and *Malgudi Days*, he has published two travel books *My Dateless Diary* and *The Emerald Route*, two collections of essays, *Next Sunday* and *Reluctant Guru*, and a volume of memoirs, *My Days*.

R. K. NARAYAN

A WRITER'S
NIGHTMARE

(Selected Essays 1958-1988)

PENGUIN BOOKS

Penguin Books (India) Private Ltd, 72-B Himalaya House,
23 Kasturba Gandhi Marg, New Delhi-110 001, India
Penguin Books Ltd, Harmondsworth, Middlesex, England
Viking Penguin Inc, 40 West 23rd Street, New York,
New York 10010, U.S.A.
Penguin Books Australia Ltd, Ringwood, Victoria, Australia
Penguin Books Canada Ltd, 2801 John Street, Markham,
Ontario, Canada L3R 1B4
Penguin Books (N.Z.) Ltd, 182-190 Wairau Road,
Auckland 10, New Zealand

First Published by Penguin Books India 1988
Reprinted 1988

Copyright © R.K. Narayan, 1956, 1974, 1987
All rights reserved

Most of these essays originally appeared in the *Hindu*. Some were also printed in
Frontline and the *Times of India*. Other essays were published in the following
magazines: 'Misguided Guide' in *Life,* 'When India was a Colony' in the *New York
Times* Sunday Magazine, 'India and America' in *Town and Country*. The bulk of the
older essays were first published in book form as *Next Sunday* and *Reluctant Guru* by
Orient Paperbacks, a division of Vision Books Private Limited. Grateful acknowledge-
ment is made to all these publications and publishers.

Made and printed in India by
Ananda Offset Private Limited
Typeset in Times Roman

CONTENTS

From RELUCTANT GURU

LATER ESSAYS

Introduction

In my BA class (we had a three-year course, then) fifty years ago, we had a professor of English who perhaps could not stand the stare of 200 pairs of eyes from the gallery and so decreed, the moment he approached the dais, "Heads down, pencils busy", and started dictating notes right away, even before reaching his chair. He taught us *Essays and Prose Selections* and dictated practically the same notes every year, which began with the sentence 'Definitions of the Essay are Numerous and Positively Bewildering...' The poor man suffered this bewilderment throughout his career.

When I began to write for a living later, I realized that definitions of the essay were neither numerous (as our teacher claimed) nor bewildering. I realized there were only two categories of essay—the personal and the impersonal or, in other words, the subjective and the objective.

First, let me talk about the objective essay. One may go through the impersonal essay for information, knowledge and illumination, perhaps, but not for enjoyment which is after all one of the purposes of literature. Unfortunately, I was compelled to read certain authors in the category of heavy essayists. My father was a fervent admirer of Carlyle, Macaulay, Froude and so on. He read Carlyle and company far into the night and felt I should also be reading them for my edification. I obeyed. To speak the truth, I found them unreadable but went through the pages as a matter of self-mortification and to show I was a dutiful son. I particularly recollect the hardship I experienced while plodding through *'The Times of Erasmus & Luther'* by Henry Froude in his volume *Short Studies On Great Subjects.* Carlyle terrified me. So did Macaulay. I could only marvel at my father's capacity for enjoying tough writing unrelieved by any light moment. So much for the heavy essay. I felt my college professor was justified in using the phrase 'bewildering'. He also probably felt dizzy and addled.

I have always been drawn to the personal essay in which you could see something of the author himself apart from the theme—a man like Charles Lamb, or more recently, E.V. Lucas or Robert Lynd (to mention some names at random) are good examples of discursive essayists. The personal essay was enjoyable because it had the writer's likes, dislikes, and his observations, always with a special flavour of humour, sympathy, aversion, style, charm, even oddity.

Unfortunately, this type of essay is not in vogue today. You see it sometimes here and there but generally it is almost extinct. Yes, we have feature writers in magazines and newspapers, astute political analysts, profound scholarly and historical writers in academic journals, earth-shaking editorials in newspapers, but not the discursive essayist. This is because the discursive essay can come not out of scholarship or research but only out of one's personality and style. The scope for such a composition is unlimited—the mood may be sombre, hilarious or satirical and the theme may range from what the author notices from his window, to what he sees in his waste-paper basket, to a world cataclysm.

I cannot claim that I fulfil all the grand conditions I have enumerated. I have written all the following essays because I had to. I had to write to meet a deadline every Thursday in order to fill half a column for the Sunday issue of the *Hindu*. I had rashly undertaken this task not (to be honest) for artistic reasons, but to earn a regular income. Three of my novels had already been published but they had brought me recognition rather than income. I had approached the editor of the *Hindu* for help, and he had immediately accepted my proposal for a weekly piece. I had not the ghost of an idea what I was going to do. As he had left me to do anything I wanted within my column I started writing, trusting to luck; somehow I managed to fill the column for nearly twenty years without a break. This selection is mainly made from the essays I wrote for the *Hindu*.

In conclusion I should say that the essays reproduced in the following pages should enable the reader to get a better sense of my idea of the 'discursive essay' than any theorizing I could do about it.

July 1987   *R. K. Narayan*

From

NEXT SUNDAY

Higher Mathematics

There recently appeared a news item that a profound mathematical discovery has been made, a solution to a problem that has been bothering the minds of mathematicians for half a century, something that will build a 'mathematical bridge' between the forces within the universe as a whole and the forces within the nuclei of the atoms. Any news that mentions the atom becomes suspect these days. I only hope this does not mean that belligerent folk are going to be in possession of a new weapon; a combination of figures and symbols with which to paralyse the thinking powers of an enemy nation. Apart from this, I view the news without emotion. This mathematical discovery may thrill some people, but it leaves me cold. Mathematics is a matter of constitution. It is like music. Some people are tone deaf and often wonder how any adult could go on sitting in a hall for three or four hours, tolerating the noise and gesticulations of a singer. In the same way I am, if I may coin an expression, "figure-blind." My mind refuses to work when it encounters numbers. Everything that has anything to do with figures is higher mathematics to me. There is only one sort of mathematics in my view and that is the higher one. To mislead young minds by classifying arithmetic as elementary mathematics has always seemed to me a base trick. A thing does not become elementary by being called so. "A rose by any other name would smell as sweet." However elementary we may pretend arithmetic to be, it ever remains puzzling, fatiguing and incalculable. There was a fashion in the elementary school in which I read to prescribe a book in which the sums were all about English life. The characters in the problems were all John and Joan and Albert, and the calculations pertained to apples and the fares of hansom-cabs. In those days we saw apples only in coloured picture-books and we never understood what hansom-cabs meant. We were used to dealing in mangoes and *jutkas* and bullock-carts, and the payments were not in farthings

11

or pence, but in rupees, annas and pies. While wrestling with the problems in this book I was always racked with the thought that perhaps I could solve the sums if they dealt with Indian life. Fortunately, in answer to this prayer, we soon had sums dealing with the interminable transactions of Rama and Krishna. But I soon found that this did not make things easier for me. The problems remained as tough as ever, and my wit and calculations remained defeated. My constant preoccupation was with the last section of the text book where one found the answers to the problems. Every time I did a sum I turned to the last section with trembling and prayer, but I always found there a different figure from what I had arrived at laboriously. The disappointment reduced me to tears. A sense of hopeless frustration seized me each time I referred to the answers in the printed book. I sometimes wished I had been born in another world where there would be no mathematics. The whole subject seemed to be devised to defeat and keep me in a perpetual anguish of trial and error. I remember particularly that the sections which made absolutely no sense to me were called "Practice." The teacher decreed. "Find out by Practice" etc. and the intelligent boys of the class at once drew three vertical lines and did something or other with them. I never understood what they did with those and why it was called "Practice." To this day I have no idea what it is all about. I also remained oblivious to the intricacies of stocks and shares and discount, these I viewed as the worst snares ever laid for a human being. I had a fear at one time that I might have to spend the rest of my life in a high school, arithmetic acting as a barrier to my exit; but in every young heart at this stage there arises a hope of redemption, through algebra and geometry. It might only be a delusion to think that drawing a circle within a triangle (or is it the other way) could be easier than calculating 3.1/4 and 7.7/8 of something or other, or that the anonymous hooded figures of algebra were easier to tackle than quantities of mangoes and percentages. Anyway, one got out of high school with a feeling of escaping from a concentration camp, the greatest virtue of university education seeming to be that unless one chose one need not go near mathematics.

I don't think years have improved my outlook or equipment in regard to mathematics, although as a grown-up I am not supposed to give out my real feelings in the matter. I have to keep up appearances before youngsters. So that the other day when I found my nephew (who has evidently imbibed my tradition in mathematics) literally in tears, sitting at his desk and chasing an elusive sum, I told him patronizingly, "Well, there is no use shedding tears over mathematics. If you read the sum correctly and think it over calmly, I am sure you will get the answer. The thing is you must not be in a hurry. You must be very calm, I tell you. At your age, do you know how we were managing it?" And I told him what I fully knew to be a cock-and-bull story about my prowess and industry in this subject. He asked, "Won't you help me do this sum?" I looked at it critically. It was something about profit and loss. As I gazed at the sum, the answer suddenly flashed on my mind. I casually turned to the last page to see if my answer was correct. It wasn't. I gently put down the book, telling the boy. "Well, of course. I can do this sum but, you know, my 'working' will be different: it won't be much use to you. You must do it in the way it has been taught in your school; moreover, you must learn to depend upon your own effort. Otherwise you will not learn." I hastily moved out of the pale of mathematics.

Fifteen Years

Language has become a profoundly embarrassing subject nowadays. The thought of it gives a peace-loving citizen a pain in the neck. I mean it with particular reference to the English language. An average citizen today is in the position of appreciating the language but not wanting it. We are not so far away from the time when people used to say as a matter of prestige, "He speaks perfect English," and a bride who could write her letters in English and who could claim to have read Scott and Dickens was considered fully accomplished. In the matter of employment, too, a young man who could draft an English letter with ease and confidence stood a better chance of being employed than the one who was proficient only in his regional language. And there were people who didn't know English, and who said with a sigh, "If I had only learned English I would have conquered the world...." This may not be a very comfortable memory for anyone now, but it would be false to pretend that such values did not exist at one time. However, various causes, practical, political, etc. have demanded the abolition of English from our midst. It is almost a matter of national propriety and prestige now to declare one's aversion to this language, and to cry for its abolition.

But the language has a siren-like charm and a lot of persistence, and (if we may personify it) comes up again and again and demands, "What have I done that you hate me so much?" The judge does not lift up his head for fear that he might weaken. He assumes the gruffest tone possible and says, "You are the language of our oppressors. It is through you that our nation was enslaved, and it is only through you that the people were divided, so that those who were masters of English could rule others who didn't know the language. Your insidious influence wrought a cleavage in our own midst...."

"You speak very good English."

"Well, well, I won't be flattered by it," says the judge. "All of

14

us are masters of English, but that proves nothing. You are the language of those who were our political oppressors. We don't want you any more in our midst. Please, begone."

"Where shall I go?"

"To your own country...."

"I am afraid this is my country. I fear I will stay here, whatever may be the rank and status you may assign me—as the first language or the second language or the thousandth. You may banish me from the classrooms, but I can always find other places where I can stay. I love this country where:

Full many a glorious morning have I seen
Flatter the mountain tops with sovereign eye,
Kissing with golden face the meadows green,
Gilding pale streams with heavenly alchemy.

"That is a beautiful Shakespeare passage. However, I cannot allow the court's time to be wasted in this manner. You have a knack of beguiling the mind with quotations. I forbid you to quote anything from English literature."

"Why are you dead set against me, sir? I have a fundamental right to know why you are throwing me out, under the Indian Constitution...."

"But it doesn't apply to you."

"Why not?"

"Because you are not an Indian,"

"I am more Indian than you can ever be. Your are probably fifty, sixty or seventy years of age, but I've actually been in this land for two hundred years."

"When we said, 'Quit India,' we meant it to apply to Englishmen as well as their language. And there doesn't seem to be much point in tolerating you in our midst. You are the language of the imperialist, the red-tapist, the diabolical legalist, the language which always means two things at the same time."

"I am sorry, but red tape, parliament and courts have a practical purpose in having a language which can convey shades of meaning and not something outright. This reminds me: have you got the criminal and civil procedure codes in the language of the country now? And have you standardized this language of the country? I remember the case of humble author who got his English works translated into Hindi but later had to put

15

away the manuscripts in cold storage."

"Why?"

"He had the translations done by a pundit who appeared to him very good. Not being very proficient in the language, the author accepted what the pundit said as gospel truth and thought that the translations were unimpeachable. But when he showed the manuscript to others, one set of persons condemned it for being too full of Sanskrit words, and another set condemned it for being full of Urdu words. Not being able to decide the issue himself the author put the manuscript out of sight. The moral of this story is...."

"You need not concern yourself with this problem. We want you to go."

"You probably picture me as a trident-bearing Rule Britannia, but actually I am a devotee of Goddess Saraswati. I have been her most steadfast handmaid."

"All that is beside the point. Even if you come in a sari with *kumkum* on your forehead we are going to see that you are deported. The utmost we shall allow you will be another fifteen years...."

"Fifteen years from what time?" asked the English language, at which the judge felt so confused that he ordered, "I will not allow any more discussion on this subject," and rose for the day.

Allergy

There are two aspects of medicine, the concrete and the abstract. The concrete used to be seen in cases such as malaria, cold, etc., unmistakable troubles for which well-known remedies were provided out of bottles. The sufferer drained off the medicine with awry face, demanded a pinch of sugar to counteract the bitterness on the tongue, repeated the procedure, and then forgot all about it. This was the good old medical system as practised in any normal L.F. Dispensary (it took me long years to understand that L.F. stood for Local Fund). The doctor wrote a great deal on the leaves of a brown register. Although the ink used was faint and dilute, the entries afforded a rough-and-ready cross-sectional view of public health. After every 'name' and 'age' there was a column for 'disease'. This column was invariably filled with malaria, influenza and indigestion, in a regular pattern, with an occasional 'general debility' thrown in, whenever something turned up which seemed to be beyond this classification. The good old doctor wrote with one hand while feeling the pulse of his patient with the other. The compounder in the adjacent room issued readymade mixtures out of gigantic bottles and placed his stamp on the prescription with an air of dismissing sickness for ever. I have lost touch with this institution, but I believe that it is not so popular now as it used to be. Nowadays people do not like things to remain so elementary and simple.

The days of glancing at the tongue and dashing off 'mist' this or 'mist' that, are past. Bitter medicines with a pinch of sugar are unacceptable to modern mind. This is an age of scientific terminology. A thing has no value unless it is clothed in respectable, scientific expression. Everybody has recognized the hypnotic value of scientific or scientific-sounding phrases. Manufacturers of various beautifying commodities nowadays are trying to attract clientele by claiming that their products contain this element or that principle or some fabulous vitamin.

Medical science is also progressing on these lines. Doctors' clinics have been resounding with new terms for over a decade now. Vitamins became very popular at one time. An elaborate vitamin-consciousness developed in people, driving them to maintain a perpetual hunt for vitamins in all their diet. It was followed by calcium deficiency. Even now the cry is all calcium deficiency, but one suspects that it has fallen into a routine and the fervour is lost. And then came a time when no doctor would look at a patient unless he had all his teeth pulled out first. The trend of medicine seems to have been all along from the seen to the unseen. Medical science is becoming more and more metaphysical.

I am saying this with the thought in my mind that we are hearing the word "allergy" too much nowadays. Calcium and vitamin seem to have yielded the place of honour to allergy. In a week I heard four different doctors mention allergy under four different conditions. A person who was suffering from rashes was said to be in a state of allergy. A person who was racked with cough was also said to be undergoing allergy. Another who was feeling fidgety was also allergic. And another nearly unconsious with high fever was pronounced to be in a state of allergy. This is a very generous and compendious word meaning anything. It is applied to every kind of symptom from sprained toes to raving mania. When a doctor says of some symptom, "Oh, it's just allergy," he seems to say in effect, "Don't bother me with this any more. I don't know how you have got it, and I can't tell you how you can be rid of it. Grin and bear it until it leaves you. God knows when...." It satisfies the doctor that he has looked over the case as best as he could, and the patient that he has had the benefit of expert advice. When a doctor says that it is just allergy he also implies that you must cure yourself of it after discovering the cause that led to it. It takes a person on through a process of self-analysis and self-discovery. Allergy has converted the doctor's room into a confessional. While you are writhing with pain or irritation you will hear the doctor say, "Just throw your mind back and see where you have erred. Just recollect all the things you have eaten, all the clothes you have worn and all the thoughts that have passed in your mind—pick out the thing that has caused this and avoid it; that's all, and you will be well again." There is a great deal of comfort in this process. It is good to think that a hammering toothache is thoroughly unreal, and is a fancied state caused by that horse-hair stuffing in the sofa you sat upon, or the attack of asthma which twists you up is an illusory condition which you could have easily avoided if you had not bothered about those unpaid bills. If this process is followed, I am sure it will be possible to say someday, pointing at a passing funeral, "That man is not dead, but is only allergic to life."

Horses and Others

I had a most illuminating conversation with the driver of a tonga
a few days ago. All along the way from the market he kept
explaining why we should have more and more horses in our
midst. His talk made me yearn for a horse and carriage. Its
economics were alluring. You could own a turn-out for an
outlay of five hundred rupees. What vehicle could you hope to
acquire for this value? You could maintain a horse on two
rupees a day and engage a driver for less than thirty rupees a
month. You did not have to visit a workshop every morning as
most motor owners do. Perhaps you might have to go to a vet or
look for medicinal leaves if the horse caught a cold or slight
fever, but one ought not to grudge this little attention to an
animal which took one about, generally without any trouble,
thirty miles a day. The horse created a salubrious atmosphere
all around, it made the surroundings auspicious enough for
Goddess Lakshmi to come and reside in.

His talk gave me a glimpse of a world with which we are fast
losing touch—the world of the horse, its trappings, the perfume
of leather upholstery, the shining brass lamps with little green
crystals stuck at their sides, the fragrance of steaming gram and,
above all, the coachman with his coat buttoned up to his neck
and his turban, and his hand lightly resting on the whip handle.
My mind went back to the days when my uncle had a carriage in
Madras. I don't know what they called it: phaeton, dogcart,
victoria, governess (or governor's) cart. It was a yellow carriage
with windows, and bench-like seats inside. You could sit
comfortably facing other passengers and also watch out of the
window. The driver's seat was screened off with a panel. He sat
high up, and you had to put your head out and tell him where to
go and when to stop. It was a beautiful experience. You had to
warn him a couple of hours ahead what your programme for the
day would be since he had much to do before getting the horse
and carriage ready for the road. He had to groom the horse

('malish', as we heard him call the process), strap on to it various leather bits, give it gram and water, and tuck a small quantity of green grass under his footrest for the way, which engendered a perpetual smell of green grass about this vehicle.

The double-bullock cart with its arched springs and matco-vered roof is another thing that comes to my mind. It may be the trick of reminiscence that endows it with so much charm now. One of the most enchanting memories of this kind of locomotion was an all-night journey I had to undertake years ago when I returned home for the summer vacation, the train putting me down thirty miles from my town. The bullock carts moved in a caravan, winding along a dark, tree-shaded highway. Robbers were known to attack such caravans about ten miles from the railway station at midnight. This menace was warded off by a simple expedient. One of the cart men walked ahead carrying a lantern and a staff and throwing blood-curdling challenges to the night air. "Hey! Keep away, prowlers, if you don't want to have your skulls pulped....Who goes there?" and so forth, the other drivers also sitting up and urging their bullocks on with the loudest swear-words. This was kept up till we passed a jutting rock beyond the twelfth milestone; the moment we crossed this spot the challenger went back to his cart, curled himself in his seat and fell asleep, the entire caravan following this example. By some strange law or understanding the robbers never seemed to step an inch beyond the jutting rock. It always seemed to me that the robbers were wasting a fine opportunity to attack with all the cart-men fast asleep and the only wakeful person being myself as I tried to sleep on a pile of straw expecting any moment to be killed. But nothing happened and we reached our destination sometime the next day, the jingling of ox bells persisting in a re-echo for nearly a week after the journey.

Death due to movement, in various forms, is an inescapable condition of living today. We move about and carry on our work, dodging an oncoming wheel all the time. 'Caution....,' 'speed limit...,' 'school zone,' 'halt and proceed' are all there, but is there anyone who takes these instructions seriously? The pedestrian is the only person likely to notice these signs, with every chance of being knocked down while pausing to study the directions meant for the motorist. In a world where the pedestrian seems to be of so little account—he is blinded by

21

motor lights, deafened by screeching horns and chased about by reckless speed fiends—it is soothing to think of a horse and carriage or a bullock-cart.

The Vandal

The real old-time vandal came in as an invader, if not a conqueror. The moment he marched in he picked up a hammer and knocked out the noses of all the sculptured figures in his new domain, and he, alas, spent considerable time breaking their arms and legs. He carried out his task as matter of routine. After this, if he saw any building of architectural value standing he lost no time in demolishing it.

This was a conscious and deliberate vandal who did what he did because he had the strength and the chance to do it. He probably told himself, "Well, there is too much art plaguing the world anyway let me do my bit to mitigate it." There is no way of remedying this man's handiwork. We have to accept it as a historical process, but the work of the not-so-historical vandal is the one that should cause us concern now. I visited an ancient temple recently, famed for the minute sculptural work on its pillars, walls and ceiling. Painstaking work by ancient craftsmen was in evidence everywhere, but even more painstaking were the efforts of those who had attempted to effect improvements later.

These should be called the real vandals. They seem to have been telling themselves, "It was all very well for the old sculptors to have attempted so much, but they don't seem to have paid much attention to brightening up their surroundings." And forthwith they sanctioned out of the temple funds the purchase of large quantities of aluminium paint, cement, lime and mortar, and plastered every cornice, wall, and pillar with lime or cement. Figures that could not be so easily dealt with were given two special coatings of aluminimum paint, with the comment, "Now there is something to be proud of. The figures look as if made of silver." Actually the figures now look as if they had been shaped out of old aluminium vessels. I noticed cigarette foils also employed for effecting improvements. A huge quantity of it was used for covering the inlay work on an inner door. I could not help asking the temple authority for an explanation of his activities. He said, "You know this is a famous temple, and our Minister visits it often. I shouldn't like to give him the impression that we are neglecting it in any way."

The vandal in authority is the person to be most dreaded today. He is capable of making a hash of the architectural pattern of an entire town. He can never set eyes on a building without wanting to do something or other with it. His words carry weight with the executives following him, with notebooks in hand, when he is out on inspection. When he points at a building and suggests improvements, those behind dare not contradict him. The building may be a concrete, streamlined modern structure, but he may order a huge lotus bud to be carved on its top, or he may demand that floral designs be carved on its pillars, or that the entire building be given a dome and Mogul turrets; or an ancient French villa-type building may suffer the addition of an utterly modernistic cantilever.

Vandalism may be direct and obvious, as in the instances above, or it may also be hidden or implied. I cannot stand the sight of unfading crepe flowers in vases. Putting crepe flowers in vases is an act of vandalism according to me. Shiny plastic curtains over doors and windows give me an uneasy feeling; also the sight of indiscriminate assemblage of ferns and potted plants in verandas, or monstrous creepers trained to cover an entire building. This is an entirely personal view. I am sure that the man who has gathered those flowerpots or hung those curtains views them as achievements and may not care to be labelled a vandal in his own home. I respect his sentiment. I shall never let him see my own catalogue listing what, according to me, are vandalisms. Each individual is free to draw up his own list.

There cannot be what may be termed a standard list of vandalisms which may be of use to those about to undertake the task of furnishing their homes and surroundings, however much we might standardize the pattern of society. Those that love calendar pictures will not rest till they cover the walls of their homes with all the calendars issued on the new year by all the business concerns in the country; a lover of group photos will cover every inch of space in his home with portraits of all the friends and relations that ever came his way; the organizer who

24

is determined to sell space in the music hall will ever hang placards announcing the virtues of asafoetida or soap on every pillar there, and the man who is bent upon painting his home deep blue and illuminating it with an abundance of green tube light must have his way. When confronted with such acts we gently avert our looks and mumble indistinctly rather than shout our views from housetops. It is in the interest of harmonious human relations. It would be unseemly otherwise. But the line must be drawn somewhere. When the vandal emerges from the privacy of his home or immediate surroundings and attempts at improving nature or art on a large, public scale, then it is time for us to start an uninhibited 'down with—'campaign against him.

To a Hindi Enthusiast

You are naturally devoted to the language which is as natural to
you as swimming is to a fish. But you do not realize that a
dry-land creature like me cannot step into the water with the
same confidence. Aquatic competence (even more so amphi-
bian competence) can be acquired only with hard practice.
Practice implies time. Time alone can mature certain things.
You feel fifteen years is a long enough time. In a matter like the
nation-wide adoption of a language you cannot fix a time-table
in advance. You cannot command a tree to put forth fruit on
such and such a date. You cannot stop the waves on a seashore,
as King Canute ably demonstrated long ago. One may multiply
instances and analogies, but the point is really this; ripeness is
all, as Shakespeare has said somewhere. Ripeness cannot be
forced by a government order or even by the recommendations
of a commission. You cannot coerce nature, and the rooting
and growth of a language is a natural process. You must first
shake off the notion that the time element is all important. It is
not. It can be altered, the more easily because it is in the
constitution. Do not look so outraged at this suggestion. You
know as well as I do that any constitution worth its name must
be amended, if not forgotten.

   Do not imagine that I underrate the urgency of the question.
That the country should stir itself from the spell cast on it by a
foreign language is a point that anyone, will readily grant,
although personally I think otherwise. For me, at any rate,
English is an absolutely *swadeshi* language. English, of course,
in a remote horoscopic sense, is a native of England, but it
enjoys, by virtue of its uncanny adaptability, citizenship in
every country in the world. It has sojourned in India longer
than you or I and is entitled to be treated with respect. It is my
hope that English will soon be classified as a non-regional
Indian language.

   You have perhaps a suspicion that we in this part of the

country are not sufficiently devoted to the cause. Let me assure you that we are in dead earnest and putting forth our best efforts. Our homes resound with Hindi declensions night and day. The domestic atmosphere is fully Hindi, let me assure you. South Indian womanhood, at any rate, has lent the cause its unstinted support. It may be that the men here are not showing equal competence or application for the task. It is because they are still entangled in the sordid business of working for a living and do not have the time or the energy for mastering a new language, but our women are forging ahead with single-minded devotion. Their zeal has made men nervous. Multi-lingualism is threatening to invade our homes too. Women flaunt their Hindi with undisguised glee; men do not understand a word of it. Presently we may need interpreters in every home for the efficient management of home affairs. The women's zeal is such that men, in their selfishness, sometimes wonder if they will attend to anything else at home, a rather unprogressive fear. Women do attend to both home and Hindi. As the season of *Visharad* or some such examination approaches, it is a common sight in any household to find the lady putting in twenty-three hours of study, all the while carrying on all her routine domestic activities. While her left hand holds open the textbook under her eyes, her right hand prepares the meal, washes the clothes and rocks the cradle. The indications are that presently an average south Indian housewife will prove an adept not only in Hindi but also in the use of a single hand for various purposes. I could not help asking a certain lady why she went through all this travail. She did not say that she felt it to be a national duty or that she hoped to be recruited to the I.A.S., but simply, "I find it interesting, that is all." This is what I would like you to note. Leave it to our good sense and pleasure and nothing will go amiss. It is not necessary to hold threats to your fellow men who, after all, belong to the same civilization. It is odious to be told, "You will not get your salary or your ration card unless you speak this tongue or that."

Here are my tips if you want Hindi to flourish in this part of the country:

Do not send us postal stationery with Hindi inscriptions on them. At the moment it only puzzles and irritates us, and wastes a lot of our time as we try to divine where to write what. Form-filling, even with the old money-order form with its payee and remitter (instead of receiver and sender), has been a trying business, always making one pause to wonder whether one was a payee or a remitter, but with Hindi text on it, it is becoming just impossible to get through any business at a post-office counter nowadays. It is childish to imagine that by sending us Hindi forms you are making us more Hindi-conscious. Shall we supply your post offices with forms and stationery printed in Tamil, Telugu, Malayalam and Kannada? That would at least give this whole business a sportive and reciprocal touch.

Secondly, try to make your textbooks attractive, not only in contents but in format. I may say without fear of contradiction that some of the Hindi text books I have seen are the shoddiest specimens of book production in the world. The *Rashtrabhasha* deserves a more dignified dress. Flimsy newsprint pages; thin, coloured covers, smudgy blocks of indifferent drawings and a stiff price are the components of a Hindi textbook as far as my observation goes. It should be possible to spend a little more on paper and production, seeing that every book of this kind has an assured sale of several thousand copies each year. Remember that half the charm of English was engendered by the manner in which its schoolbooks were produced, at least in the old days. I still keep with me an old Nelson Reader, nearly forty years old. I still get a peculiar delight out of turning its pages: Its exquisite coloured frontispiece showing some London bridge and river and towers in a fog, its thick and smooth pages, its typographical excellence and, above all, its carefully selected content with relevant black and white pictures, all these have in a subtle and unseen manner helped the language in this country.

'No School Today'

By the time one comes to the stage of being called an adult, one has left behind all the travails of school-going. One does not entertain any worry on that account. It is one of the few compensations of age. One could afford to look on with detachment at all the children hurrying along with their satchels. And then one forgets one's past so much as to admonish some child who may show reluctance to move in the direction of school. Most of us are guilty of such forgetfulness. It makes us say, "It is a pity that the present generation is developing on these lines. In our days, school was something which we looked forward to with pleasant anticipation. In fact we used to hate our holidays and vacations." Sheer falsehood. Adulthood may be defined as a phase of self-deception. Nowhere is it carried to a greater extent than in statements beginning: "In those days...." The listener, inevitably not a contemporary but one of a younger generation, has no courage to contradict the man nor has he any means of checking the veracity of his statement. No adult ever speaks the truth about his schooldays, partly out of bad memory and partly out of diplomacy. The man does not want his child to take his schooling casually. But the fact remains that no child with red blood in its veins could ever think of its school with unqualified enthusiasm. It is no use asking why it is so. It is so and it is to be accepted as an inevitable fact. The Monday-morning-feeling is a solid reality. An adult experiences it as keenly as a child. He reflects in bed, "I wish I had no office today." It is a routine sentiment for a Monday morning. The adult may be the sort who loves his work excessively. He may be the sort who cuts short his holiday because he cannot keep away from his desk too long and does not know what to do with his leisure hours. Even he cannot help feeling, "Oh, the wretched Monday again." It is subsequently suppressed, rationalized and sublimated, so that the man moves down the rut smoothly the rest of

29

the week. It is a creditable performance of will, worthy of an adult, but to expect the same application from a child would be unnatural.

Shantha, six years of age, is sent to a convent school across the road, but she has no enthusiasm for studies, nor does she believe there is anything wrong in expressing openly her views on education. She is the happiest person on earth on any Saturday or Sunday. Fortunately for her, in her total self-absorption, she never bothers about the coming Monday. The Sunday evening is not ruined for her either by the prospect of Monday or by the thought that the holiday is dripping away. It is just lived through, fully and completely. When someone takes the trouble to remind her, "Go to bed early, tomorrow is Monday, school in the morning," she answers, "Oh, no. We have no school tomorrow," and lives happily in the belief till she is actually pulled out of her bed and out of her dreams the next day. As soon as she is up she complains of vague pains and indisposition in the desperate hope that she may return to her bed, but the adult world does not leave her alone. With a frown on her little face she resigns herself to her lot, muttering all the way to school, "I tell you, we have no school today." It is all nature's balance, the child's aversion to school and its elders' zeal for it. No one can object to it. But what I really find objectionable is the adult's horror at the thought that a child should hate its school. With devoted parents, school is an obsession. They are dismayed at the attitude they see in their child. I know a parent who started a separate establishment twenty miles away from his working place because he wanted to put his child in school. Four-year-old Ramu was to all appearances enthusiastic about the scheme. He liked the change and the new satchel and books bought for him. The first day Ramu went to the school he insisted upon standing all the time in the veranda and watching other children going through their drill and games in the quadrangle. Next day he was persuaded to enter an infant section but he insisted upon his father's coming up and taking his seat beside him in the classroom. They prodded and persuaded and made him go to school every day: each day it was a trial of wit, strength and patience between him and his parents. Thus he attended the school for a few weeks and suddenly one Monday morning announced his unshakable resolve, "I won't go to school." His father was nearly in tears when he reported to me, "I have taken a house on seventy-five rupees a month only for his sake, although it means driving back to my factory twenty miles every day. I wouldn't mind any trouble or expense if only Ramu could be made to like his school." They were very kind there: they even tried to tempt him with chocolates and toffee, but that didn't work. It seems Ramu told his teacher, "My father has ordered me not to eat sweets. They will do me harm." I told the father, "Why do you despair? This is probably a child's happiest stage, when every nook and corner at home looks rich, mysterious and soul-satisfying; no school-room, however well-organized, however psychological or well-behaved the teachers might be, could ever compare with the quality of the home. It's the best period of one's life to be home in." In this respect all schools are deficient. Until we adopt the view point of a child and reorganize our educational system, our schools will continue to repel children. They may overcome it, get used to it or resign themselves to it—but love the school, never.

The Non-Musical Man

The man cannot understand why so much fuss should be made about music. He can never make out how people could sit in their chairs for hours in a hall gazing on a musician and shaking their heads. In his view the whole thing is a piece of hypocrisy practised by a group of persons who wish to look different.

In a sort of superior way the musical enthusiast feels a pity for this man. Says he to himself, "Ah, this poor fellow is deaf to music. What a lot he misses in life!" And he goes to him with the idea of improving his outlook. He tells the one deaf to music, "You must come and hear so-and-so's music on Sunday," peremptorily, with the air of a physician forcing a draught of quinine.

The other looks scared. The prospect is frightening. He tries to withdraw, but he is compelled to spend the Sunday evening at the music hall. The most unacceptable thing there for him is the mournful silence that he is expected to maintain. He cannot discuss weather or politics with his neighbour. He has to speak in whispers, if at all, and generally conduct himself as if he were in a Presence. His democratic nature does not permit him to tolerate such restrictions. He sits silently fretting in his seat. He feels bored. He tries to count the electric bulbs in the hall. He studies the faces around him. He spots a friend across intervening heads, far off, and feels like shouting, "Hallo, long time since we met!" but he swallows the greeting. He studies a watch on someone's wrist four chairs off. He reads an advertisement board stuck on a pillar, forward and backward, spelling it out letter by letter. He feels bored with all this activity very soon. He sits back in a mood of profound resignation. He looks at the dais.

The programme is attaining its zenith: the singer and his accompanists are negotiating their way through a tortuous *pallavi*. Our friend notices that the drummer is beating the skin off his palm, the violinist is jabbing the air with his elbow while attempting to saw off the violin in the middle, and the vocalist is uttering a thousand syllables without pausing for breath. A triangular skirmish seems to be developing among the three on the dais. Evidently someone seems to have emerged a victor presently, for the audience which was watching the fray in rapt attention suddenly breaks into thunderous applause. There is a stir in the crowd and a general air of relaxation as the instruments are being tuned and touched up after the terrific battering they suffered a while ago.

Our friend hopes that this is the end of all trouble, but he notices, to his dismay, that it is only a pause. The audience shows no sign of leaving. The musician clears his throat and starts once more, and involves himself in all kinds of complicated, convulsive noise-making. Our friend, who had a brief moment of joy thinking that it was all over, resigns himself to it again, reflecting philosophically, "Everything in this world must end sometime, even music." A most consoling thought.

When the performance ends he leaves the hall with an iron resolution never to go near music again. If he remains an unknown, insignificant man he may exercise his fundamental right of keeping away from music; but if he becomes a man of consequence he will have to bow to other people's will. He will be invited to attend an eminent artiste's performance. He will be received at the gate by the organisers of the show. He will be conducted to an honoured seat while an audience of a thousand watch his movement with wonder and respect. The programme will not start until he is well settled in his seat.

Why they want him to attend this musical function is a question that can never be precisely answered. It may be for a variety of reasons. His presence may lend weight to the occasion; he may be in a position to cast favours, such as ground for a building, or funds; there may be a dozen reasons why they want him there, all except that he likes music or knows anything of it. He has to sit through the music fully conscious of his own suffering. He knows that he is imprisoned in his own status. He is not a whit changed inside. His bafflement at the goings-on on the dais is still the same. He still wants to break out into chatter or call up a distant friend. He still feels the same impulse to rise and dash out of the hall at supersonic speed (to quote a young nephew of mine addicted to comics and science fiction), but he simply cannot do such a thing. He cannot afford to hurt anyone.

If he gets up, it is feared, the musician may lose his inspiration, it may dishearten the organisers, or throw the audience into a confusion.

Usage makes him a hardened music listener in due course. He can sit through a four-hour performance without turning a hair. Gradually, he wreaks a subconscious vengeance on those who have dragged him into it, by beginning to talk about music in public and in private. He can explain what is good and what is not good in music. He classifies music as classical, heavy, light, bantam, folk, meaningful or meaningless, compares their respective values, and prescribes what is good for whom. This may safely be taken as the point of danger for music as a whole.

On Humour

"If you love humour don't talk or write about it," said an eminent guru to his disciple. Commendable advice. For, nothing evaporates so swiftly as humour the moment it is examined or explained. Nothing kills it so successfully as analysis and study. I am happy, and feel repeatedly happy at the thought, that humour is not made a subject of study in our universities, which has spared us from the predicament of having Ph.Ds. of humour in our midst. I often speculate what question a 'theory paper' on humour might have contained if it had been a university examination subject: explain with diagrams the anatomy of laughter; distinguish between chuckling and grinning; trace the relation between gravity and humour; explain the origin of smiles; write short notes on buffoonery, sally, clowning, quip and innuendo. The 'practical paper' might probably have asked the candidate to apply his theory and make an attempt to move at least one of his examiners to emit a loud guffaw.

Humour is still not a public speaker's theme. Had it been one, eminent men presiding over the celebrations of the national humour week might be found exhorting their audience, "Be humorous. We must all strive to wear out grimness wherever we may meet it. Remember grimness is our national enemy number one. Humour lightens the burden of existence, and so let all the good citizens of our country exercise their sense of humour (without detriment to their avocations) during their weekly holidays and all other recognized government holidays." As our good fortune will have it, no government on earth has bothered to create a ministry of humour, although some have come perilously near it with their zeal for cultural activity. Humour fortunately still remains an individual business. Otherwise we should be having experts, bluebooks and statements of annual turnover of jokes emanating from various secretariats.

I have a secret conviction that the Posts and Telegraph, more than any other government department, possesses a sly sense of humour, and arranges its affairs in such a manner as to enjoy a quiet chuckle now and then in its contacts with the public. Otherwise how could we explain some of the most bewildering things we see them perform now and then? A bridegroom receives a greeting telegram on his wedding day with just the message, "Number Eight." I have found this mysterious message creating quite a lot of speculation and bewilderment in an otherwise peaceful household just setting down to a restful afternoon after the wedding festivities. "Number Eight" assumes all the sinister quality of a message in code passing between deadly conspirators until one goes to the nearest post-office and finds out that it is just the code number of a greeting which calls upon heaven to shower its choicest blessings on the happy couple.

Further, one may notice the presence of small metal discs on the footpaths of any city, stuck at regular intervals. Each disc rears itself up like an angry cobra, a foot above ground: the inscription on the disc explains itself as a 'C.T.D. cable,' placed there by the telegraph or telephone department. Only a dull, humourless mind would protest against it. If you watch closely you will find dozens of feet coming on proudly and then suddenly stumping on one or the other of the discs: some go limping forward, some step away in surprise, some execute a tango in sheer pain. When the traffic police compel pedestrians to walk on the footpath—ah, that is the time when the C.T.D., discs fulfil their mission without a doubt. This piece of humour is no doubt of the class of circus clowning, but nonetheless it is some kind of humour and let us give the credit where it is due.

Humour is such an individual matter that it would be difficult to generalize about it. I feel distressed whenever I find serious, solemn persons enquiring, "Have we a sense of humour?" The question will have to be answered by each according to his capacity. But there is also this danger: one might think oneself humorous, but others may not perceive it. There is none so tragic as the man who has delusions in this respect. There is nothing on earth more miserable than the man of anecdotes and constant jokes studiously learnt and cultivated. I know of a public speaker whose most cherished possession is a bulky book containing quotable anecdotes and jokes. He picks up a couple of them at a time, carefully rehearses himself before a mirror and brings them out in the evening. His audience anticipates all his humour and enjoys it unreservedly, although knowing fully that it is all derived from a vast storehouse of quotations. When the lecturer pauses to say, "I am reminded of an anecdote…" the audience laugh in advance. It only proves that the public loves to laugh and that it possesses a better sense of humour than its humorous speaker.

Our cartoonists, humorous writers and columnists are now fully alive, deriving their inspiration from the absurdities and contradictions seen in public life: in the pomposities of self-important men, the elaborate pageantry surrounding the arrival and departure of a V.I.P., the ridiculous fuss bureaucrats make everywhere, and above all the plight of the modern unknown warrior, who is the middle class common man, and who is unable to bear all the improvements and benefits that his would-be champions attempt to heap on his head. It would be impossible to survive these if we did not possess a sense of humour: that itself is a proof that we have an abundance of it.

Reception at Six

Not too long ago the South Indian marriage was a five-day celebration. Festivities went on day and night. It was great fun, the chief entertainers being the newly-wed couple. It was all very well as long as there were child marriages or near-child marriages. As civilization advanced the old type of festivity and fun became unacceptable. The bridal couple were not of the age to face all this tomfoolery. In fact the bridegroom uttered this word a great deal! He looked askance at every ceremonial and punctuated it with, "Why all this tomfoolery?" He liked to give an impression of being sophisticated and extremely modern-minded; and this being the one occasion when people listened to the words emanating from him with every show of respect, he indulged in a rather free commentary on the irrationality of most of the functions going on around him. At this the priest and the elders begged him to put up with their eccentric ways, promising to abbreviate the proceedings as far as possible: the bridegroom grunted and let them go on. But he drew the line somewhere, and it was where the old type of wedding fun was concerned. He refused outright to go in a procession or amuse his audience in any manner and discouraged giggling children from gathering around him; but it took away from the whole function all entertainment. People were invited, and when they gathered together some excuse had to be found to keep them on for a while. In order to achieve it,there began to appear at the bottom of the invitation card the legend: 'Reception 6 p.m.'

Now it is a well-established institution, and no one needs to be told what it is all about. In fact the complaint is that it is too well-established. The business part of it is well-set: festoons of lights, arrays of folding chairs, a musician on the dais; and tea and cool drinks in one corner, and the couple safely placed on a sofa facing (somehow) both the dais and the auditorium. Invitees arrive at the other end and proceed along in a variety of walking styles, stumbling over chairs, extending their hands towards the bridegroom and bestowing a simpering smile on the bride. To save the visitor all this strain, stage fright and awkwardness, there is now the considerate practice of stationing the couple at the entrance itself, where the visitor may shed his good wishes and possibly presents, and go forward, spot out his friends in that wilderness of folding chairs, and enjoy himself. But at this point it is worth asking: does he meet anyone and get all the expected enjoyment out of the situation? It is a delicate point. Actually it seems as though one has little to do in the place after one has thrown a smile at the bride and bridegroom. The visitor feels restless and bored and waits for a chance to clear out. At the time he received the invitation he told himself, "I must attend the reception, otherwise so and so will be wild with me," a piece of self-flattery. And so he presents himself under the decorated entrance in due course. The master of ceremonies is of course there. The invitee runs up to him with. "You see, I could not come earlier, what happened was...." He does not complete the sentence, the other is not listening, he is busy bestowing a smile of welcome on the next visitor and then on the next, as invitees are pouring in in an endless stream.

It is evident that the man, the chief host, has been meeting and has had to be nice to too many persons since the beginning of the day, greeting and welcoming on a mass scale, and it has rather worn him out. Full of sympathy and understanding, the invitee, the man who considered himself his particular friend, proceeds to relieve him of his presence and drifts to a nearby chair, exchanges some banalities with someone in the next chair, takes to bits some nondescript buttonhole flower given to him at the gate, smells the back of his hand and notes the scent of sandal paste, and tries to listen to the music. But there is too much babble. He notices the master of ceremonies officiously leading a V.I.P. to a chair in the first row, saying something agreeable all along the way. The invitee who has so far engaged himself through his own efforts, suddenly realizes the futility of the whole business; he feels that there is a lack of cohesion somewhere and that he need not have come here at all. If he is a hardened, happy-go-lucky type and manages to catch his host's eye again, presently he finds himself in a group drifting towards a dining chamber, but if he is the retiring sort he leaves unobtrusively, snatching the paper bag with coconut at the gate, and melts into the night. It is likely that when he meets his friend the host again, many many days later, he may be asked, "How is it that you did not attend the reception at our house the other day? I remember having sent you an invitation!" And he must have a suitable answer ready, which is neither untruthful nor too offensive.

In the Confessional

A writer feels pleased when he meets one of his readers. It is a piece of vanity which is generally forgiven in a writer. People generally think, "Probably it is the only reward the poor worm receives for his work, let us tolerate him." A writer feels gratified when a stranger nods knowingly at the mention of his name, but he soon pays the price for his satisfaction. "Oh, yes," says the stranger, "You are so and so. I have heard a lot about you." If the writer is wise and experienced, he must leave the stranger alone at this point and go away, with the flattering thought that his words are really read. But he probes further and gets the answer. "You write on astronomy, don't you? I have read every word that you have written. I never miss it. Very illuminating, very illuminating," and you, as one who cannot locate even the Pole Star realize that you are being mistaken for someone else. You feel like a miserable pretender to a throne, about to be denounced.

There is the reader who displays the utmost enthusiasm on meeting you. He appears so warm and gratified that you think that here, after all, you have met your ideal reader. It has always been your hope that you would come across this ideal person some day, a man who by his very warmth would make you feel that you have been doing some important work, vital for human welfare. But it turns out to be a very short-lived gratification. Disillusionment is actually around the corner. While you are hoping that you are about to have the pleasure of listening to his reaction to your latest weekly effort, he asks suddenly, "I am proud to meet you, but may I know what you generally write about?" This is an unanswerable question for a writer. You blink for a moment and reply. "Well, mostly fiction..." and he asks with a slightly sour face, "Fiction, what sort of fiction?" You feel that you are now with your back to the wall. It was bad to have met this man and encouraged him to talk, now there is no escape; you will have to face it fully, and

41

you mutter a feeble explanation of your outlook on fiction. It is a sort of rambling explanation. All the time you are talking, you have a feeling that you are issuing a self-certificate. But mercifully your explanations are cut short by the other's remark, "I never read fiction. I have done with fiction in my adolescence. However, I am glad I have seen you, having heard so much about you, and you know I love to meet writers." And so at the next chance of meeting a reader, you carefully avoid any reference to fiction and when you have to explain what you do, you say, "I write sketches, essays and skits, and light commentaries on contemporary matters," only to rouse the man into saying, "Yes, yes, I am sure I have enjoyed reading your short bits, but why don't you attempt something bigger, say a novel? I am sure you can do it. They say there is a lot of money in novels," and you take the line of least resistance and say, "Thanks for the suggestion. I will try if I can make good there."

There is another type of worry from a reader who overrates you. You have perhaps written a few bits which have touched off your reader's sense of irony or humour, or lampooned or attacked something which happened to be also his pet aversion. It has tickled him so much that he views you—that most dangerous of reputations to acquire—as a humorist, and when he meets you he is prepared for a hearty laugh. He watches your face and lips anxiously, and you cannot say, "Rather a hot day, isn't it?" without sending him into paroxysms of laughter. He discovers a sly wit hidden in the statement. He has made up his mind that your very look, your very breath is humorous. He views you as one who performs clowning feats in print. One person went to the extent of saying to me with a lot of patronage, "Continuing to amuse humanity? Very good!"

There is the type of reader who demands to be told, the moment you are introduced as a writer: "What books have you written? Give me a list of your works." And you recite the names of your books, the handful of titles you have produced in your decades of writing, only to provoke the other into saying, "Only ten books for so many years! Can't you write fifty books a year? I have heard that the late Edgar Wallace used to write two books a week....Anyway please let me have a complete set of your books; of course you must send the bill along! I like to encourage Indian authors. I also want our children to read books by modern Indian authors." You promise him your co-operation, although you might perhaps do him a service if you told him that you are only an author and not a bookseller, or that the books you have written may not come under the definition of children's books. This man may also display his partiality for facts and figures. He will demand to be told what you were paid for that film story or how much per column you get from such and such paper or what royalty your books fetch. You might probably answer that these facts ought to interest only your income-tax officer, but still you give a reply, out of politeness, as near the truth as possible. He is frankly disappointed that your sales are not on the million level.

The trouble is that the writer, unlike others who have anything to do with the public, works blind-folded. The stage actor has the chance to see how the public reacts to his performance, the musician has unmistakable response shown to him, the painter can stand aside at his own exhibition and listen to the remarks of his public, but the writer alone has no chance of studying his reader's face or hearing his immediate comment. It is well it is so. It is nature's protective arrangement, I suppose. For it is a well-known axiom that either the writer proves superior to his work or it is the other way round. A meeting of a writer and his reader invariably produces disillusionment, which might as well be avoided. I remember one person who went away in chagrin after coming to see me. He had found in my shelves other people's books, and not my own in golden editions as he had expected. My talk was not scintillating and, above all, I was different from the picture he had of me in his mind.

Bridegroom Bargains

The stock of the bridegroom is rising again. He is again displaying bullish tendencies. It must be a heartening situation for the speculator who has been nursing the stock for a little over two decades. I heard an optimistic father declare that next to investment in housing, whose value can never go below a certain level, the most secure 'gilt-edge' is a son who is unmarried. All that is advantageous in the case of a father with a son naturally turns out to be otherwise for one with a daughter. It may be put down as a safe axiom that the satisfaction felt by the father of a girl is in inverse ratio to that felt by the one with a son. It is naturally so considering that one is a seller and the other a buyer; and matrimony today remains a seller's market. The father of a girl always prays that matrimony should cease to be any sort of market, and that he should be in a position to say, "My daughter is a priceless possession I have had with me for sixteen years now, I don't know how I am going to be without her. She is invaluable as far as I am concerned and even if you pay me a price of ten lakhs, I would still feel unhappy to part with her, and so I am not selling her; I shall give her away provided you satisfy these two conditions. I must have a confidential report from one of the daughter-in-law of your house, on the outlook and conduct of the elders at home, and I want a psychologist to examine your son and give him a certificate of soundness."

The reality of course is otherwise. The parent who has groomed a son properly, so that he sweeps the honours in all examinations and has been selected for an administrative career, is the actual dictator of prices today. This market was temporarily dull, or nervous, owing to various political causes, when the Indian republic was newly established, and there was some uncertainty in the services, when the system of recruitment and prospects were undefined. Old values were falling and new ones had not risen. In that brief period trading was cautious. It was an interim period when one heard a bridegroom's bargain agent declare, "Dowry! Never. We don't want anything. We care for only a good alliance, all else is secondary. We don't want any dowry, but since you are pressing it on us, it is enough if you give us something to meet our actual expenses." This 'something' might mean anything from eight thousand to twelve thousand rupees, most of it supposed to be utilized for defraying the expenses of travel of the large army of relatives and friends accompanying the bridegroom. The bad word *Varadakshinai* was avoided; instead it was called expenses. But now it is a sign of returning confidence that the word is coming into vogue once again. One might note a new directness in demands. The demands today for an eligible bridegroom are beyond the wildest expectations of a former generation. Says the bargainmaster of the prospective prize boy, "I want a cash dowry of forty-five thousand rupees and a motorcar." This is a new trend in bargains, this addition of a vehicle to the cash dowry. If the girl's father thinks that he can palm off a second-hand 8 H.P. to 10 H.P.* he will be told presently, "My son has to maintain his status, you know, and he must have a car big enough to seat at least six at a time; and you know he is a very sensitive boy, he is very keen on these things; he has an aversion to driving any car manufactured earlier than 1953." Some may throw in along with their other demands a refrigerator or a radiogram, as an afterthought, explaining, "You know my boy likes ice cream," or "You know he is a great music lover." The poor man, the would-be father-in-law of the boy, is too timid to ask, if the young man was so fond of ices or music, why he should have waited so long to provide himself with these amenities; but he cannot speak out since, to repeat the position, he is in a seller's market. It almost looks as though the inspiration for these demands is derived from the advertisements of crossword competitions, which sometimes make special seasonal offers of a phenomenal cash prize plus a car plus a refrigerator plus various other inducements. The poor man sadly reflects whether he should hold out so many inducements along with his daughter in order to make her acceptable. The limit was reached I think recently in a case where, following the announcement of the competitive examination results, the hopeful father of a daughter knocked

* This essay was written in 1959.

on the door of a successful candidate, whose father opened the door and asked not whether the girl was good looking or accomplished, but whether the man was prepared to buy an 'A' type house in Gandhinagar for himself and his wife, in addition to other items to be memtioned later.

I don't think there is going to be any effective way of abolishing dowry, the victim himself being often an abettor. If it is made illegal, a black market is likely to evolve from the repression. I often think a sales tax may be levied on the transactions involving a bridegroom, but this may again be shifted on to an already overburdened father of a girl. So it is just as well that we recognize the institution and work out a table of payments and presents which will provide at a glance what liabilities a would-be *Sambhandi* is likely to incur: first class in competitive examinations: Rs 45,000 plus a 20 H.P. motor-car, model not earlier than October 1953; engineering graduate: Rs 15,000, Jeep, plus a miniature locomotive in solid gold; M.Sc. (nuclear physics): Rs 15,000 plus five acres of land containing thorium, lignite, etc.; pilot with 'A' certificate: cash, plus a helicopter for private use; third class B.A., without any property: Rs. 5,000 plus a bicycle or an autorickshaw (if he chooses to make a living out of it). Marriages are, of course, made in heaven, but they are a business in our part of the universe, and why not run it on efficient lines?

The Scout

I remember I was very proud of being a scout. I spent several sleepless nights revelling in visions of myself in a scout uniform : Khaki shorts and shirt, green turban (those were still days of turban), colourful shoulder-straps and the mighty staff in hand. There was really no need for me to spend my time in mere dream but for the fact that my scout teacher seemed to have told my people that they could take their own time to provide me with a uniform. I don't know why he said it, but probably he felt that my novitiation was incomplete; he must have had a better measure of my stage and worthiness than I. I thought no end of my accomplishments, although now looking back, any competence I exhibited must have been only in regard to the holding of the staff, and in giving the scout salute. But this was obviously not enough: If I had been asked: "What is the fourth law of scouting?" I am sure I should have felt flabbergasted. Or, "What are the three promises?" I was sure to bungle because the easiest thing that came to my head was, "On my honour I promise to do my best for god, crown and country." But we belonged to an association which had decided to drop the *crown* in their promise, deftly substituting something else; perhaps *truth,* in its place; but I always stumbled on to crown, under the strong influence of a friend from another troop, which followed the orthodox line. In addition to my own handicaps another important reason why I could not have the uniform was that my people at home believed that good khaki could not be easily obtained except by using someone's influence. Their line of thought was: "I know someone who knows someone who alone can get the best khaki at the cheapest price." This meant agonising trips for me, up and down, and waiting on the arrivals, departures and moods of a contact man who, beside this business of finding me the best khaki on the easiest of terms, had plenty of other things to do for himself, and so could not view or remember his promises with the single mindedness I expected of him. But all this meant only delay and not actual frustration.

Eventually the khaki pieces arrived, to be followed by countless journeys on my part to the tailor, who was probably unused to the business of stitching shorts and the scout shirt, with so many pockets and straps and flaps; finally he did produce something approximating our design. It turned out to be a little prolonged here and a little curtailed there, but by judicious tucking-in, slicing-off and re-stitching, he gave me something that might have seemed a little ill-made to impartial eyes, but enough to fill my heart with pride and satisfaction when I viewed myself in a mirror; khaki turban and streamers at the shoulder. The picture that the mirror gave me was so imposing and self-inspiring that I had no doubt I was one of the pillars of the nation. I would give anything to feel that again now with such genuineness and intensity. I had a feeling that I had ceased to be just a boy hanging around fringes of the world of elders, but someone of consequence. I belonged to a very vital group. We stood at attention, turned right and left, saluted each other and uttered patrol calls. When we marched in the streets in a file we had a feeling that we were the objects of envious watching by the whole town. We had certain esoteric, secret training and abilities; by glancing at the marks on the ground we could say where a companion had gone or where a buried treasure could be located. We knew what to do if someone was drowning, how to light a fire in a storm with a single match stick (I never passed this test), how to tie a reef knot, the mysterious purposes of sheep shank or clove hitch, how to bandage a cracked skull. All this knowledge filled us with the pride of accomplishment and performance. And how anxious we were to place our knowledge and training at anybody's disposal, always waiting to be asked to regulate crowds, help people out or watch over something. It was incumbent upon a scout to record at least one good turn a day in his diary. It was not at all as easy as it might sound. I can recollect the desperation some days where the world seemed to be so perfectly organised that one looking about to perform a good turn hardly got a chance. It was harrowing to feel that perhaps the page would have to be left blank for the day. Driven to desperation, one did all sorts of things. If one could somehow salvage my good-turn diary of years ago one would find therein such profound entries as "Chased away a big dog when it came to bite a small dog." or "Saw the old lady in the fourth house suffering from stomach ache, ran to the opposite shop and fetched a bottle of soda water," and "Guided a stranger to the toddy shop."

Of course there were badges and decorations for special achievements, but they were not the chief source of inspiration for the performance of shining deeds. The important thing was finding an occasion for performing a good deed; all else was secondary.

Gardening without Tears

A little gardening goes a long way, and I view with apprehension the recent outburst of horticulturism that is evident everywhere. What one needs is not a mere garden, but a garden which leaves one in peace. If someone will draw a blueprint for gardening without tears I shall be the first to support it. The gardening enthusiast is the most anxiety-ridden person on earth. He is constantly racked with the feeling that he has to contend against evil forces all his life. He visualizes himself as a victim of all the malicious forces in the universe which are ever ready to frustrate his dream, coming to him in the shape of straying chickens from the neighbourhood looking for seeds, seedlings or sprouts; or a laughing child dancing on a patch of soil cultivated with blood, sweat and tears, or just a dignified visitor whose dignity would be injured if told not to let his finger play mischief with the foliage on the way. Every fervent garden-maker becomes a cranky neurasthenic full to the brim with complexes. There is something in gardening which affects what may be called the norms of human temperament.

There are at least two gardens within every compound—the seen and the unseen. What a visitor sees in the first round is only a small portion of what the proud gardener actually has in view. The lover of plants lives in a sort of fourth dimensional plane. Many things that you as visitor will not notice are already there: that plot of turned up earth is just a forest of roses, the small twig sticking out a green shoot a tenth of an inch long is not actually a stick but *plumeria, poinciana or spathodia*, rare and noble trees which have transformed the landscape. Their very names possess magic and poetry. There is much to commend in the use of botanical names, which apart from other things act as passwords among the community of plant-lovers, shutting out the Philistine who cannot distinguish between cacti and cannae: and which also keep alive in our midst Latin, probably the only language which has not spread widely enough in our country to create a problem.

There are at least as many types of gardens as there are temperaments. Our tradition is to start a piece of gardening, whatever may be the size of the area, with a coconut seedling on an auspicious day, and follow it up with other things. The coconut is for posterity, hibiscus and jasmine for the gods in the *puja* room, vegetable for the kitchen, and lastly come those that afford merely visual pleasure. It is in contrast to the quick gardening that, for example, a foreign visitor taking a house for a few months would plan: pansies, asters, phlox and zinnia, and this and that, which come up within a few weeks, brightly wave their multi-coloured stalks, and as swiftly wither away without a trace. I once observed an American who took a house for a few months; he hustled the earth with phosphate, sulphate and compost, and grew lettuce for salad, maize (corn on the cob) for snack, and cut flowers for table decoration, and gave an impression of creating a garden overnight, but it was a strictly utility garden that would not outlast the lease. I observed that there was no semblance of a garden left a week after he vacated the house.

A plant, no doubt, can be a man's best friend: silent, unobtrusive and (more or less) responsive. The great thing about plants is that they don't move or make noise, the two great evils that beset us in this world of ours. We are all the time so much battered by noise and movement that it ought to prove a tonic for us to watch things that don't move or talk. But we must first examine ourselves and ask, "Are we worthy of this great company? Unless one makes sure of it, one is likely to suffer (and also cause suffering) by contact with plants. Who is the happy gardener? It is he that hath the hope and resignation of a gambler, the nerves of a circus acrobat, the unfading wonderment of a growing child, the detachent of a seer and, above all, the forbearance of the eldest of the *Pandavas*.

Private Faces

It is a well-known condition of modern times that any man who is a public figure has to live two lives: one for public view and the other something not so public. The trouble is that this arrangement is not always successful. It is as though those who were supposed to be looking at the front plate-glass window were all the time looking for a chink through which they might get a view of the backyard. Otherwise there is no reason for the interest and curiosity that people display in the private life of a public man. While he is all the time striving to convey a particular impression of himself, the public is all the time consumed with curiosity as to what he is and what he looks like off stage. In effect the public seems to say, 'Well, we have seen you with paint and costume and your set declamation, but we feel that it cannot be the real you. We are interested in watching your show to a reasonable extent, no doubt, but what we really want to know is how you spend your time at home, how you take out your family for shopping, what you do with that naughty son of yours and so on; in short our interest is in seeing you as a normal human being." Out of this curiosity a particular kind of journalistic feature has in recent times developed, presenting a personal angle on eminent men through photographs and interviews. It is nice to see the great man at home in his dressing gown or *dhoti* and shirt. He is mounted on the hall sofa, with his children, grandchildren or little nephews around him, happily looking at their picture-books. I once asked a great man how he actually enjoyed the company of children, for the caption under the picture said, "So-and-so generally relaxes in the company of the little children at home, whenever he wishes to escape the stress of public life". He replied, "It is just as true as the picture of my playing cricket with my little nephews which you see there. To be frank, I loathe cricket, but the photographer made me go through it as a sort of *mamul*. And secondly, when I wish to forget the stress of public life, you

52

may rest assured that I won't invite the stress of life with children. I love children no doubt, no one can help it, but I don't seek them unless I am sure that my nerves can stand their noisy, restless company. I like to leave them alone if they leave me alone...." Many other things that the great man does, such as his interest in plants, his taking a thoughtful walk in his garden at five a.m. and his meticulous attention to correspondence are all routine things that a great man is expected to do in his private life. The whole thing has become more or less standardized. It is almost implied that unless a great man shows an interest in cricket or reads nursery rhymes or looks sentimentally at the flowers in his garden, he will lose the esteem that the public has for him.

In a recent book I came across an interesting grouping of public men: cabinet ministers, successful authors, prize fighters, cinema actors and bishops. Each category has a public front to maintain and at the same time satisfy public curiosity in regard to its unseen life. The public is always curious to know if the successful author gets his inspiration before or after writing his piece, whether he writes before or after lunch, whether he writes on a long sheet of paper or on the back of an envelope, whether he cares for his wife and children or prefers to live a Bohemian life and, above all, what he earns out of his work—all of which is entirely irrelevant to an understanding of his writing; but somehow the public seeks these bits of information, and has to be answered in the most cordial manner. So also with the politician: the public likes to know if his domestic life is also full of challenge, harangue or table-thumping; and in the case of a prize fighter, I suppose, if his wife ever thinks it safe to ask him to hold the baby. Out of all this a convention has developed of what we may broadly call public relations. Although the ideal is to have a single show for private and public view (a state attained by saints alone), ordinarily, in the nature of things, it seems an impossibility. It is very well illustrated by Oliver Wendell Homes in one of his Table Talks:

....there are at least six personalities distinctly to be recognised as taking part in that dialogue between John and Thomas.

Three Johns: (1) The real John; known only to his maker; (2) John's ideal John; never the real one and often very unlike him; (3) Thomas' ideal John; never the real John, nor John's John, but often very unlike either.

Three Thomases: (1) The real Thomas; (2) Thomas' ideal Thomas; (3) John's ideal Thomas.

Only one of the three Johns is taxed; only one can be weighed on a platform balance; but the other two are just as important in the conversation.

Coffee Worries

For a South Indian, of all worries the least tolerable is coffee worry. Coffee worry may be defined as all unhappy speculation around the subject of coffee, as a habit, its supplies, its price, its quality, its morality, ethics, economics and so on. For a coffee addict (he does not like to be called an addict, the word has a disparaging sense, he feels that we might as well call each other milk addicts or food addicts or air addicts), the most painful experience is to hear a tea-drinker or a cocoa-drinker or a purist who drinks only water hold forth on the evils of drinking coffee. He views it as an attack on his liberty of thought and action. Even a misquoted Parliament report (as it recently happened) on the coffee policy of the government can produce in him the gravest disturbance, temporarily though.

It is not right to call it a habit. The world 'habit' like the word 'addict' has a disparaging sense. One might call smoking a habit, one might call almost everything else a habit, but not coffee. It is not a habit; it is a stabilising force in human existence achieved through a long evolutionary process. The good coffee, brown and fragrant, is not a product achieved in a day. It is something attained after laborious trials and errors. At the beginning people must have attempted to draw decoction from the raw seed itself or tried to chew it; and then they learnt to fry it, and in the first instance, nearly converted it into charcoal. Now people have developed a sixth sense, and know exactly when the seed should be taken out of the frying pan and ground, and how finely or roughly it must be ground. Nothing pleases a normal man of South India more than the remark, "Oh, the coffee in his house is excellent. You cannot get the like of it anywhere else in the world." Conversely no one likes to hear that his coffee is bad, although the truth may be that the powder he has used is adulterated, the strainer has let in all the powder, and there is every indication that they have (a horrible thing to do) added jaggery to the decoction. In this instance the thing to appreciate is not the coffee itself but the spirit behind it. South India has attained world renown for its coffee and every South Indian jealously guards this reputation.

Coffee forms nearly thirty per cent of any normal family budget. The South Indian does not mind this sacrifice. He may beg or run into debt for the sake of coffee, but he cannot feel that he has acquitted himself in his worldly existence properly unless he is able to provide his dependents with two doses of coffee a day and also ask any visitor who may drop in, "Will you have coffee?" without fear at heart. This is the basic minimum for a happy and satisfied existence. Here and there we may see households where the practice is more elaborately organized, and where coffee has to be available all hours of day or night. There are persons who call for a cup of coffee before starting a fresh sentence while writing or conversing. Perhaps all this may be too much. These are likely to come under the category of addicts, but their constant demand is understandable. No man asks for a fresh cup of coffee without criticizing the previous one. "It was not quite hot.... It seemed to have too much sugar. Let me see how this is...." It is only a continuous search for perfection, and let no one spoil it by giving it a bad name. Anyway, it cannot be called an addiction since anything that takes on that name brings forth evil results. Coffee has produced no bad result. It is supposed to spoil sleep, but there is a considerably growing school of thought that it is very good for insomnia. For one person who may say that coffee keeps him awake there are now at least three to declare that they can have a restful night only when they have taken a cup before retiring. All moralizing against coffee has misfired in this part of the country. "Coffee is a deadly poison, you are gradually destroying your system with it, etc." declares some purist. He may lecture from a public platform or on a street corner but people will listen to him with only a pitying tolerance, with an air of saying. "Poor fellow, you don't know what you are talking about, your don't know what you are missing. You will still live and learn." In course of time this prophecy is fulfilled. Many a man who came to scoff has remained to pray. Coffee has many conquests: saints, philosophers, thinkers and artists, who can never leave the bed unless they learn that coffee is ready, but not the least of its conquests is among those who came to wage a war on it.

Looking One's Age

Honestly speaking, one is never satisfied with one's own photograph, the feeling always being that it could have been better. One puts the blame on the photographer, light, some unexpected distraction that brought on that stunned expression, and so forth.

Photographers advise their subjects to look pleasant, casual or unconcerned. But nothing helps. Among facial expressions a smile is the most risky one to adopt. "I never realized how ghastly I look till I saw that snapshot of mine taken when I was supposed to be smiling," confessed a friend to me recently. "One feels sympathy for a world that has to go on looking on this face." The only consolation in this is that it is mutual and universal. The feeling is one of uneasiness in any case, whether one thinks that one's photograph might have been better or worse. No photograph can be said to be perfect: it always overstates or understates one's personality. One's thoughts are either, "I wish I deserved the compliment the photographer has paid me!" or "What a bother! This man has caught me while I am simpering like a moron." I have met very few persons who have the hardihood to hang portraits of themselves in their studies or at the entrances to their homes.

A photographic impression is perhaps the most fleeting of impressions. A photograph caught in a fraction of a second is valid only for that fraction of a second. Even as the spool is being wound the personality changes. In this sense a mirror can hardly confirm what a camera presents. I do not refer here to the young person who gets into the habit of deep contemplation of his or her own features with due appreciation of the reflected image, but of a normal person on whom Nature has started her operations unmistakably.

One goes on living in a fool's paradise, visualizing oneself as one used to be, never acquiring a sense of reality, always blaming the photographer or the mirror for anything that may seem uncomplimentary. If others do not give out the actual state of affairs, it might be because they are considerate or have not noticed the changes. This state continues until one day someone, whom one has not seen for a long time, turns up, and exclaims, "I say! It look me time to recognize you. I thought it was someone else, possibly your uncle." "Why? Why?"

"Oh, you have...." he hesitates, "you used to be so slim and your hair probably was not so grey." However indifferent one might be, there comes a time in everyone's life when one hears it for the first time. Depending upon the type of person to whom it is addressed, it comes as a shock or a pleasant surprise. It is not everyone who is likely to feel depressed at the thought that he has lost his original youthful apprence. It is only an abnormal person who will cling to a vision of himself as he was years before. Most persons, after they get over the initial surprise, will settle down and accept the position with a good deal of cheer. That is how Nature has intended it to be taken. Within reasonable limits one ought to look one's years. There is a certain propriety about it: that girth is inevitable at that age or that degree of greyness. To be rosy-cheeked, curly-headed and slim at fifty! You have only to think of this picture to realize how incongruous it could be. It would be in the nature of an insult to the age, as unacceptable as at attaining the rotundity and baldness of middle age at eighteen. Nature seems to have arranged it all with great forethought. That receding forehead, that greyness at the temple, that filled-in shape are all divinely ordained, and succeed in producing a wonderful picture of serenity and wisdom, and lend weight to the personality. I have come across persons who are bothered by their youthful appearance: that shock of youthful hair, that smooth chin, that unwanted slimness are greatly distressing, especially when the man has to keep up an appearance of authority or pugnacity in order to get some work going. He attempts to remedy the deficiency by nurturing fierce whiskers or by wearing heavy blackrimmed glasses, masks which are expected to overawe an onlooker.

It is good to acquire the appearance that one's age warrants and to know how one strikes others, without any feeling of shock or surprise. This thesis, however, is intended mainly for men and not for women, about whose psychological reaction in these matters I dare not speculate.

The Great Basket

In a new order of things I hope the wastepaper basket will receive the recognition and status that it deserves. It is not just a receptacle that you keep under your table for flinging unwanted papers in. Unwantedness, in any case, is a relative term. The urgent paper of today becomes the unwanted one of tomorrow. If a new symbol is needed to indicate Time it should be neither the hour-glass with falling sand nor the hands of a clock, but a wide-girthed wastepaper basket into which all papers vanish and attain a final equality. This tax notice, that cinema folder, that reminder of an old bill, even letters from friends or foes whose contents have been read and digested, and invitation cards so laboriously prepared and printed, where do they end?

I have discovered a most practical way of dealing with unnecessary correspondence. I suffer from the privilege of receiving letters from strangers, most of whom desire to tell me how to write or what to write about. I go through them with reverential care, but I am never able to acknowledge them. It is not because I am not able to appreciate the brilliance of the advice or the spirit in which it is given, but, having to write for a living, it is impossible to engage oneself in the same activity at the end of day's labour. If a writer does not always display the courtesy of acknowledging a letter it must be put down to nothing worse than the psychological difficulties of his profession. And so what happens? I read the letter, send up a silent thanks to the writer and then gently toss it under the table. I know where it will fall. By long practice I know exactly how far a gentle fling will carry a piece of paper. I don't have to look a second time. It is rarely that I overshoot or undershoot and find the letter or paper lying under the table. When that happens it means that the missile must be an abnormal one, of an unusual density or volume, such as a questionnaire form or a catalogue. It may seem unjust that this should happen to the most carefully composed forms and lists, but no one who is reasonable can ever object to this disposal. What else can one do with them? It is with reluctance and regret that I consign such papers to the basket, constantly asking myself what else I could do about them. If I keep them in sight on my table, they will go on bothering my conscience. I don't wish to go through existence with a gnawing conscience all the time. By putting that letter out of sight I remove one possible strain on my conscience. I make the wastepaper basket my conscience-keeper. I never crumple a letter while slipping it into the basket. I leave it whole with all its postmark intact on its envelope. I never have my basket cleared except once in a while. This helps me take a second look at my correspondence when occasion calls for it. I remember quite a few occasions when I have pulled out a letter from the basket and written a reply on second thoughts.

Apart from other considerations there is the question of space. You may have the largest study and the most capacious table but yet, day by day, there is bound to be gradual and steady encroachment on all the available space, and a time may come when (to quote Shaw in a favourite saying that also appears elsewhere in the book), "The dead may crowd the living out of this earth." The word dead must not be resented by anyone. Keep any letter for a week and it becomes dead, and then the only thing to do with it is to put it out of sight and no one is the worse for it. When examined after a week what seemed pressing and inescapable seems just cold and inconsequential. Only government offices enjoy the unique privilege of keeping in ponderous files what had better be entombed in the great basket. Their fear is that all sorts of papers may be necessary for some reference at some future date. My view is that this world would be a better place to live in if there were fewer references available on any question. No question is valued on its own present worth but in relations to a deadweight of its past.

I feel that a little more liberal use of the W.P.B. will also solve all accommodation problems in this world—everywhere there is a cry for more accommodation—not for human beings alone but for papers and files. It is just here that the W.P.B. can help humanity.

The basket is an equally good place for sudden and voluminous literary effusion. There is a cold impersonality about its reception of literary matter which always appeals to me. I have sometimes found it necessary to consign to it several thousand words of a new novel representing weeks of hard work, and I have felt the better for it. When one can bring oneself to the point of doing it, one feels light and free and able to resume an obliterated chapter with a better perspective.

Apart from its association with much paper, the great basket is an article worth possessing for its own sake. It is the shapeliest article ever made by human fingers. It has symmetry, poise, accessibility and balance, and it certainly deserves a better place than the dark regions under a desk.

Of Trains and Travellers

I have a weakness for odd trains, some shuttle or passenger
which will crawl through the countryside and stop long enough
at unknown stations to enable one to gain an idea of the life and
habits there. I like to reach my destination by a series of such
hops rather than by a masterful, purposeful mail rushing along
to its terminus without pausing to look this way or that. The
disadvantage of travelling by such a strict train is that one glides
past most places at dead of night. For instance, Salem or
Jalarpet are stations which I have crossed hundreds of times
these many years, but without any idea of what they look like.
In order to remedy this deficiency in general knowledge, I have
taken to travelling by unspectacular day trains. Not the least
part of the delight of such a journey being that you find the
human element within the compartment as attractive as the
landscape without. During a night journey, preoccupation with
the problem of sleep distorts the human personality.

The bearded *sadhu* who occupies a corner with scorn on his
face for all worldly goods including railway tickets; the meek
paterfamilias taking his wife and numerous children somewhere, always consumed with anxiety lest they should be
crowded out of their seats; the businessman and his friend
lounging back and continuously shouting over the din their
prowess in market operations; the bully stretching himself out
on a complete seat in full luxury, daring anyone to approach
him; the glutton who can never allow a single edible pass
outside the window without stopping and buying one, every
time haggling over price and quality and showing no inclination
to produce his cash till the train actually begins to move,
compelling every vendor to trot beside the train; the season-
ticket student showing off his familiarity with the railway by
perching himself precariously on the footboard or at the
doorway; these are familiar characters one meets in any
journey.

There is one other type of person who grips everybody's attention the moment he enters a train. He is the loquacious man. He can never leave anyone alone. His air of assurance and friendliness wins him a new listener, if not a friend, every moment. It may be said that this man attempts to guide the life and thought of everyone in the compartment. There a child may cry. Our friend will not only persuade the child to remain quiet but also explain to the mother how children should be brought up, what should be done if they suffer from stomach ache, how to treat a cold, how to tackle bad temper or mischief. If need be he can move everybody and clear a space for the young mother to spread out a piece of cloth and put her child to sleep. He once cleared a lot of space for elders by persuading all the children to sit in a row on an upper berth. One might take him to be a child specialist until one sees him turn his attention to the next subject. He may happen to notice the glutton eat his orange when he will yell out, "How much did you pay for the orange?" and follow it up with a discourse on the ups and downs of the orange trade, the method of its cultivation and the geography of the country where it is grown. If he happens to see the actual transaction, this or any other, you may rest assured he will throw his weight on the side of the buyer and force the vendor to bring down his price. If he overhears some others in a corner talking among themselves of political matters, he will step in and put an end to their conversation, compelling them to listen to his own talk. He is one who knows all that goes on behind the scenes at New Delhi. He can explain why this policy is being pursued or why the other one is dropped. He knows who is at the back of everything. He may even claim to be the one who originated the Janata Express, Shatabdi Concession, or the Hindusthan Coach, through his mysterious agencies in the proper quarters. When he mentions the Parliament he assumes the look of one who bears it like a burden on his back. He knows all the persons that pull the strings that move the puppets in the Parliament and in the Cabinet. His hints about his own participation in various political activities builds up a background to whatever he says and gives them a touch of credibility. He can mention most of the personages at Delhi by their pet names; it may take time for an ordinary man to spot them out under his terms. Not for him the word Prime Minister but just Jawahar; for most of the others in the Government he employs mystifying initials and abbreviations.

This man gives one the impression that he travels for no other purpose than to gain first-hand impression of how people are faring. He demands very little from others except a hearing which he will get anyway. He hardly keeps a seat for himself, always surrendering it to anyone who may look for more space. I have always wanted to ask whether he possesses a ticket or not, but could never muster enough courage to put the question to him.

A Library Without Books

I am generally put off by the expression 'library movement.' The very word movement endows the whole business with an abstract, unreal air. It produces in one's mind a picture of humanity, jammed together, moving in a mass towards a goal—a very impressive picture, no doubt, but having nothing to do with the business of reading. Or am I mistaken in thinking that the champions of the library movement are interested in the business of reading? Library science seems all concerned with systems of classification, shelves, furniture, locks, keys, registers, vouchers and statistics, everything except reading. The most noticeable deficiency in any library today seems to be a lack of propaganda for books themselves. It would be useful to inscribe on every library wall the motto: "Books are meant to be read and not merely to be classified and preserved." In every library elaborate rules are being framed for the borrowing and returning of books. There is a university library that I visit where there are so many regulations for book-borrowing that few ever find the time to go in and borrow a volume. You have to spend half-an-hour before you get through the formalities of picking up a book from the shelf, and another half-an-hour before you can get through the various entries and signatures and go out of the library. Compared to this the ceremony of getting through a custom's inspection looks child's play. In every library there are so many involved technicalities for this transaction that I sometimes wonder if they would not do better to keep dummy books with gilt titles in sealed *almirahs,* so that they may only be seen and counted and never taken out, which seems to be the best way of keeping a library secure, above reproach from auditors and with unimpeachable stock register.

The great handicap for the libraries now is that governments have begun to take an interest in them, and eminent men utilize them as themes for grandiose speeches. As a result of it, most library efforts get entangled in red-tape and become a matter of cess, authority, statistics and funds.

Recently when I visited a certain important town I saw a new library building coming up at feverish speed. The name boards of the architect, contractor, electrician and sanitary engineers stood up on all sides of the compound in letters of gold. The ground was swept, lawns were laid and watered desperately and all workmen were finishing up their tasks by gaslight. I felt pleased. The thought that someone was hurrying on at a desperate speed to provide cultural amenities to the townsmen was a very pleasant and sustaining thought. I felt that you couldn't see that zest in any other part of the world. I felt that the friendship of those who were responsible for it was worth cultivating. I sought them out and expressed my feelings. They were naturally pleased with the compliment and were willing to give me all the facts connected with it. I learnt that the building was costing them two lakhs of rupees. They gave me the names of all the technicians who were at work there, and concluded "According to the terms of the contract the building must be handed over to us by the tenth of this month."

"Why such a firm date?"

"Otherwise it will be no use for us. Sri...will be passing this way on the tenth and he has agreed to perform the opening ceremony. If the building is not in our hands on that date it will be practically useless for us afterwards." I could not accept the statement. "Why do you say it will be useless? You may always stock the books and start using the building any moment, irrespective of whether an eminent man is passing this way or not."

"Oh, books!" he said. "We are not bothered about that now. We are thinking only of the opening ceremony." I could not help asking: "When are you going to bother about it, anyway?"

"Oh, can't say. It will depend upon the funds available at the end of all this."

"If and when you decide to admit books into the library what will be your procedure for acquiring them?"

"We will probably call for tenders for the supply of books. We want to encourage the local booksellers and distribute the patronage evenly."

I couldn't help asking, "How are you going to select the volumes?"

"We shall leave it to the booksellers. We shall first measure the total shelf space, get an approximate idea of the number of volumes required to fill them, and call for quotations for the supply of this quantity. Anyway we are not going to worry about this detail now. Our first requirement is building and furniture. After that we must find funds for sending up someone for library training, for which we are already receiving numerous applications."

And so I gathered the following facts and figures about the library:

Building Rs. 2,00,000; lighting Rs. 15,000; plumbing, etc., Rs. 12,000; garden layout and supervisors' charges Rs. 5,000; counters, shelves and furniture Rs. 30,000; opening ceremony: printing of invitations, welcome address, president's speech and secretary's report Rs. 2,000; *Pandal* and tea Rs. 4,000, and books: no budget yet.

A Writer's Nightmare

A few nights ago I had a nightmare. I had become a citizen of a strange country called Xanadu. The Government all of a sudden announced the appointment of an officer called the controller of stories. All the writers in the country sent up a memorandum to their representative in parliament, and he asked at the next session of the house: "May we know why there is a new department called the controller of stories?"

From the Government benches came the answer: "Through an error in our Government printing section five tons of forms intended for the controller of *stores* were printed controller of *stories*, an unwanted 'I' having crept into the text. Consequently the Government was obliged to find a use for all this printed stuff."

"What sort of use?" asked the member.

"Since the stationery was inadvertently ready a department of stories was started."

"Was a new incumbent entertained for the post of controller of stories and, if so, will the Honourable Minister quote the public services commission circular in this regard; what is the cost of this post and where are you going to get the money for it and under what head is it going to be charged and who will be the deciding authority and will you place on the table a copy of the auditor-general's remark in this regard?" went on the Parliament member, trying to get the Minister into an entanglement of linked-up questions. The Minister was familiar with such tactics and curtly replied, "The answer to A is in the negative, B the Government is watching the situation, C the question does not arise, D see B, E it will not be in public interest to answer the question at present...." He spoke so fast, without a pause, that the questioner got derailed and lost track of his own questions. Undaunted, he asked again, "Will the Honourable Minister explain if this is in keeping with the Government's recent economy drive?"

"The answer is in the affirmative."

"Will he kindly explain himself?"

"Yes. In the first place we have managed to utilize a vast quantity of printed paper. Anyone who is familiar with the world shortage in paper will appreciate this move, and in the second place there is no extra expenditure involved in starting this department since the controller of stores will be *ex officio* controller of stories and will generally conduct the affairs of this department, for after all stories are also stores in a manner of speaking."

"May we know the why and how and what-about-what and wherefore of this department?"

"I am glad to have an opportunity to speak on this issue. The Government is becoming increasingly aware of the importance of stories in our national life. Since this is a welfare state the Government is obliged to keep a watch over all the activities that affect our citizens. It has come to our notice recently that sufficient attention is not being paid by the authors in this country to the subject of story. The Government has observed that next to rice and water, stories are the most-demanded stuff in daily life....Every moment someone or other is always asking for a story. It may be a child asking his teacher or a novel-reader his author or a magazine-buyer his editor or a film producer who has spent lakhs and lakhs and has every equipment ready except a story, and of course all our radio stations and theatres, too, demand stories. The demand is far in excess of supply, and may I add even where a story is seen it turns out to be deplorably bad stuff? The Government has made up its mind that they will not tolerate bad stories any more."

At this point the question-master interrupted with, "May we know what is meant by bad stories? Will the Honourable Minister quote instances?"

"No. I cannot mention any specific bad stories at this juncture, since that would lead to the suspicion that invidious distinctions are being made, but I would like to point out that bad stories are stories that are not good, and our honourable friend must be satisfied with it for the moment."

"May we know how this department is to function?" asked the member.

"Presently, the controller of stories will undertake the

formation of a body called the Central Story Bureau which will immediately go into the business of formation of a Chief Story Officer for each state."

"May we know what it will have to do with the story writers in the country?"

"Every story writer must fill up Form A, obtain a local treasury certificate for ten rupees, and forward both to the Central Story Bureau (general branch), and he will receive an endorsement entitling him to call himself a registered story writer. Thereafter, whenever he has an inspiration for a story, long or short, he will have to send a synopsis of it in quadruplicate to the C.S. Bureau (technical branch), and obtain its approval before proceeding to expand the work further."

"Why should it be in quadruplicate?"

"For facilitating procedure. The Central Story Bureau (technical branch) will consist of four directorates, one each for plot, character, atmosphere and climax, and each section will examine the proposed story in respect of its own jurisdiction and may suggest emendations and improvements in respect of the story before issuing a final authorization certificate to the author, which must be prominently displayed in his study. Any author who attempts to write a story without proper authorization will be fined five hundred rupees and imprisoned for a period not exceeding eighteen months.... The Government has every desire to avoid these extreme measures, its sole aim being improvement of national culture, and we have every hope that all this will bring about a revolution in story writing within the next ten years. Incidentally I wish to inform the house that we are presently inaugurating a national story week which will see the birth of a write-better-stories movement all over the country...." He concluded, "All this is in the nature of an effort on the part of the Government for improving the standard of story writing in this country. We shall watch the results, and let me say," here he raised his voice, "let me warn all bad story writers that I shall not hesitate to smash their ink bottles. We don't want bad stories in this country in any form. We shall watch the situation and see how it develops, and if writers fail to show any improvement, which we shall be in a position to judge from the quarterly reports submitted by the regional story officer, I have no hesitation in saying that we, on this side of the

house, will take to story-writing ourselves...."
And, at this stage, I woke up.

Umbrella Devotee

I read with great pleasure the recent news that the prices of umbrellas (why not 'umbrellae' for plural in order to add to the dignity of the subject?) have fallen. I am one of those, I believe it is a somewhat select group, who believe that every adult should have a minimum of three umbrellas: one for personal use, one for lending and one for reserve in case all the umbrellas suddenly vanish from the face of this earth through some freak action such as an atomic blast. Deep within, the umbrella devotee is a prey to all kinds of phobias. And not all the phobias are unfounded, if we remember how well-founded is his impression that all are frantically attempting to get at his umbrella all the time. He cannot leave it resting in a corner and be sure that he can find it there when he wants it again. Everyone thinks that he can pick up any umbrella that he sees. The man who would hesitate to pick up my ring never hesitates to snatch away my old umbrella hanging in its stand. It is this utter disregard for ownership in umbrellas that is responsible for all the confusion and irritation that we notice in the umbrella business today. I heard a friend confess recently, "I have five umbrellas and five hundred enemies." He explained, "I make enemies this way: I have five umbrellas because I like to have five, that is all. I have as much right to have five umbrellas as I have to have five fingers. Anyone who questions why I should possess five umbrellas sounds impertinent to my ears and gets the appropriate reply. And then when they ask me to lend them my umbrella I invariably refuse to do so; that makes people call me selfish and I retort appropriately. People are sometimes persistent and will plead and cajole till I give them my umbrella. Of course it is given with stern warnings and stipulations regarding time and place of its return, but I am yet to come across a single creature who remembers this injunction; ninety out of a hundred will not remember their obligations. In the end I have to undertake a trip to retrieve my umbrella, and then I do not hesitate to tell a person what I think of him. Moreover, it is a well-established fact that ninety-nine out of a hundred do not know how to hold an umbrella: when I find a tear in the cloth or a loosened rib or handle, I tell the borrower plainly that he ought to be sent to jail for it. People do not appreciate forthright comments. I am sorry to say that most persons do not know how to handle an umbrella; some have the distressing habit of twirling its handle while walking, or holding it too high or too low, right over their skulls as if it were a cap; all this will ruin an umbrella.

"There is a technique in using an umbrella as in all things. There should be neither stiffness nor too much flexibility at the wrist of an arm that holds an umbrella; it must be adjusted properly to the pressure of the wind. Wind is an insidious enemy whose effect is most wearing; the ribs may be made of iron but it is as a broomstick to the wind. What must protect an umbrella is an understanding wrist. How can everyone understand this subject, when most people never think of an umbrella except when it rains? I wish they would include a course in umbrella-holding in all educational institutions. Just fifteen minutes a day for two or three days in the week and it would produce wonderful results. It must be based on the same footing as compulsory military training. Another reason why all these unpleasant things exist about umbrellas is that there are far too many persons in each of our households and too few umbrellas. In a normal joint-family household there are at least ten persons in a house, but how many umbrellas are there to be found? Just one, where it ought to be really thirty on the basis that everyone should have at least three umbrellas. What happens is this; one umbrella probably belongs to an enthusiast, but everyone has his eye on it whenever he wants protection from sun or rain. It is either sunny or rainy, one or the other, and the umbrella is in danger of getting into circulation. Fortunately nobody asks for your umbrella when there is the moon. I believe it is due to that wonderful proverb which says that only an upstart will hold an umbrella over his head at midnight. We need more and more of such proverbs. I believe one way in which people may be induced to own their umbrellas is to include the question in every form that is to be filled out. Form-filling for one purpose or another is a necessity for ration, passport, education, employment or anything, in which a lot of questions are asked regarding age, ancestry, etc. of every person, and among all that host of irrelevant questions why not add one more, 'Do you possess an umbrella? If so, how long have you had it? How do you manage to keep yours?" This may not always bring forth truthful answers but it will at any rate put people into a proper frame of mind. Nowadays umbrella lovers are viewed as cranks, which is most unfortunate. People openly brag, 'Oh, I cannot think of carrying an umbrella in the streets; Oh, no, I would never be seen with one.' This is a very unhealthy attitude. They go even a step further and say, 'I have lost nearly twenty umbrellas this year.' Somehow this is said in a tone of pride. Why should it be made a matter of boastful talk rather than one to be ashamed of? If this braggart has lost twenty umbrellas, you may rest assured that the losses are someone else's and not his. Existence will not be perfect until it becomes as impossible for a person to carry another man's umbrella as carrying another man's driving licence. "I do not accept the statement that the slump in the umbrella trade is due to the successive failure of monsoons. No true umbrella devotee will ever be put off by such fickle causes as weather. A man loves his umbrella for its own sake. He would hug his umbrella, whether it is a London-imported variety rolled to look like a stick or whether it is the heavy-canopied flabby one with a cane handle, not because it is hot or rainy but because he has true affection at heart for it."

Next Sunday

Sunday is the day most looked forward to by everyone. It is the one day which suddenly evaporates before you know where you are. Everyone knows the Saturday-evening feeling, with all the pleasures of expectancy, and the Sunday-evening feeling already tainted by thoughts of Monday. What happens to the day? It is the day on which so many items are thrust—promises made to children for an outing, promise of a little shopping, calling on someone, and so on and so forth, all promises, promises. There is no way out except by stretching the twenty-four hours to do the work of forty-eight. Before one notices it the forenoon is gone.

In the morning one decides to stay a little longer in bed and one does it till one is worried out of bed by the noises which start earlier than usual, because it is a Sunday. A radio enthusiast in the next house who has been waiting for this day to tune in an hour earlier, a motor-car with its engine going to pieces, children's shouts of joy because they have no school today; all this goes on while the Sunday devotee is planning to spend an hour longer in bed. The man gets up in a slightly frustrated mood and that is not a very good way to start the day. It knocks all charm out of existence at the very start itself. When one has got up in this mood it is no use hoping for a good life again. It is better to accept it for what it is: that the Sunday is nearly gone. Next, one begins to notice things. On other days one has no time for all those scrutinies and examinations. I know a person who is a very gentle being on all working days but completely turns a somersault on a Sunday. He becomes ferocious and difficult to deal with. He sees that everything at home is going wrong. He is a hobbyist, one who likes to repair things with his own hand. This man draws a heavy schedule of work for Sundays. Hanging a picture, fixing a leaky tap, choking off the squeak in the radio, or oiling the watch or bicycle, are all jobs for a Sunday. All through the week he keeps making a mental note of what he proposes to do on the Sunday. If he could have his way he would have to work far into midnight and a part of the Monday morning also. But he never gets through this arduous programme. No doubt he opens up a radio or a watch the first thing in the day, and squats down like a great god in his workshop. Francis Thompson said of Shelley, "The Universe was his box of joys." We are reminded of this picture when we see this man sitting amidst his toys; but with this difference: Shelly was pictured as being lost in the delight of creation, while this man is unable to do anything because he finds so many articles missing. A nail which he cherished, a piece of string or wire which he reserved for future use, a precious nut or bolt, and something or the other is always missing, and it enrages him. He has a number of children and his losses are in direct ratio to their numbers. This is not a thing that this irate man can take casually. The children have been helping themselves to various articles all through the week. A blade for pencil mending, a wire for tying up something, something else for something else, and a nut and bolt because they look nice. This man's anger knows no bounds. He calls them, lines them up and starts an investigation. The investigation may lead to useful results or it may not. It is in the laps of the gods. One child, impressed by his father's manner, may give up his loot and another may out of a desire to earn a certificate, or they may do nothing of the kind but remain unyielding of their treasures. The man sitting with his box of toys is clearly frustrated. His suspicion is roused and he now proceeds to take stock of all his losses. He hurriedly gets up and opens his cupboards, and presently the household keeps ringing with, "Where is this?" or "What has happened to that"? in varying degrees of petulance. But like Jesting Pilate's, his questions are destined to perish without an answer. People would answer if they could. Others know no more where that hammer is gone, which no one has ever seen, than he does. He realizes that he lives in a most unhelpful world. He shoots his question apparently in the general air, but actually aims it at his wife who is busy in an inner part of the house, and at the children who are gleefully watching their father's tantrums and are only waiting for a chance to run away. One child of seven years, an intuitive escapist, with apparent innocence suggests that probably such and such a thing is in such and such a place, and should he go and look for it? The irate man falls a prey to this guile. No David more easily vanquished a Goliath. Before the man knows what has happened the young fellow is gone, and once the line-up is broken it is broken for ever. The man gets absorbed in something else, probably a book or magazine on his table, and forgets all about it for a while, till he sees the same children unconcernedly playing in the next house. He calls them back by a lusty shout through the window. They all troop back, and the man opens the offensive by asking about their books and schoolwork, clearly a sadistic design. This leads to an examination of their educational progress and propensities. He discovers that his children have not been developing on the right lines at all; he had not noticed till now how badly they were growing up—an oblique reference which at once brings down a hot denial from an inner part of the house. He bullies the children for a while and grows tired of it very soon. Now he discovers that half the Sunday is irrevocably lost. There are only a few more hours of sunshine left. He is now reminded of all his promises for this day after he had his midday meal and has acquired a pleasant mood. He promises to fulfil his obligations after a short nap. When he gets up after his rest he realizes that he simply cannot take his family out today. He simply will not spend the balance of this much-battered Sunday at bus stops. He recollects how sometime ago he had to spend two hours at a bus stand with all his children howling with hunger, and all of them had to trek back home late at night. He shudders at the memory and suddenly cries, "Please, let us stay at home. I will take you all out next Sunday."

The Sycophant

Sycophancy is one of the oldest professions in the world. Old King Cole was a merry old soul because he could afford to be so. He would have felt choked by his surroundings but for the sycophant who stood by and helped him attain peace of mind. The sycophant may well be called the provider of peace of mind for those in authority. He acts as a shock absorber—even this word is a little ahead of the sense: it would be nearer the mark to say that he acts as a shock repeller. The sycophant is ever watchful and manages to keep his chief from feeling unduly bothered by conscience or commonsense. The sycophant's genius lies in showing a feeling that is not his own but his master's. He cannot afford to assume any colour of his own. His survival depends upon his capacity to take on the hue that his master is likely to assume at any given moment. Hamlet points to the sky and asks Polonius: "Do you see yonder cloud that's almost in shape of a camel?"

Polonius: "By the mass, and it's like a camel, indeed."

Hamlet: "Methinks it is like a weasel."

Polonius: "It is backed like a weasel."

Hamlet: "Or like a whale?"

Polonius: "Very like a whale."

I quote this because it seems to me a masterpiece of sycophancy, although Polonius has perhaps other aims, such as wanting to humour a madman, in making himself so agreeable.

The essence of a sycophant's success lies in his capacity to remain agreeable under all conditions. He may not be a lover of children, least of all his master's favourite, the seven-year-old devil. He may feel like spanking him and putting him in his place whenever he sees him, but his first sentence, his opening line for the day, always is: "How is the little charmer, sir?" He has to show a keen interest in the boy's games, books, hobbies and friends; and cherish for timely use one or two quotations from the young man's speeches which display his wit and wisdom. There is a certain amount of self-abnegation involved in it. The sycophant is one who sacrifices much and bears much, and it is no small strain to remain agreeable under all conditions. After all, when we come to consider it, what is his personal gain in all this? It is not much. All that he seeks is that he be allowed to bask forever in the sunshine of his master's presence. This gives him a reflected glory and an authority which seem to him the most important acquisition in life; the material and other advantages that may arise therefrom are mere by-products. He practises sycophancy for its own sake, for the pleasure it gives, for the sense of well-being that it spreads all around. This man I would place at the summit of the category. One who practises this fine art for the sake of obvious gains can take only second place in this hierarchy. It has all the difference that we observe between one who is a devotee of art for art's sake and the utilitarian who uses art for propaganda. When we see a man employing sycophancy for some cheap purpose we are seized with the same sense of bathos as overwhelms us while seeing a film, perfectly made in every way, but out to show only the virtues of the caterpillar wheel or of chemical fertilizers.

When the history of mankind comes to be written more fully, I expect a great deal will be included about the sycophant and his influence on human affairs. How many rulers of men, how many despots, lived in worlds of their own, unperturbed by contrary views and outlooks? In the *Fall of Berlin* there is a historic instance, which may be of questionable accuracy, but the portrayal itself seems significant. Hitler is told that the fall of Moscow is imminent, a matter of a few minutes. He keeps looking at the time and frets and fumes. A military adviser suggests that Moscow may, probably, never be taken since, in the course of its history, many an invader has had to turn back from its gates. This man is dismissed instantly and a courtier who blindly assures Hitler that the German troops are at the moment marching in the streets of Moscow is promoted very high. We may question the propriety of this presentation but it is a perfect example of the sycophant's role in human affairs.

The American colloquial expression for it is more direct: 'Yes-man'. It seems to me that this expression may not exactly mean sycophancy but something more. 'Yes-man' appears to be a democratic word. Sycophant was quite adequate for one-man

79

rule, when the ruler did not have to worry about public opinion, but nowadays the ruler has to get through his business with the backing of his yes-man, which alone can give it a democratic touch.

The yes-man's role is not necessarily confined to politics. Of late he has made his appearance in the scientific world also. When a scientist becomes a yes-man he will assert that the earth is square or flat or crooked, just as it suits his master's mind. Galileo's trouble was that he could not show this accommodating spirit and hence suffered persecution all his life. Now in some places the scientist obviously avoids the folly of Galileo, and is ready to assert that man and not nature should decide how much time wheat or some other corn ought to take to grow and ripen, if his master shows any signs of annoyance at the time-table followed by nature.

I have tried to trace the origin of the word 'sycophant'. The dictionary says: 'perh. orig.' "one who informed against persons exporting figs," from *sukon* 'fig', see *'Syconium'*, which injunction I could not lightly ignore. I looked up *Syconium* to know that it was Greek for fig or a near-fig-like fruit. I have found it very illuminating on the whole. I realized that we have after all been bandying about a word without being aware of its association with the fig business, its export restrictions and possible controls, the men who profited by flouting the law, and the greater profit that other men derived by watching (and informing against) the men who profited by flouting the law, and these last were known as sycophants. This is all only an incidental discovery. My original purpose in turning the pages of a dictionary was to know if sycophant had a feminine form. I am sure it will be a heartening piece of news for many to know that there is no 'sycophantess' just as there is no such thing as yes-woman.

The Maha

A judicious admixture of Sanskrit and English, I find, produces sometimes a marvellously handy idiom. It may not have the approval of pundits of either language, but I think it is effective. For instance, how fluently speaks one whose sentences fuse into Tamil and English alternately: the tongue naturally selects the easy way. This is not say that the mongrel breed is the best in a language, but sometimes it is the most effective. English, at any rate, has been so pliant and absorbent that it has become the most resilient language in the world.

I wish to add to this language a new phrase, maha superiority. *Mahat,* the Sanskrit word, seems capable of going in harmoniously with any word in any language; and it is just the word that can add a degree to superior. We want now a word which is above the ordinary superlative; it is achieved by coining 'maha superiority.'

What is maha superiority? It is a state beyond the ordinary standard of snobbery. The ordinary snob pales before this man. The common snob may like to show off his wealth or wit, but his horizon is apparently bounded by another class which can show off more wealth or brighter wit. This is the secret sorrow of every snob. He is ever conscious, through all his preening and measured swagger, of a higher snob, to reach whose place is the secret hankering in his heart all the time. He has a sense of superiority to a certain class of persons around him but he has not that absolute sense of superiority which is the privilege of one who comes under the 'maha' class. The maha superior man has no secret misgivings about his eminence. He feels that the world is at his feet. His uniqueness, he feels, can rouse the envy of gods.

You can generally spot him by his cigarette holder which is the only one of its kind in the world, by his pocket screw pencil of which only a dozen are known to exist in the world. He may not play cricket or any game in the world, but he has a cricket bat given to him by Bradman himself with his autograph. His familiarity with all the names which are only newspaper names for the rest of mankind is breath-taking. Don't be surprised if you hear him say, "Once, when I put my hands into the Aga Khan's pocket at Nice, do you know how many diamonds I could pick up in a handful?" Or he will talk of the various personal comments made by Clem, Winston or others. "When I ran into them accidentally at Prague last time...." or "Franco is not really a bad sort. He once told me...." or "At that time I was in a hurry to catch the plane but neither Chiang Kai-shek nor Madame Chiang would let me go without supper, and their chief of air force phoned the airport to delay the plane for three hours." He is a walking autograph book. He refers to most celebrities by their first names so that most times you may not recognize to whom he is referring. If he says Ingrid or Cecil or Harry, he is quite clear in his head whom he means, though his listeners may take time to sort out the famous star, the famous producer, President of America. America? You will never catch this gentleman using the word. He will always refer to it as the States. "When I was in the States...." You, a simpleton, are likely to think that unless you say U.S.A. or America in an obvious heavy style, you will not be understood (remembering your political-science definition that a state is one which has an area, population and government, and that there are thousands of states in the world), but this man has no such doubt. He has a mind free from any kind of misgiving or doubt. His conviction is that what is clear to him ought to be clear to the rest of mankind. What he does not notice is not worth noticing. His talk has always an international background. He is a product of too much travel. He is the sort to say, "My second son is in Manchester, training in textiles....My daughter is in Cambridge; I put her there directly after she passed her high school; I had to rush up to see about her admission personally although I was busy in Rio de Janiero at that time. After all we must take the trouble to settle our children's lives.... I have always been keen on my children getting a cosmopolitan outlook. Our standards must become international in all matters."

The air-travel bag has now taken the place of the Kaiser-i-Hind medal or the old decorations of Dewan Bahadur. The maha superior man's contempt for the slow-witted land-or sea-travellers is unbounded. He is ever trying to impress on them the casual ease with which he performs his journey. "Do you know I never carry anything? I go on with just a *dhoti* and a *banian*...." You are astounded. You thought in your innocence that one had to put on a tie or a long coat or things like that. It is all for lesser folk; here is the man who has a feeling of ownership with the airlines. "You mean to say you can go with a *dhoti?*" you ask innocently. "Why not? It is our national dress; I always like to attend even formal dinners.... For instance, when I was in Paris last year.... where many ambassadors were present, I sat down to dinner in shirt and *dhoti*. People stared at me, that is all; let them, he concludes. He likes to have people stare at him; in fact, he thrives on it. If others value elaborate dressing up he at once advocates simplicity. He is bound to strike out an independent line for himself. "Don't imagine we can go up before others like clowns. We have to observe certain proprieties, remember." He advocates an international outlook till a lot of others also joined his way of thinking, when he might suddenly say, "All this talk of internationalism is all very well, but we must first think of own homes....I have seen these folk at conferences; each is interested in his own affairs. I tell you they are no good. We must set our house in order before we think of anything else."

Headache

Of all the blessings conferred on mankind by a benign providence, the most useful is the headache. But for it there would be many great embarrassments in life. Factual explanations are not always either palatable or feasible. In such circumstances a headache acts as a sort of password. I remember at school, the very first letter-writing lesson I was taught was: "Respected sir, as I am suffering from headache, I request you to grant me leave...." I always wondered what made our headache as an excuse, even in a specimen letter. I think it was very much in everybody's thoughts, useful alike to the pupils, and their master. For us a headache was a boon. We used to have drill after school hours (which I still think is an unfair and undesirable practice). We disliked this hour. On the drill ground almost all appeared to be afflicted with "Splitting headache, sir," and our drill instructor put an end to it by decreeing one day. "Those suffering from headache will hold up their arms." It raised our hopes, but he added, "Since I wish to detain them for some special exercises that will cure their headache." Not one lifted his arm, at which the instructor declared, "Now all of you take off your coats and get through the usual drill. I am glad to find that the class is going to exercise in full strength today."

Headache gives the sufferer a touch of importance. All other aches sound crude and physiological, and sensitive people would not mention them. No other ailment can be so openly mentioned with impunity. You could mention headache in the most elegant social gathering and no one would be shocked by it. The only expression which is superior to headache is 'indisposition'. Whenever I see that word I wonder what it exactly means. It is one of those curious words (like 'inanity' which has no 'anity'), which do not necessarily mean the opposite without the 'in'. You cannot say, "Owing to disposition I am not taking the medicine," whereas you can say,

"Owing to indisposition I called in the doctor." What exactly in this indisposition? I have never been able to understand it, except that it sounds very well in press notes or health bulletins or in messages from eminent men to gatherings to which they have been invited. 'Indisposition' cannot generally be said by the person directly afflicted. It does not sound very well for anyone to write directly, "Owing to indisposition, I am not attending your meeting." It sounds unconvincing. It sounds better in the third person. It implies that the gentleman is an eminent one, has a secretary or a deputy who can speak for him. "Mr. so-and-so regrets his inability to attend the meeting today owing to indisposition." People will understand and accept the statement and will not question, "What is that indisposition? Is he down with flu or malaria or cold or rheumatism? I know a doctor who can cure it...." On the contrary, they just accept it at its face value and pass on to the next item. Indisposition could be used only at a particular level, not by all and sundry. A schoolboy who says, "As I'm indisposed, I want to be let off," will have his ear twisted for his precociousness.

I think I should shock mankind if I suddenly said. "There is no such thing as headache or indisposition. It is all just an excuse, an elegant falsehood, for have I not seen dozens of headache cases walking or driving about gaily, to be seen everywhere except where they ought to be at the particular hour!" The world is not yet ripe for such outspokenness. A man cannot say, "I am not attending the meeting today since I don't feel like it." A clerk who writes to his master, "I am not attending office today because I am not inclined to look at any paper today," will lose his job, whereas he is quite at liberty to say that he is down with headache.

A headache is essential for maintaining human relationships in working order. We cannot do without it either at home or in public. In any normal household one can see a variety of headaches, curtaining off a variety of uncomfortable situations. The mother-in-law, who forswears her food on the plea of a splitting head, is clearly not on the best of terms, at least for that day, with the daughter-in-law or her son; the son, who pleads headache, may want to keep away not only his friends and officers but would like his wife not to press him too much to fulfil his promise to take her out; the little man who pleads headache has definitely skipped his homework, and would like the tutor to be sent away. As I have already said, it will not do at all to be bluntly truthful on all occasions. The sign of cultured existence is not to pry too deeply, but accept certain words at their face value, as expressed by the speaker.

Headache has become such a confirmed habit that a huge trade has developed in providing a cure for it. Some people feel lost unless they carry a tube of some headache remedy in their pockets all the time, and opticians give glasses guaranteed to relieve headache. These are instances to show that mankind easily begins to believe in its myths.

The Critical Faculty

The critical faculty is most potent one in the human make-up. Its pervasiveness and force have not properly been recognized because, like breathing, it is so much a part and parcel of human activity. The difference between a simpleton and an intelligent man, according to the man who is convinced that he is of the latter category, is that the former wholeheartedly accepts all things that he sees and hears while the latter never admits anything except after a most searching scrutiny. He imagines his intelligence to be a sieve of closely woven mesh through which nothing but the finest can pass.

The critical sense is essential for keeping social transactions in a warm state. Otherwise life would become very dull and goody-goody. The critical faculty is responsible for a lot of give and take in life. It increases our awareness of our surroundings; it sounds dignified no doubt, but it seems also to mean that we can watch someone else's back better than our own! We never know our own defects till they are pointed out of us, and even then we need not accept them. We always question the *bona fides* of the man who tells us unpleasant facts. On the surface it is all very well to say, "I want an honest criticism; that will help me, not blind compliment." I wish people would mean it. In my experience I have met only one person who took my views literally and tore up the story that he had brought to me for an opinion. He could very well have turned round and said, "The stories you write are certainly no better. I see no reason why I should accept your judgment," but he tore up his manuscript into minute bits and scattered them out of the window, and turned his attention to other things immediately, and later became a distinguished anthropologist.His book on the subject, a respectable demy size volume priced at thirty shillings, is about to be published by a famous press. I sometimes flatter myself with the thought that perhaps it was my critical sense that helped the young man turn his energies to a vocation that suited him best. However, it is an isolated insance and not likely to occur again. No one ever accepts criticism so cheerfully. Neither the man who utters it nor the one who invites it really means it. Any artistic effort has a lot of ego behind it and can never admit criticism. The only two categories that a writer or a musician recognizes are those that admire and those that do not have the wits to understand. It takes several years of hardening experience for a writer to become really indifferent to what others say about his work, but at the beginning of his career every writer watches for reviews of his book with a palpitating heart. If the review is all praise, then the author feels that the reviewer is a clever fellow full of subtle understanding, but if it is adverse he cries. "These fellows lack elementary intelligence and discrimination! I don't know why some papers give the reviewing work to their office boys."

I have discovered that a lot of interest that people show in each other's affairs comes just out of a desire to exercise their critical faculties and to measure how far below one's own the other's achievement is. It is particularly applicable to those in the same profession. It is only an engineer who can properly deprecate another engineer's handiwork. I have noticed that anyone who has recently built a house shows an undue zeal in inspecting every new house that he can possibly reach. It gives him a lot of pleasure to be able to say, "Oh lord! How that contractor has cheated the poor man! What a lot of space they have wasted, and what hideous pillars on the verandah! I wish he had seen my house before starting on his own!"

The democratic machinery is kept going through the exercise of the critical faculty. If someone should ask, "How should an opposition function?" the best answer would be, "In the manner of a traditional mother-in-law who watches the performance of household work by a daughter-in-law and follows her about with her comments."

Beauty and the Beast

It has become a fashion to choose the beauty queen of the year in each place, but her majesty's reign is strictly limited in tenure and jurisdiction. For instance, the beauty queen of 1951 may be forgotten an hour after the 31st of December, I suppose. Or the beauty queen of, say, California, may hardly receive recognition in Calcutta. Presently we may have a beauty queen selected for each month, who will not be looked at when her hour has passed. A surprising philosophical admission seems to be implied in this scheme—the utter evanescence of all appearance. It seems a rash, impractical activity all the same. Even for the briefest duration, how could anyone fix 'the most beautiful?' "The young one is a golden pet for even the cow," says the Tamil proverb. What a parent sees, others definitely don't. It is not merely confined to appearance, but also to accomplishments and quality. "My little fellow, you know, is very smart; oh, that fellow is terribly mischievous." This may be said of an infant which still lies flat on its back, kicks its legs and emits gurgling sounds. The fond parents are able to interpret so much in that sound and movement and look, although to a rank outsider it may mean nothing. A parent is openly boastful when his offspring is only a few months old, and he keeps it up till the child is five or six years old. Thereafter he adopts a little reticence, and gradually gives up openly boasting of his son's unique qualities. The parents may be reticent, but you may be sure they have not, inwardly, moved a jot from the standpoint they assumed when they declared to a polite-minded rank outsider, "See him, don't you think he is too clever and understanding for his age? And I'm sure he is the most lovely." And the rank outsider peeped into the crib with the appropriate show of agreement, although having his own views in the matter.

But a rank outsider has no place in the assessment of beauty of either personality or person. That is why any elaborate beauty contest, with judges, fills me with wonderment. How can beauty be judged by means of tape and weighing machine? Perception of beauty seems to be an entirely personal matter, peculiar to each individual and even to each country. This is the reason why we remain unmoved when we see in our newspapers photographs of beauty queens of other lands. What is beautiful in one country or in one part of the country may be viewed differently in another. Among certain aborigines piercing the upper lip and rivetting on it several layers of metal discs is considered indispensable for any lady of social standing. In our part of the country nose-ornaments are very popular, and not so in the north; green eyes and red hair are probably considered masterly touches of nature in the West, while we think they handicap a girl's future.

It's not only in a perfectly measuring figure, but also in features that real beauty is to be perceived; and this perception may turn out to be a highly individual view. For this reason a photo-finish for deciding beauty is not feasible. The eye of the camera, though perfect in judging neck-to-neck of horses, is no better judge than the human eye, where human beauty is concerned, for the simple reason that its data, once again, will have to be verified and accepted only by us. The camera cannot be an absolute instrument of perception. Sometimes people look better than their photographs and sometimes photographs are better than the originals. It is for this reason that any astute would-be bride-groom refuses to be led away by photographs when he has to make up his mind, but insists upon holding over his decision till he has a chance to view the girl, which becomes really a turning point in any young man's life. It is all, as anybody knows, elaborately staged and arranged. The girl is decked and dressed in her best. She is induced by her parents and sisters to come forward and show herself properly. The young man has to watch the curtain or the doorway through which she has to come with the greatest anxiety and curiosity, and yet not seem to watch for the sake of propriety. The girl may come up and take a seat opposite, but it does not help the young man. He is afraid to stare and judge. He is for the moment a beauty judge, but handicapped by proprieties which will not let him stare and assess. All his impressions will have to be finalized by darting looks and side glances, while keeping up a general flow of conversation with a lot of uninteresting people around. When the interview is over, the man is tortured with the feeling that he wasted precious moments which ought to have been spent in proper scrutiny. "I didn't notice whether her nose was slightly arched or straight." He wishes he could have another look before saying yes or no. But few get such a chance. And even if a man says yes with a lot of secret misgivings, he never displays any regret later in life. He has no doubt that he has made the right choice. It is this that led a cynic to define beauty as something we derive when we have got used to the beast. There must be some degree of truth in this statement. Otherwise no one except a handful of universally acclaimed paragons can ever have a chance of marrying and settling in life.

It'd be interesting if somebody sponsored a world ugliness contest. If ugliness, too, could have a commercial value I'm sure it would find its sponsors: a sweater-making company which can declare, "We will make you look like the devil," a draper or outfitter who can say, "We will make you look like a tub," a railway or a bus service claiming, "A two-hour journey on our lines will transform you into an ogre," a film producer looking for ghoulish players or a hat-manufacturing company intent upon making people look like fools. In due course many may sigh for that bulbous nose or the tapering forehead which gave the winner of the contest his holiday in Europe, his photograph in the papers and the film contract at the end of it all.

Memory

It is said of Faraday that he was so absent-minded that he was constantly writing on slips of papers reminders of what he should be doing next. His pockets were stuffed with hundreds of these slips; there they rested untouched, for there was no way of reminding him of the existence of the slips. Men of genius are particularly absent-minded. They have reason for it; their minds are engaged in noble pursuits. It is understandable. But why should we ordinary mortals also be afflicted with it? Faces of persons: "Your face is familiar," is the elegant formula which covers an unpardonable lapse. A face seen every day behind a counter in a bank or a post-office becomes unrecognizable in the street. "He is a pleasant and helpful person, but where have I seen him before?" you wonder secretly. It would be a pity if this caused any bitterness, for no one is to be blamed for it. We are all at the mercy of an erratic faculty: memory. It proves particularly treacherous where proper names are concerned. You go about feeling confident that all the names you need are properly labelled and stocked in your mind, and that you can call up any at will. The occasion arises. In the middle of a dignified and fluent sentence you realize that you cannot get at a particular name. Your ideas scatter, and you become incoherent while you frenziedly pursue the name that recedes like a chimera. Others look on and smile half sceptically as you tear your hair and wail. "It was on my lips a moment ago." You are now in an awkward situation, as if you had been tripped from behind. Later, when there is no occasion for it, the name will intrude upon your attention and will not leave till you repeat it irrelevantly.

There are numerous suggestions as to how memory can be developed. I have found none of these tips practicable. Most of them are based on what may be called associative thinking. It works in the following manner: I am unable to remember 14. All that I have to do now is to remember 13 on one side and 15 on the other. Or, taking another instance, if I cannot recollect where I left my bunch of keys, all that I must do is to sit back and mentally go over every place I visited in the last three or four hours. This exercise will leave an ordinary man so exhausted at the end that he will have little interest in his lost possession, and by itself it seems such a feat of memory that those who are capable of it are not likely to misplace things.

The child under four is acknowledged on all counts to be an ideal being—a creature who has an almost unearthly delight in living. He is able to attain this grand state because he is unaware of the existence of the thing called memory. He has no clear-cut notions of past and future. Many of his plans and aspirations are placed in a tomorrow. He hardly remembers anything that has happened in the last hour. If he only remembers the admonitions given him by his elders, the physical ills he has suffered and the frustration of his little life, he would cease to be a child. However, he is not left in this happy condition very long. Presently the home tutor comes along with his multiplication table and rules of grammar; henceforth he must study and remember. From this moment existence becomes an endless hide-and-seek between him and memory till old age overtakes him. By the time he reaches seventy-five his mind has turned itself into a vast jumble of memories which makes the immediate life around entirely unacceptable to him.

It is for this reason, I suppose, that poets have always cried for the mercy of oblivion. For, in our present stage of evolution, we have not yet understood the precise use of this power. It is like having a storage battery on hand for no special purpose. The result is that we constantly suffer from too much of it or too little of it, and have no clear notion as to whether we are the masters of this faculty or its servants.

Street Names

In the India of post-1947, the most marked feature is the passion for changing names of streets, towns, parks and squares. Our men in authority seem to have come to the sudden conclusion that old names, like old clothes, are not good. We must first understand that a street is not born with a name. It is given one, say, by a donor who financed something or the other or a municipal councillor who had the pluck to manoeuvre his name into it, or the first gentleman who dared to take his residence there. Through a street name one often seeks to immortalize a personality. This immortality, however, is more imagined than achieved. In the fancy of the man whose name is given to a street the public, as he thinks, will stop to ask every time the name board is seen, "Who is this Shri X.Y.Z., after whom this place is named? Must have been an outstanding personality to have his name gracing this locality." But actually usage is deadening. However grandly a name might have been devised, it is hardly noticed after some time. A Minister, of course, might have presided over the function and might have unveiled the name with his own hand with a speech dwelling on the importance of streets in the five-year plan, and the important role played by Shri X.Y.Z. in the nation's life, with garlands slipping over heads, and with nearly a public holiday thrown in. But with all this, it is unfortunate but true that in course of time every passer-by will see the name of Shri X.Y.Z. but will not bother to know who he might be.

Generally speaking, a name grows up with a street and no one bothers to think what it might signify. All the significance is forgotten in the very first week following the naming ceremony. The friends and members of the family of the man may remember it for some time, and feel a glow of pride whenever they see it or think of it. But even they will get used to it in course of time, and they, as well as everyone else, will look at the name coldly, till it sheds all its significance and association,

94

and the name stands by itself on its own authority, a pure name. This may not be so tragic after all. It is only a name which acquires a status, independent of all its associations and significance, that could be said to possess real vitality. For years I have been seeing a certain Ramaswami Street. Till this moment it has never occurred to me to question who he might be. It may refer to an eminent local personage, or a national figure, or an unknown, forgotten municipal councillor, or a bullock-cart driver who fell off his seat, or a first-class mathematics student who was denied a seat in engineering and stood on his head till his grievance was redressed. None of it is remembered when the name is uttered; it is just Ramaswami. No one could ever associate the street with any other title. Ramaswami becomes the street. It begins to sound almost like a common name, something like door, chair or bottle, and no one bothers to analyse why these have come to be named so. No one goes into the origin of these terms. They are just accepted as they are. When a proper name becomes common as a common name, then it may be said to have vitality, if not immortality. People must not bother to ask who was that person.

While proper names are thus reduced to insignificance, think of the actual common names which somehow come to pass. No one gives them a thought. Katcheri Road never provokes any one to ask, 'Whose *Katcheri?* Vocal or instrumental or what *Katcheri?"* It's just accepted. Or Salai Street or Solai Street never provokes anyone to demand the sight of the lush vegetation that the appellation conjures up in one. There is above all the instance of Broadway. I do not think anyone has so far demanded that the irony of this term be ended and that the place be given its rightful name. It is accepted without question, not because of its rational association, but because it seems to have grown up with it, however meaningless it may be. And of couse there is the classic Barbers' Bridge (which I hope now is not going to be changed to Bharat Bridge or something similar).

There must not be too much rationale in the naming of a street. This is just where members of municipal bodies and perfervid patriots go wrong. They attempt historical aptness or the righting of a historical wrong. This is generally seen in changing foreign names. Smith Lane, for instance, is always in danger of being attacked by righteous-minded persons. Some-one will suddenly discover that Smith was an odious colonial administrator and transform the lane, with every pomp, to Jagadguru Lane. Apart from confounding a familiar, used landmark, it only achieves one object: it gives an extra-job to a signboard painter. If the authority thinks that it is likely to gratify the Jagadguru, he is grievously mistaken. The Jagadguru can well afford to ignore this honour. He has reached an eminence where this honour cannot in any way be taken as an addition to his glory. Nor, on the other hand, is this change likely to make the ghost of the old despot go pale with shame and remorse. Even if it does affect the ghost, would it be legitimate to achieve the end in a country nurtured on *ahimsa*, the essence of which is that we should not hate our enemies, much less our dead enemies? On the contrary, the despot's name should be left untouched just to show how his despotism has proved futile in the long run. Acrimony, contemporaneous-ly or in retrospect, can have no place in a nation nurtured on *ahimsa*. And will you remember, you passionate changer of street names, the tradition thus started by you may be continued by someone else coming to your place later, whose views may be different from yours? He may take down the very names which you put up with such veneration now, elevate his own candidate and give out an equally rational explanation for it. And then what is to happen to the man who tried to find his way about the town depending upon familiar landmarks?

From

RELUCTANT GURU

Reluctant Guru

When I accepted an invitation to become a Visiting Professor at a certain mid-Western University, I had had no clear notion as to what it meant. I asked myself again and again what does a Visiting Professor do. I also asked several of my friends in the academic world the same question. No one could give me a concrete or a convincing answer and so I contented myself with the thought that a Visiting Professor just visits and professes and if he happens to be in the special category of 'D.V.P.' (Distinguished Visiting Professor) he also tries to maintain and flourish his distinguishing qualities. Well, all that seemed to suit me excellently.

I had plunged into the role after warning my sponsors in the initial stages of our correspondence that I was a mere novice in academic matters and that it'd be up to them to see that I did not make a fool of myself on their campus.

So, on the first morning, I reported myself at the English Department of the University. The Chairman of the Department who had arranged my visit was a distinguished scholar and critic, who, among other things, had also made a detailed, deep study of my writing.

I asked him what I should do now and he kept asking in his turn what I would like to do, the only definite engagement for the day he was aware of being that I was to be photographed at two o'clock. I sat brooding.

'Yesterday this time, Bangalore...Bombay...Rome...London...New York...or was it the day before? Time gets lost in space.' I was still jet-dazed after thirty-six hours in the air.

He called up his secretary and told her, 'Here is Narayan. Please give him a room where he can feel comfortable, meet people or read or write as he may like. Please also find out if any of the English classes want him, and schedule his visits.' So on the first day I had nothing much to do except pose outside the building for a photographer against the signpost announcing

'English Dept'.

Most of the days following, I was left free to walk, think, or read, and generally live as I pleased.

The secretary busied herself and ultimately produced a time-table for me. She would telephone me in my room to say, '11.35 tomorrow, Professor —'s class at—hall—'.

'Where is it?' I would ask, slightly worried how to locate it in this vast sprawling campus and reach it in time, punctuality being my nightmare.

'It's on 52nd and anyway you don't bother about it. A car will come to fetch you.' She arranged it all with precision and forethought, not demanding more than a couple of hours a week of my time in the coming weeks.

On stepping into my very first class I felt startled, as it consisted of elderly women, each one holding a copy of *The Guide* in her hand.

I was pleased no doubt at finding my book in so many hands, but I also felt uneasy. If they cross-examined me on my book, I should feel lost; they had the advantage over me of being up-to-date with the details of my story. I stiffened into a defensive attitude, and became wary, as I took my seat.

I was also struck with their enthusiasm—elderly women who doubtless had their families, homes, children and grandchildren (one member was eighty-six years old) to mind, but who still found the time to take a seat in a class-room and study English literature, which was how my book was classified.

I sat wondering where to begin and what to say. But luckily for me their regular professor who had fetched me, eased the situation with an introductory speech, and straightaway invited the members of the class to ask questions. This is always a good method as it gives an audience something to do instead of sitting back, passively watching the speaker's predicament. One member asked as usual whether I had based my novel on some actual experience or if it was pure fiction. A familiar question, which I generally answer evasively, since I myself do not know; and also I don't see how it should make any difference to the reader. Next question was if the town Malgudi (the setting of my novels) was imaginary or real. I played the ball back by asking what was the difference between the two. Next I was asked if India was full of saints, and whether the hero of *The Guide*, who is mistaken for a saint, and later compelled to become one, was typical, and if my novel itself was 'typical' of India (Typical—did it imply that my readers expect the majority of the 550 million citizens of India (as it was over a decade ago) to go through a phase similar to the one portrayed in my novel?) I had to repeat here, and later, everywhere that a novel is about an individual living his life in a world imagined by the author, performing a set of actions (up to a limit) contrived by the author. But to take a work of fiction as a sociological study or a social document could be very misleading. My novel *The Guide* was not about the saints or the pseudo-saints of India, but about a particular person. I do not think that my explanation carried any conviction as they continued to ask in every class, outside the class, at the quadrangle, the university centre, the roadside or anywhere, the same question. Added to this the city newspaper took a special interest in my visit and featured me and my work. A reporter interviewed me, and tried to elicit my views of life after death, which happened to be the theme of my novel *The English Teacher* (known in the U.S. as *Grateful to Life and Death*). I was asked if I believed in death. I was asked if I thought it possible to communicate with spirits. I was asked if I had seen a ghost, if I was prone to mystic experience. I answered the questions candidly, emphasizing the fact that I wrote fiction. When the interview appeared in the paper I found it charmingly written but over-emphasizing my mystic aspect! This led to a very complex situation for me during the rest of my sojourn on that campus. More and more people began to ask, 'Do you believe in mysticism?' 'Can anyone practise yoga?' 'What are the steps to a mystic state?' The words—mysticism, metaphysics, philosophy, yoga and ghost contacts—all came to be mixed up. At first it was amusing but day after day when I found people on the campus looking on me with awe and wonder, perhaps saying to themselves, 'There goes the man who holds the key to a mystic life!' I began to despair how I could ever rise to that sublime level. Apart from the students, I realized that even some of the staff members were affected by this notion. A senior professor of the English Department approached me once to ask if I would meet her students. I agreed, since that was the purpose of my sojourn on the campus. Nearer the time of the actual engagement, I met her again to work out the details, 'What am I expected to do in your class?' I asked.

She replied promptly, 'My students want to hear you on Indian mysticism.'

I told her point blank, 'I know nothing about it.'

'That shouldn't matter at all', she said.

'Of course it matters a great deal to me. When I go to a class I should like to speak on a subject which I know or at least have a pretence of knowing. I do not wish to parade my ignorance in a class-room.'

She seemed to think that it was an extraordinary piece of diffidence on my part and said encouragingly, 'Please, half-an-hour will be enough. You can tell them anything you like about mysticism, just for thirty minutes.'

'Not even for half-a-minute. Why did you commit me to this engagement?'

Her answer was startling. 'Because they have demanded it. They want you to talk on Indian mysticism.'

Two points emerged from this conversation:

(1) The word 'demand' arising from the students' side as to what was to be taught. (2) Mysticism.

These were the real pivotal points on which the entire academic situation seemed to revolve. I heard later that the students' representatives met the faculty members in order to specify what they wished to be taught in the class-rooms. They wanted to brighten up (and also broaden) English literary studies, with a lot of interesting; though not relevant, additions to their reading lists. This was the basis of their demand for Indian mysticism from me. I had a chance to observe how some teachers were trying to rise to the occasion. I knew a couple of young men from India, doing their post-graduate course in English, also holding assistantships, who spoke on a different theme each day to their students. One day it'd be Fitzgerald's translation of *Omar Khayyam,* another day Ramakrishna, or Vivekananda, a third day on Yoga or the theory of incarnation, a fourth day on Buddhism, and on the fifth back to English literature. It was amazing with what agility they managed all this, while the seniors pored over 'black literature' and tried to include it in their talks, discussions and seminars. In all this process there was an apparent widening of knowledge, but it actually produced shallowness. I could not help wondering if all this show of adaptability and resilience on the part of the teacher was not creating an amorphous, diffuse academic climate and if they were not becoming responsible for creating a set of hollow minds, echoing the mere sound of book titles, and regarding themselves as being versatile. Finally I questioned them, how in such a world of hotchpotch studies any examination could be conducted. I realized immediately that I was sounding hopelessly antiquated, as promptly came the reply that the examinee could frame his own questions and write the answers. I did not know if this was a universal practice or only peculiar to this university. Or if this particular Indian lecturer was joking about it. In any case, I found that these two young men were extremely popular. One of them grew a tiny beard and the other left untended his nape-draping tresses, and both looked and sounded so convincing as versatile semi-(demi)-mystics that they were keenly sought after by their students. Their weekends were crowded with social activities, in addition to a regular schedule of dating. I asked. 'What is dating? How far does one go?'

'It depends, anything from sitting around eating and drinking to making love', came the reply.

I asked, 'What of the responsibilities after dating?'

They replied, 'None. I and my friend have decided not to go steady under any circumstances, but marry only in India after we get back.' I visited their apartment and found it bare, with a few rolls of mat on the floor; and books all over the place. I suppose there was an aroma of incense. One of them constantly said, 'I am much interested in Yoga and am teaching my boys Yoga.'

I asked him, 'Have you studied Patanjali's *Yoga sutra?*'

He looked a little bewildered and said, 'Not yet but I will...' He finally said, 'What does it matter what I read or teach? Whatever book I may recommend they will read only Vatsyayana's *Kama-Sutra*. The campus book store can hardly keep up with the demand, boys and girls devour this book and seem to know nothing else about India, nor care.'

Whether through *Kama-Sutra* or mysticism, India is very much in everybody's thoughts, particularly among the American youth. And this was not a passing phase or a mere affectation. I realized presently that there was much validity in this search and I met many young men here and there, invited them to my room, and answered their questions about India. I give here a composite report of my talk to various persons at different times.

Young friend (I said), perhaps you think that all Indians are spiritually preoccupied. We aren't, we have a large background of religion and plenty of inner resources, but normally we also have to be performing ordinary tasks, such as working, earning, living and breeding. In your view, perhaps, you think that in an Indian street, you can see bearded men floating about in a state of levitation. Far from it. We have traffic, crowds, shops, pimps, pickpockets, policemen and what not as in any other country. We have our own students' agitations—but they are for different causes, sometimes political, sometimes personal and sometimes academic, and sometimes inexplicable. Your opposite number in our country would not be wearing beads and beards and untouched long hair as you do (how smartly your Barbers' Association withdrew a rather rash resolution to increase the rate for a haircut-from 2.50 to 3 dollars!), but tight pants and coloured shirts and 'Beatles' crop-cut. The Indian student would not normally bother about eternity, but about his immediate employment prospects after graduation. You have to realize that unemployment among the educated classes is a grim reality in our country; and a young person has to overcome this deficiency before aspiring for the luxuries of a mystic state.

Of course, you are fed up with affluence, gadgets, mobility and organization, and he is fed up with poverty, manual labour, stagnation and disorganization. Your search is for a 'guru' who can promise you instant mystic elation; whereas your counterpart looks for a Foundation Grant. The young person in my country would sooner learn how to organize a business or manufacture an atom bomb or an automobile than how to stand on one's head.

As a matter of fact, if you question him, you will find that our young man has not given any serious thought to Yoga and such subjects. Perhaps at a later date he may take to it when his more materialistic problems are over and when he begins to note that it's quite the fashion in your part of the world. At the moment the trend appears to be that he is coming in your direction, and you are going in his. So, logically speaking, in course of time, you may have to come to India for technology and the Indian will have to come to your country for spiritual research.

The belief in my spiritual adeptness was a factor that could not be easily shaken. I felt myself in the same situation as Raju, the hero of my *Guide* who was mistaken for a saint and began to wonder at some point himself if a sudden effulgence had begun to show in his face. I found myself in a similar situation. My telephone rang at five o'clock one morning and I scrambled out of my bed. The man at the other end announced himself as a scientist, a research scholar, and said, 'Do you know what has happened today? The Chairman of our department summoned us and announced that he was not going to renew our assistantships next term , which may mean that I cut short my stay and return to India. Do you know if this will happen?' I could not understand what he was saying or why. I even wondered if I might be listening to a telephone in a dream!

'How should I know', I asked and added, 'But my immediate curiosity is to know why you have thought fit to call me at this hour?'

He answered, 'Don't you get up at four for your meditations? I thought that at this hour, you'd be in a state of mind to know the future.'

Evidently this scientist had caught the general trend in the atmosphere. While I could appreciate an average American's notion that every Indian was a mystic, I was rather shocked in this instance, since I expected an Indian himself to know better. But here was this young man from India convinced that I was an astrologer and mystic combined. He dogged my steps. Although he gave up calling me at dawn, he followed me about with requests to impart to him the secrets of my attainments, to show him the way, to tell him whether he was destined to get his doctorate, whether his wife's impending confinement (in India) would be safely gone through and so on and so forth. Actually, after lunch one afternoon, he took me aside to ask, 'What should I do to get a glimpse of Goddess Kali? Will she appear before me?' in the tone of one who was trying to know the T.V. Channel on which a particular show would be coming. When I denied any knowledge of it myself, he just looked pained, but he also looked determined to get at me ultimately when he would gather in both hands all the secrets of meditation, astrology, and spiritual powers that I now kept away from him, for reasons best known to a 'guru' of my stature.

105

My Educational Outlook

My educational outlook had always differed from those of my elders and well-wishers. And after five or more decades, my views on education remain unchanged, although in several other matters my philosophy of life has undergone modification. If a classification is called for I may be labelled 'anti-educational'. I am not averse to enlightenment, but I feel convinced that the entire organization, system, outlook and aims of education are hopelessly wrong from beginning to end; from primary first year to Ph.D., it is just a continuation of an original mistake. Educational theories have become progressively high-sounding, sophisticated and jargon-ridden (like many other subjects aspiring to the status of a science), but in practice the process of learning remains primitive. In the field of education, the educator and the educatee seemed to be arrayed in opposite camps, each planning how best to overwhelm the other.

In my boyhood, the teacher never appeared in public without the cane in hand. I used to think that one's *guru* was born clutching a cane in his right hand while the left held a pinch of snuff between the thumb and forefinger. He took a deep inhalation before proceeding to flick the cane on whatever portion of myself was available for the purpose. I really had no idea what I was expected to do or not do to avoid it. I could never imagine that a simple error of calculation in addition, subtraction or multiplication (I never knew which) would drive anyone hysterical.

I notice nowadays a little girl at home always playing the school-game in a corner of the verandah, but never without a flat, wooden foot-rule in hand, which she flourishes menacingly at the pupils assembled in her phantasmagoric class-room. On investigation, I found that the cane, being discredited, has yielded place to the foot-rule, especially in 'convent' schools. The foot-rule, has the advantage over the primitive birch of mauling without marking (which could count as an achievement in torturing technique) and it also possesses the innocent appearance of a non-violent, pedagogic equipment. A modern educator, naturally, has to adapt his ways to modern circumstances, and put away obsolete weapons. The flat-scale is employed only at the primary stage: at higher levels of education, torments to a young soul are devised in subtler forms progressively; admissions, textbooks, and examinations are the triple weapons in the hands of an educator today. In June every father and son go through a purgatory of waiting at the doors of every college. Provision of seats planned in a grand musical-chair-manner keeps every applicant running frantically about, unless, as in certain well-geared technical colleges, the parent could make a bid in the style of a competitor at a toddy auction of old times. Five thousand rupees for an engineering seat is considered quite reasonable nowadays. I recently met a hopeful father who had just written a cheque for ten thousand rupees for two sons in the first year B.E. in a certain college. He is a businessman fully aware of the debit and credit value of his action, and must have undertaken the financial sacrifice after due consideration. Those that cannot afford it have to queue up in the corridors of colleges, hunt and gather recommendations, plead, appeal, canvas, and lose weight until they find (or do not find) their names in the list of admissions. At the next stage the student will once again queue up, beg, beat about, and appeal—for textbooks this time (especially if it happens to be a 'Nationalized Textbook',which may not be available until the young man is ready to leave the college). Finally the examination. In a civilized world the examination system should have no place. It is a culmination of all sadistic impulses. Learned commissions and conferences meet and speculate why young men are always on the verge of blasting street lamps and smashing furniture. In technical language it is known as 'student indiscipline'. It has always amused one to note the concern the problem causes and how it always ends in woolly, banal resolutions such as: students should be given compulsory military training, asked to perform compulsory rural service, and compulsory what not. Students should keep out of politics (a great many others ought to keep out of politics too; in any case, it's too late to suggest this as students were inveigled into politics not so long ago in our history). The real wrecker of

107

young nerves, however, is the examination system. It builds up a tension and an anxiety neurosis day by day all the year round, all through one's youth, right into middle age (for some). I remember the desperate nervousness that debilitated me from January to April every year. After four decades, I still jump off my bed from nightmares of examination. I feel convinced that the examination system was devised by a satanic mind. The anxiety and sleeplessness, the gamble over possible questions, the hush-hush and grimness of the examination hall, the invigilators (the very word has a Grand Inquisitorial sound) watching like wardens at the gallows, the awful ritual of breaking open the seal of the examination papers, the whole thing now appears ridiculously ritualistic and out of tune with a civilization in which man is capable of taking a stroll thousands of miles above the earth towards the moon.

If I became a Vice-Chancellor, my first act would be to abolish all secrecy that surrounds question papers. Instead of permitting wild speculations or, as it happens nowadays, advance sale of questions in the black market, I would take advertisement space in newspapers and publish the questions in every subject, adding under each a credit line: 'Set by Professor so and so'. I would not hesitate to announce with courage the names of those who are going to evaluate the answers and decree failures and successes. I would add a postscript to every question paper: 'If you cannot answer any of the above questions, don't despair. Remember your examiners are not infallible and may not do better if placed in your predicament. Your inability to answer will in no way be a reflection on your intelligence. We apologize for the embarrassment. Also remember, if you expect a first class and do not secure even passing marks, don't rave against your examiner, he is also a human being subject to fluctuating moods caused by unexpected domestic quarrels or a bad digestion just when he is sitting down to correct your papers; also, not being an adding machine, occasionally he may slip and arrive at 7 while totalling 8 and 3. Please forgive him.'

At a certain university in America I met an advanced soul. He taught Political Science. One month before the annual examination, he cyclostyled (or 'xeroxed') the questions and distributed them among his students, who thereafter spent nearly twelve hours a day in the library in the 'assigned reading room'. I described to him our habits of hiding the questions till the last moment. He remarked, 'Why on earth keep the boys in the dark over questions that after all concern them?' I explained, 'We believe in mugging up; on an average 200 pages per subject, and fifteen subjects in a year. One who can demonstrate that he can recollect three thousand pages in the examination hall will be considered a first-class student in our country, although he need not understand a word of what he reads, or remember a syllable of what he has read after the examination. The whole aim of our education is to strain the faculty of memory...'

'Your system must have been devised before Caxton, when there was no printed book, and handwritten books were chained and guarded. Memory is not so important today. Our need is for more libraries and multiple copies. The only condition I make for my boys is that they spend at least six hours a day in the library a month before the examinations, and while writing their answers I permit them to refer to the books. My only condition is that they should write their answers within the given time.'

In my college days, I had a professor of history, who said, 'It's a pity you have failed. If you didn't know the answer, you could have written any answer you knew; if you didn't know anything of the subject, you could just have copied the question paper. If you couldn't do even that, you could have told me and I would have given you marks.'

'I didn't know you were an examiner, sir'.

'What a pity, they ought not to keep it a secret. All our troubles are due to it. After all, you have listened to my lectures for a year and that's enough.'

I had another professor from Scotland who taught us English; an enlightened soul, who marked a minimum of 35 per cent on all papers, and raised it on request. He was accessible, and amenable to reason and even to bargaining. He would ask, 'What marks do you expect to get?'

'Sixty, sir'. He would pick up the answer paper, glance through it, shake his head ruefully. 'I have given you the minimum, of course, but I'll raise it to 40.'

'Sir, please make it 52, I want at least a second class.'

'All right. I hope your interest in Literature is genuine'.

'Undoubtedly.'

Oh, but for this noble soul, I'd never have passed in English.

Here is an instance of memory without intelligence. A story of mine called 'Attila' has found its way into Pre-University prose in a certain university. I had a chance of learning how questions on the story were answered. A few answers were just line-by-line reproductions of the original, but nowhere could I see that they had realized that the story was about a dog. I was even asked once, 'When did Attila do all that you describe? I searched European history and the encyclopedia, but nowhere do I find this episode mentioned. What is the source of your information, sir?'

Two more gems to conclude this piece:

'R.K. Narayan was a romantic poetess who died in 1749.'

Long after getting his B.A. Degree, a person met his old teacher and confessed, 'I am sorry, sir, I never knew till today that Lady Macbeth was a woman.' Another teacher was asked, an hour before the literature paper, 'Is *King Lear* a tragedy or comedy, sir?'

I mention these without comment. If our educational system is not to continue as a well-endowed, elaborately organized, deep-rooted farce, a remedy must be found immediately. I dare not end this on a note suggesting crisis, as before the ink on this sentence dries, academic experts and ministers of education are likely to pack up and leave for New York, Rio de Janiero or Toronto, in accordance with an almost superstitious belief among our leaders (in all fields) that when there is a crisis at home the thing to do is to buy a round-the-world air ticket and leave.

Trigger-Happy

The word 'trigger-happy' is applied to one whose finger can pull a trigger without the mind being bothered about the consequences. Some are born that way. Of late, in most parts of the world, the air is kept lively by those who may be good at heart but who can never realize that what their fingers release may end the existence of a lot of people at the other end. The American gangster films (of course shown not in order to teach the rest of the world the finer points of gangster technique, although this is more readily appreciated than the ultimate moral, that crime does not pay) have familiarized us with trigger-happy folk. The gangster solves all his personal problems simply by shooting. If he has a passing doubt of the trustworthiness of a colleague, he clears it just by shooting; if he has to borrow urgently a motorcar in which an unwanted owner happens to be sitting, he just settles the question by pulling out his revolver; and of course professionally, too, he has to be employing it constantly. Whether for persuasion, profession, expediency, or escape, the gangster pulls the trigger with the unconcern of a health department attendant spraying D.D.T.

I have also classified another type also as trigger-happy; this type of person is less harmfully employed but he has the same faith in his gun. His virtue is that he does not shoot the human species but he is ever ready to shoot all other things that move on this earh. He is never happy unless he is planning what to shoot next. The classics that he studies are mainly arms catalogues detailing the comparative virtue of different bores; his dreams consist of tigers finished off at point-blank range, a brace of ducks falling from the sky like confetti, bison with lowered horn arrested within a split second (the posture to be immortalized by the taxidermist later): and his constant hope is that the newspapers will carry every week photographs of himself in the company of dead tigers lying at his feet. But dreams are seldom realized in real life. And this man's life becomes just one continuous effort to grasp this vision. I remember the sad, frustrated look that an enthusiast generally wears after his regular week-end efforts in the jungle. 'The thing came just within range....I was about to pull but someone seems to have breathed a little heavily....' Absolute noiselessness is the most important condition for the success of his enterprise. And so when he takes his companions for his forest expeditions, he takes particular care to see that they are the noiseless variety; it will not at all do to have persons around who are likely to sneeze or clear their throats.

It is for this reason that the hunter himself, through long contemplation, acquires a feline style in walk and general demeanour. Soft-footedness is a basic necessity. Otherwise, and this is the saddest phrase in their dictionary, the thing will 'get away'. All sorts of cunning knowledge is attributed to the beast. 'I tell you,' said an enthusiast in all earnestness, 'these things are becoming too canny nowadays. For instance, if an ordinary lorry is passing the jungle road they just laze about unconcernedly, but if the sound comes from a jeep, such as the one I drive, they just slip out of the area and go miles away.' This man's greatest worry is the 'bait'. He generally 'borrows' a sheep or a goat from the people in the nearby village, ties it up, and awaits the arrival of the tiger or the leopard. Villagers who have made a business out of this, charge exorbitantly when the bait is mauled or, as it sometimes happens, carried off before a shot is fired. In such circumstances the hunter is racked with the thought that he has only been providing a costly meal for a tiger who has not been bagged. This is a major worry for the perfervid hunter: it is both economic and psychological.

I saw a person solve this difficulty by recording the bleating of sheep and the barking of mongrels on discs and playing them on a battery-worked gramophone in the depths of a jungle, with loud-speakers concealed on tree-branches. These records are expected to attract any normal tiger with the same certainty as any live bait since the gentleman who has devised this novelty is convinced that tigers are attracted by sound and not by smell. With all this elaborate arrangement he may succeed or he may not, but in any case there can be no such thing as satiety for him. I once saw a hunter return home with four medium-sized tigers. As they lay stretched side by side in his garden, every passerby congratulated him on attaining a possible world record, but he just mumbled cheerlessly, 'It should have been actually five, but the fifth disappeared into a ditch and I could not reach it....'

'You must have seen the one that got away' is a chronic state of mind with him, and all his life he is planning to get at it. The man that is trigger-happy keeps his gun in trim for this ultimate achievement by just shooting anything that comes into his view—it may be a brightly-plumed bird just alighting on a branch, or a spotted deer, or a wild boar. It is all the same to him. But there can be no doubt that this type of man with his insatiate mind and deadly weapon is a menace to wild life.

Better Late

A young student who habitually went late to his class, when asked to explain his conduct, answered breezily, displaying the latest piece of learning, 'Better late than never, sir,' and needless to say got what he deserved. The teacher, of course, stressed the point that he would not hesitate to make it rather 'Never' than 'Late'. It would be an interesting pastime to analyse and catalogue activities that may, with impunity, be performed late and those that must be dropped altogether. There are certain things that cannot survive unpunctuality, there are certain things that are in fact all the better for a little delay and the consequent ripening. Personally speaking, I feel, under normal circumstances, most things can survive a little delay. One ought not to develop into a watch-gazer all one's waking hours. This is a purely personal philosophy. I don't expect anyone to agree with me, at any rate, not the man who has been kept waiting for an engagement.

I know a gentleman who refuses to talk to anyone that arrives late for an appointment. He has classified it under the head of wantonness, villainy, and like qualities. The gentleman owns a very expensive and accurate watch, and I fear he often looks at it sternly in order to know whether it is itself behaving property. But, unfortunately, he is in the wrong country for this attitude. In a country like ours, the preoccupation is with eternity, and little measures of time are hardly ever noticed. A wristwatch becomes a mere ornament and not a guiding factor.

I have no wish to mend this state of affairs. I think the ideal time-indicator is one on which you cannot read the time in a hurry, such as a lady's watch. Except for setting right a fracture or catching a train or the post, I feel that one might conveniently live within a certain margin of well-regulated unpunctuality, without much damage to oneself or to one's surroundings. This is the safest attitude to develop in our country: otherwise one will be inviting shocks of all kinds. The gentleman I mentioned trusts all the promises made by tradespeople and artisans, and is chagrined whenever he finds things not arriving in time. When you expect too much from others, even the most innocent carpenter can give you a shock. If you ask him when he will deliver the article, he will reply without any hesitation, 'Of course, tomorrow,' but he has said the same thing to a lot of others. You should not take him literally. The way to meet the situation is to give everyone an unasked for margin of fifteen days with possibility of extension, and keep up regular visits to see how things are going. Sooner or later the man will have done his job—for his delay is unplanned and his intentions are always to get through the job and earn a living. Only he is not able to keep time; such an attitude is inborn and we can do nothing about it. We must take it with resignation, as one must all national and international traits.

Wisdom is a thing that dawns habitually late; and no one can force its pace. How often that stinging reply, or the crushing rejoinder, or the brilliant repartee occurs fifteen minutes after the occasion, when it is past all stage of real utility and the person to whom it is to be addressed is no longer there. Even in practical affairs I suffer from delayed wisdom. There is no man who has faced greater hardship than I through lack of on-the-spot judgment. Sometimes it seems to me that a blind, unvarying denseness is preferable to the wisdom that torments us by its late arrival. Every practical transaction for me is a painful ordeal. I can't say 'No' easily. I can't say 'Yes' to anything without a legal expert looking through what I have done, and saying later to me, 'This is a pretty bad case. No harm in your saying anything you like orally, but whatever made you write all that down and sign it?'

I suddenly find myself in a position in which I can go neither backward nor forward, nor stand at ease. When I said 'Yes' and appended my signature, it never occurred to me that I was signing away my peace of mind, and my liberty of action. I signed it because I felt that the man before me might otherwise feel hurt. It might spoil the genial air all around; the air was full of smiling confidences and the utterances of mutual regard. If I showed finickiness in giving him my autograph where indicated, I feared I might look mean and calculating. I admired him when he declared: 'Do you think that if this does not turn out to our mutual satisfaction I'll be going to a court to enforce it? Not at all...I'd be the first to tear it up. It's after all, a gentleman's agreement.' I have not the wit to ask at that moment why all the elaborate conditions and terms and stamped receipt and what not, between real gentlemen. The question occurs to me very much later in the day, long after the event has passed. Fortunately for me, I've been on the brink of various involvements, but have always been pulled back in time. Fortunately, in actual life, no situation is irremediable although in theory it may be so. Otherwise I shudder to think where I should have gone by now.

There are many checks and balances to fill the time till wisdom should dawn, before a decision is made. It is conveniently done, mostly in joint families, by referring to someone who is not three, maybe an elder brother, or an aunt or a 'distant' cousin. The man who wants to mark time explains: 'I'll speak to my brother. Not that he is going to say "No". In fact he does not interfere in our affairs at all, but still, as a matter of courtesy, I like to tell him and then proceed in all our family matters. It's a general courtesy in our family, you know.' And then it turns out that this man is not easily met, and several days pass—time given for initial enthusiasms to cool, and cold reason to take its place. Reference to an absentee relative is one of the traditional methods of putting off a decision; it may pertain to the leasing of a house, loan, marriage, contract, or anything. The implication is that one needs time for a correct judgment, and neither a 'yes' nor a 'no' could be precipitately uttered. In a business firm it is done by referring to a partner: the absent one is ever the grumpy and cautious one, who has to be propitiated before anything can be done; this is a well-known business principle, but conjunction of partners proves, at crucial times, as hard as the conjuction of desirable planets.

In municipal, government or democratic organizations, time (for wisdom to dawn) is gained through the forming of committees. By the time the personnel is settled, correspondence got through, agenda drawn up, luncheons eaten, and the report is ready   passions have cooled and the burning question has lost its heat. Luncheons are the most effective sub-device for achieving delay. I'm on a certain advisory body, where the tiffin forms the most impressive item on the agenda. Nearly two hours of the meeting-time is taken in attacking the fare on the

116

table, When we have managed to leave the cups and plates empty, and chewed the *beeda,* we are in such a festive and forgiving mood that all burning questions begin to look silly, and some violent remark that one intended to make is just said in a generous, 'advisory' manner, which is further emasculated in the reported version popularly known as 'minutes'.

It'd be ungracious to call such a highly evolved condition by the name of delaying tactics. It is only a recognition of the fact that wisdom comes late.

The Winged Ants

The swarm comes in the evening. We don't notice it at first, but as soon as the lights are on, there comes along the first member—a pale little body poised on flimsy transparent wings. It circles round the light. One would think that it had a purpose or limit, but its circumambulations grow beyond count. Before you say, 'Here is another!' there are five more, and very soon, imperceptibly, as many as thousands have gathered round the light—quite a cloud of them, like the photograph of bombers poised over a doomed city. They go on circling round and round the light at a giddy pace, hitting us in the face, dropping into our food, and becoming a general nuisance. They gyrate till their wings drop off and then trail along the edge of the floor behind one another helplessly, 'Eyeless in Gaza'. When the flight nuisance is at its height, as any householder knows, a basin of water placed under the light draws away most of the circumambulating crowd to a watery grave. Their attempt to reach the light within the bulb has itself been an illusory pursuit, their attraction to the reflection in the basin of water has proved a disaster! Here is sufficient stuff to keep a philosopher thought-stricken!

For all the flutter it creates, the ant's whole existence lasts only an hour or so. God knows why they come out at all. Any evening, particularly if there has been a downpour of rain, we may anticipate the coming of the swarm. If we watch the crows and sparrows in the garden, we should see them engaged in a lively activity: they have found their ideal dinner, also a limitless one, coming their way, emerging from the ant-holes in the ground, and they catch them in flight. Not many of the winged creatures have a chance of coming out further until the birds retreat for the night. And then they come out full-fledged towards every source of light and flutter their brief life out.

Millions arrive, fly about, and get destroyed in various ways. What is Nature's purpose in devising this extravagance?

An entomologist has given me the answer. Millions come out and perish so that an elect may survive. Out of multitude the queen is protected and led back to their subterranean home, where she is fed and pampered and encouraged to breed. Once this aim is achieved, it does not matter how many are trampled under human feet or swept away with a broom.

Why has Nature made the white-ant so prolific and important? Some day, I hope people will give sufficient thought to the subject. I feel there must be some purpose in having in our midst a creature who will destroy anything. Consider the termite and its activity. First and foremost, it builds laboriously a home—perhaps not for itself but for the deadliest enemy of man: the snake. Tunnelled, sheltered, full of passages—an architecturally ideal home for the snake. Should we view the white-ant as the sworn enemy of man, one that provides a concealed home for the viper and then proceeds to nibble away everything that a human being values? The importance that Nature attaches to the breeding and welfare of the white-ant ought to give us food for thought. Man should once for all get rid of the presumption that the universe is created for his convenience.

Imagine for a moment a world without the white-ant. The possessiveness inherent in man will crowd the world beyond all reckoning. There will be no standing room owing to the accumulated junk everywhere; old newspapers, government records, classics in ancient editions, and old furniture. Once I removed to the garage a basketful of classical works whose pages had become verminous. A month later when I opened the garage door and peeped in I found not only the classics gone but also the basket in which they had been heaped. I felt depressed at first, but the impartial annihilation that the white-ant had effected struck me as something cosmic.

In my profession I accumulate too much paper; review-cuttings, typescripts, galley proofs, correspondence which makes no sense now, manuscripts in various stages, mementoes of various kinds, all things that should have been dumped into a disintegrator ages ago but weren't because of a vague irrational thought that they may have value or utility some day. Observing myself with honesty, I realized that I had not touched any of it a second time in twenty years, while they went on choking all the available space in every room, shelf, desk, and drawer. Twenty years is an adequate period for testing the usefulness of anything. Now when I wish to clear up I put everything into a basket, leave it in the garage, and forget about it. And in less than a week I won't even remember what I have lost. There is something to be admired in such a consummate corroder: it saves the world from becoming clogged.

Taxing Thoughts

The uppermost thought in anyone's mind today is, "What new taxes shall I wake up to, tomorrow?" Of course this is a very unenlightened attitude to adopt. In a modern welfare state with such complex and well-defined aims as are generally to be noticed, the least that any person could do to show his appreciation of the troubles that his rulers take, is not to grumble at the notion of taxes. In an ideal State, according to any tax-deviser, the moment a budget is announced there will not be *Hartals*, protest meetings, and acrimonious exchanges in Parliaments, but rather processions, public thanksgiving, and prayers. Every normal citizen will cry in joy, "What a privilege it is going to be to pay a rupee more per yard for every cloth I buy! How grateful am I that I am going to pay an anna extra for every match-stick I strike! Oh, why don't they tax my breath also at so much per lungful! I am happy and proud to be a tax-payer." He may even go to the extent of telegraphing his representative in Parliament, "Pray suggest Finance Minister increase my income tax fifteen annas in rupee." Following the proceedings in Parliament he will demand to be told not why there are so many new taxes but why there are so many glaring omissions in the budget speech. For instance why have they not thought of a four-anna levy on every bunch of coriander leaf in the market, which ought to yield three crores?

This is only in the nature of a vision and is hardly likely to be realized in the near future. But let us hope that the speed of political enlightenment will be such as to enable us to witness the transformation within our lifetime. But as things are, it must be very depressing for our tax-devisers to note the public reaction. It is so because people have developed a selfish tendency: they are more preoccupied with private finance than with the public one. Public finance, of course, in the view of any statesman, should take precedence over every other kind of finance. But the private citizen has not yet got over the dark and uncivilized habit of thinking that his own finance is all-important and should be left untouched. He hates all association with tax. Income-tax upsets his digestion, excise levy affects his sleep, something else frays his nerves, and the multi-point sales tax is an abomination and a nightmare to him. He indulges in dreams of a tax free universe. This is the normal constitution of a citizen, and how could any State run its administration and carry out its plans, with such a psychology always there to neutralize its efforts? We have to admire the pluck and sense of duty of persons who pilot the ship of the modern State. Public administration is becoming a costly business; river-valley schemes, railway links, cultural projects, national theatres, building new radio stations or transferring old ones to new places, all these are activities to be paid for not in thousands but in lakhs. It is no one's business to suggest, 'Why not hire a building for the national theatre instead of constructing one at a cost of seventy lakhs? Why not hold the assembly in the old town hall instead of raising a new building at a cost of sixty lakhs? Why not let cultural activities wait? Why not leave the old radio station where it has been making its noise all these years?" The typical public agitator is likely to put all these questions to his rulers, but he will be dismissed with the succinct statement, 'It has all been decided upon already.'

I read somewhere that in ancient times the prestige of a kingdom depended upon the number of taxes it was able to levy on its people. It was very much like the prestige of a head-hunter in his own community. The ruler who had not the wits to devise enough taxes was considered to be weak and spineless. And so we read of seventy-eight different taxes in an ancient State. Birthdays and death-days were taxed alike. The most lucrative tax was the one levied on any person found swinging his arms while crossing certain streets of the capital: in certain other streets tax was levied on folk with their arms folded across their chest or locked behind. By the operation of the law of averages all citizens were caught one way or the other. This was based on the principle of the pincer-movement in taxes; taxes should leave no one out. If you taxed every false tooth worn, you should assure yourself no one went scot free by displaying a sound set of thirty-two teeth. It ought to be covered by the provision that whoever displayed sound dentures beyond certain years should pay a certain sum into the treasury. A creative mind can extract a tax almost out of anything.

My pet phobia is that some day the tax authorities may suddenly realize that while they are sufficiently penalizing those who move in motor cars and other vehicles, those who walk do not contribute anything to the treasury. To remedy it, they may suddenly say that every declared walker must submit a statement of the mileage covered on foot. This is likely to produce a very large figure for tax purposes. I walk five miles a day, one-hundred-and-fifty miles a month, one-thousand-eight-hundred miles a year, and nine thousand in five years. Now let the experts calculate what it would mean in terms of revenue!

Elephant in the Pit

At dawn we motor to a village about fifty miles from Coimbatore and reach a lonely farm-house in the shadow of the Anaimalai Hills. From there we travel in a bullock cart towards the hill, bumping over boulders and wading through little streams. Columns of people are seen moving along under the bright sun to the foot of the hill. Presently we find that a camp has grown up where the vendors of plantains, oranges and coloured aerated water are carrying on a brisk trade. The aerated water is being manufactured on the spot—the available water (in the puddles and cesspools) is strained through old, discoloured Turkish towels into large pans, then bottled and given a dozen turns on an aerator riveted to the edge of a wooden handcart, and sold at once to thirsty customers besieging the handcart: the only difference between this and the water in the nearby pond being that this is coloured and you have to knock off a tinsel lid before drinking out of the bottle.

People are crowding around a pit into which an elephant has fallen. I have never seen an elephant looking more bewildered and miserable. We are generally used to seeing an elephant in a better state—walking majestically with calmness and assurance in its eyes. But here it is in a most undignified position, thrust into a pit and made to look up at a vast, curiosity-stricken crowd.

The people in these parts seem to have perfected the technique of elephant-catching. All along the foot of the hills they have dug circular pits about fifteen feet deep, covered with bamboo, camouflaged with leaves and grass. Away from these pits they have cultivated many acres of *cholam*, whose green, waving stalks tempt the elephant in the hills to come down when he looks about for something to munch at dusk. Treading the ground anywhere here is risky and sooner or later he goes down. The moment he has fallen, hundreds of persons, who have watched his movement from the treetops, surround the pit and get busy. Heavy logs are drawn over the pit and lashed together in several cross-layers. The elephant is now bottled up. They then manage to pass down ropes and loop them around his neck and feet. Presently heavy ropes, thick as temple-chariot tugs, emerge from the pit and go up a hundred feet or more, out into the hands of nearly two hundred persons ranged about the mouth of the pit. They have the appearance of a tug-of-war team. They are now able to steer and turn the elephant in any direction they please. They are able to prevent his getting entangled in the ropes and also his attempts at knocking down the sides of the pit with hefty kicks. Yelling, shouting human beings, running hither and thither, gaping at him, and interfering with every movement of his, must seem to him peculiarly monstrous creations of God.

They keep throwing at him pots of cold water, not only to keep him cool but also to create enough mire to make his foothold slippery. In a short while, his head and trunk are covered with clay, his feet are in a mess.

Very soon the information spreads to all the surrounding villages that an elephant has 'fallen'. A vast crowd turns up in buses, bullock carts, cycles, and jeeps, and spreads itself about in picnic groups.

Now the next big event is the arrival of a trained elephant from a jungle eighteen miles away. Everyone knows it by name and mentions it with respect—a famous elephant named Ayyapan. They expect him to arrive at ten a.m. but he is really sighted at three in the afternoon. He presents a perfect picture of an elephant, very tall and slightly arched on top—the prototype of the one we used to see on the covers of illustrated journals of old times. Matters get brisker now. A most elaborate roping of the captive goes on. It is tethered on all sides.

Ayyapan comes up and in a businesslike manner unties the logs, lifts them and puts them away in a neat pile. The excitement and shouting are tremendous. People are ordering and directing and making a deafening uproar. Most of the logs have now been removed. In a moment the captive will be out and will try to run away, but Ayyapan will pilot him into a steel enclosure in the farm-house, where two veteran trainers whose equipment seems to be unlimited elephant lingo and a thin cane will cajole and bully the captive into entering the world of man and living on good terms with him. But unfortunately just when the climax is reached, there comes a sudden lull. Ayyapan is driven away in haste a furlong off, the swarm of workers withdraw from the pit, and the tug-of-war team slacken their hold. All shouting ceases and a silence falls on the gathering. The sun is going down. The captive elephant is dead. In the melee of instructions and counter-instructions, the rope was tugged too violently in a wrong direction: it wrenched the neck of the elephant and probably snapped its spinal column. It raised its trunk a moment ago in a readiness to come out, but the next moment dropped down dead. I shall never forget the fixed stare in its eyes as it lies back half-submerged in the mire, its trunk lying limp across its tusk. The crowd turns back and files away across the *cholam* fields in a solemn silent mood as the night comes on.

The Lost Umbrella

I realized at about eleven in the night that I and my umbrella were parted. While returning from my evening walk I had stopped by at a little shop for buying cloves. It did not seem a particularly appropriate moment for this transaction, as the Sales Tax department had descended in strength on this particular shop, and an inspector and his minions swarming around the counter. The shopman who was normally genial and communicative could do no more than throw a hapless simper in my direction, over the shoulders of the officials hemming him in. It was like a class in zoology practical with enquiring minds crowding over a disembowelled specimen on the table. There could be no doubt that it was an inauspicious hour for replenishing one's stock of cloves. No one in that shop was free to look at me, every hand being pressed into service for propitiating the gods with offerings of day-books, stock-registers, and ledgers. But I preferred to wait: the cloves of this shop were reputed to be genuine 'Zanzibars'—any connoisseur of spices knows what it means, cloves of ebonite shade, sheeny with oil, and each perfectly designed in miniature like a Greek column supporting a four-pointed cupola. A quarter of this pristine specimen placed on the tip of the tongue would be enough to sting and to tingle the nervous system. At other shops cloves looked anaemic, enfeebled, and tasted like match-stick. This was the shop for cloves. It is human nature to have faith in one shop rather than another; going out to buy something becomes not just a casual act but a profound undertaking. The same brand is displayed everywhere, the same labels are arrayed on the shelves; you could pick up the articles you need anywhere but still the matter is not so simple. Even if one's favourite shop fails to hold the price-line too tautly, still one prefers it, for various reasons, to an officious cooperative store. Among the multitudinous *avatars* of our Government, the latest one is that of a shopkeeper. I wonder if the red-tapist at the counter is going to appreciate the psychology of an average shopper and treat him with the considerateness he is accustomed to at his favourite shop. People on their side have no reason to expect that multi-storeyed, multi-purpose, super markets and mighty 'price-line' holding establishments will ever do better than our State Banks, Telephones, Airlines, Railways, Cooperatives, Corporations, or Coffee Boards, where a customer is reduced to the rank of a supplicant or petitioner, unless he proves influential or aggressive in one way or another. The ordinary man, the unknown soldier in civic life, the meek one blessed though in the next world has enough trials in the present one, and whose only source of power is the single vote to be revived and cast quinquennially, would prefer his accustomed shop.

I waited hoping to catch the shopman's eye, deriving meanwhile what entertainment I could from watching the Sales Tax operations. In a state of mild beguilement I hung up my umbrella on an awning-rod projecting from the shop doorway. I have recently got into the dreadful habit of unconsciously hanging up my umbrella on any projection, leaving my spectacles and pen on any available ledge, and half my time is spent in searching for something. I waited, hoping that the Sales Tax men would leave but they seemed determined to outstay me at the shop; so I left. At eleven in the night I remembered my umbrella and immediately drove back to the shop. The shop was shut and deserted. I examined the awning-rod for any trace of my umbrella. After an uneasy night of sleep, I went to the shop again just when the shopman, who still looked battered and dazed from his Sales Tax encounters, was unlocking the door. He complained, 'There was such a big crowd to watch last evening's *tamasha*, anybody could have walked away with your umbrella. Even the Sales Tax people carry away articles from shops, rather forgetfully I think'.

I have filed a detailed complaint with the police, fully describing my lost property, in case they want to identify it in the hands of some gentlemen who unfurl a new umbrella every night and perambulate around the clock-tower at the market offering a bargain to the crowds. I myself propose to frequent the clock-tower and watch like an F.B.I. agent. The police officer who took my complaint happened to be a reader of my books as well, and was overjoyed to see his author in the flesh. I have no doubt he will do his best for me. Meanwhile, I turn a searching look on every umbrella handle hooked on any arm in the streets, sometimes hurrying up close to the side of any that may appear suspicious but most of them on scrutiny prove un-American—that is, no push-button, automatic opening (in order to facilitate the opening of an umbrella with one hand while the other is holding the loaded grocery bag, evolved specially for a coolie-less society).

Even supposing that I noticed my umbrella in someone else's hand, how could I claim it? Invite him to the police station? Or shadow him to his address and hurry back to tell my inspector friend, or just snatch it back? What would happen if I found it in the hand of our local wrestler, who might have negotiated for it at the clock-tower or got it from an admirer happening to visit the clove shop last evening soon after I left? Fresh and unsuspected phases of the problem unfolded themselves to me every minute as I planned the strategy to retrieve my umbrella.

Finally, I think, I should fall back on philosophy. In a country where ninety-five per cent can't afford an umbrella, I have enabled some poor creature to shield himself from the sun and the belated monsoon. (I only hope he knows how to open my umbrella without dismembering it.) Our *shastras* enjoin upon every individual to perform umbrella *dan* on every possible occasion. The bridegroom's umbrella on his wedding day is just as important as the one given on less auspicious occasions to the priest as a possible insurance against inclemencies in the next world for a departed soul. An umbrella is a highly-prized possession. An umbrella devotee will not hesitate to cover the black cloth with white cloth, as a reinforcement, and carry his umbrella into the innermost sanctum of a temple unable to leave it out of sight even for a moment, or nurse it on his lap while listening to great music. No one takes amiss the words of warning or caution uttered by one who is about to lend an umbrella. In England, the sleek silk umbrella rolled to a rapier, could almost be a part of an Englishman's limb, while he walks down Regent Street holding it a few inches away without touching the ground or his person. In America, that automobile land, they are terribly casual and indifferent; when the wind becomes sharp the man just thrusts his umbrella into a trash-can on the roadside, and hails a taxi. Unthinkable in our country, where the umbrella-repairer is regarded as a saviour and sought after. The American economy may be termed a 'throw-away' one, since mending is a millionaire's privilege costing ten dollars an hour, while ours is based on a Cherish and Mend philosophy.

On the fourth day of my loss I am feeling actually elated, being filled with a sense of redemption. Forty years ago, I acquired an umbrella as someone else has done four days ago at the clove shop. My first umbrella must have belonged to one Mr. Bettiah; the man coming in to deliver an invitation had left it hooked on our gate and later must have looked for it everywhere else.

The Newspaper Habit

The morning paper in the city (and possibly the afternoon one in the "mofussil") has grown on us as a habit. There are many whose vision of paradise is a high and soft cushion, long couch, and a newspaper to which one is accustomed. It is not enough that some newspaper is read but it must be *the* newspaper. Everyone has his own taste in this: some persons like to be dragooned by strong headlines, and some like their paper to leave them alone, ever suspicious of anything that is clamorous. The advertisement pages too are a source of great delight. The variety of life that is presented therein gives one the same pleasure as going through a crowded bazaar; here is one asking for a suitable person for some job, there one demanding a place under the sun, here a car for sale and there someone trying to dispose of a house or a horse; jobs to be filled up, jobs to be had, lawyer's notices to defaulting debtors or of ex-parte proceedings. It is indeed a composite reflection of the world. It gives one reclining in his couch the feeling of being in the thick of life and the same sensation as of pacing before shop windows.

The man-in-a-hurry glances at the headings and summary and puts away the paper for a thorough study later in the day; but unless he is a tyrant before whose dark moods humanity quails, he is not likely to find the paper again. The daily paper gets buffetted about in the house and rests, if at all, in bits in the various corners of a house. It is one of the causes of the numerous minor skirmishes that occur in a normal household everyday, but so far no one has been able to enforce a general code of observance in regard to the handling of a newspaper at home. The boy of the house will always detach the sports page, the young lady cannot help tearing out ruthlessly any portion of the paper that interests her: it may be anything—beauty-tips or about a pudding or the weather conditions in Simla or the birth of a baby in a royal household. It is no use the zealot crying out,

"Oh, keep the sheets neatly folded back so that others may also read." It becomes a routine statement to which nobody pays any attention. There is a widespread belief that every copy of a newspaper belongs to all humanity irrespective of who pays the subscription. Its boundary certainly is not limited to the doorsteps of the house on which the newsboy drops it. There are people always on the alert for the arrival of the newspaper in the next house. In harmony with this condition there is the subscriber who is so tolerant that when he wishes to see the day's paper, he sends a messenger around to investigate its whereabouts in the neighbourhood, and resigns himself to it if the hardened borrower sends back word that he has still not finished reading the paper. Often this good man will have to content himself with reading the day-before-yesterday's issue. For it must be said that while we cannot always get at the latest issue, the one a few days old turns up spruce and tidy a dozen times during a search. This constant turning-up of an old issue may drive some mad with rage till they snatch it up and fling it out of reach on to a loft, but the man of patience may accept it as a design of fate and take it to bed with him.

Personally I must confess I am not thrilled by the usual news items however important they might be. Not for me the obvious excitements. I keep an eye on the politics of the country and glance through the messages pouring forth from ministerial quarters, but the real delight for me is the news tucked away, printed in small type, without a heading. It is this type of news that stirs in me the profoundest reflection. As an instance, some days ago, I read a three-line news item at the bottom of a column, used as a space-filler, which said, "Turbans will be one of the prizes which the Government of India proposes to give to successful farmers in the crop competitions. This item is estimated to cost the Government Rs. 2½ lakh." Now I gazed upon this items with the profoundest interest. It was like looking into a smooth-faced crystal with its polished surface. Now, I wondered, what made the Government select the turban for a gift, and not some other item of dress? When did they learn that our farmers were fond of turbans? How many turbans could one buy for two-and-a-half lakhs of rupees? Anyway, actually, who thinks up these things at New Delhi? Are they going to give the Mysore lace-turbans or the Punjab ones or the Poona style? What will they do to secure turban-cloth in the present textile position? Is it a sign that the textile position is improving and that the black-marketeers have been successfully choked and buried? It stirred up in my mind a most pleasing picture of the Indian peasant. He wore a loin cloth, his body was bare and was baking in the sun, his feet were unshod while he patiently walked behind his plough, but his head was resplendent with a turban that was placed there by the Minister with his own hands....

This is only an instance to show how I read a newspaper. I fear it is an extremely subjective experience. I hope everyone will perfect his own technique of drawing the subtle essence out of every item of news he reads.

Castes: Old and New

I fear that foreign observers of Indian life would feel frustrated if the caste system should completely disappear in our country. They will have nothing left to talk about. The caste system has always offered a convenient handle for foreign observers. In my opinion, next to Russia, India is the most visited and the most-commented-upon country in the world. I am afraid that the abolition of caste will affect the tourist traffic, on which so much anxious thought and discussion is being bestowed at present. If a notice should be put up at Santa Cruz aerodrome or on the Gateway of India announcing, "There is no caste system in this country," I believe, many a tourist would turn back home with the feeling that he has been cheated of legitimate entertainment for which he has paid a heavy fee in the shape of air or steamer fare.

Once a visitor from a far-off country called on me. When I asked her what I could do for her, she replied, "I should love to take Indian coffee in Indian style." This was an understandable request in this part of the country. After coffee she said, "Now I want to see the caste system. May I see it in your house?" I blinked for a while and then told her that the caste system was not a curio in a glass-case to be displayed on request. "Then what is it?" she asked, cross-examining. I explained, throwing into my sentences a proper sprinkling of such words as *varnashrama dharma*, etc. She was properly impressed. "What caste are you?" she asked. I told her. She would not believe it. "You can't tell me that! If you were really a Brahmin you would not have drunk coffee with me, don't I know so much?" I felt that there was some justice in her observation, and explained to her how the caste system was disappearing in our country and how our national aim was to create a casteless society. She was aghast. "What, no more caste system!" She looked as if I had told her that the Himalayas were to be shifted to another location. Presently, she asked, "What will you give us in its place, for people like us who come thousands of miles to see your country?"

"Perhaps fertilizer factories, river valley projects, hydro-electric...." She would not allow me to finish my sentence. "I have seen all kinds of factories and projects in all parts of the world. I don't have to come to India to see them. I would not have taken all this trouble to come here if I had known there would be no caste system. I wish I had known it earlier." Then, out of sheer pity, I took her to a Sanskrit college: there she saw people wearing tufts and caste-marks, wrapped in colourful shawls, sitting on the ground and reciting their lessons. She took several photographs of the classes at work, and then told me, "Now show me where the other castes are. I want to photograph the entire caste system." "Why?" I asked her.

"I have signed an agreement with a lecturing organization to tour America and lecture on the caste system in India." She went away greatly pleased, and I am sure she has gone through a heavy lecturing programme. I do not know whether she abused or complimented this country on this subject, but anyway it brought her here.

We hear that several thousand tourists are likely to visit India in the coming year. In the interests of this traffic would it not be advisable to start a model caste-system village, kept in full swing, if need be with a subsidy from the tourist department?

The old caste system is wearing away, no doubt, but who is to check the development of new castes? Breathes there a man, except a saint, with soul so dead that he does not attempt to show off his learning, possessions, contacts, and so forth? The reason why a certain person adopts the nursery-picture-bush-coat seems to be, not that he could not secure any other cloth, but that he attempts to remove himself from a group wearing bush-coats made of non-spectacular material. I recently learnt that among bush-coat wearers there are twenty-five sub-sects. Among motor-owners there are said to be forty different sects, depending upon the length of the whip-like aerial on the mudguard, the variety of little plastic birds stuck on the glass inside, and so on. New lamps for old seems to be the law of life. Old or new, lamps serve the same purpose. It almost seems as if all change is illusory. We seem to be repeating the same set of old things, but under a new guise and a new denomination. It would be an interesting pastime for anyone to observe and classify the new castes that are springing up all around.

Curiosity

If I had the time and the resources I should soon be starting an organization called S.P.C. This is an age of multitudinous abbreviations. The United Nations Organizations have appropriated most of the letters in the alphabet. If someone says, "I am working on behalf of N.A.A.F. which as you know is a branch of E.E.Z.F.", we do not bother to know what it means. We are getting used to many abbreviations in daily life. I feel that I might add, without anyone noticing it, just one more to this wealth of abbreviations. Mine is going to consist of only three letters S.P.C.—Society for the Promotion of Curiosity.

One of the saddest developments in recent years is the attitude we are adopting towards curiosity. It is one of the undesirable results of urban standards of social life. One is supposed to be behaving properly as long as one does not display any curiosity towards another. I think we have been misled by the old saying, whatever may be its origin, "Curiosity killed the cat." It is possible that the cat owes its nine lives to this .virtue.

The old type of question that an aged lady puts a stranger, "How many children have you? What is your husband's salary? How much has he saved?" is one of the most spontaneous acts on earth. The modern tendency is to shudder at such 'personal' questions. What question is worth asking unless it be personal? When it is discredited, naturally, a lot of coldness creeps in, and all intimacy and warmth goes out of human relationship. When two persons meet, they are obliged to talk of the weather, test-scores, ministerial crises and such other impersonal matters, and waste precious hours of existence. When all topics are exhausted and there is nothing more to speak about they suppress the yawn (bad manners to yawn openly), and look bored. In spite of all the suppression that sophistication decrees, one's instinct keeps clamouring inside one all the time. One may outwardly be engaged in discussing political questions with a friend, while really wanting to know what are the latest antics of that pugnacious brother demanding a share of the ancestral estate. One might spend an hour elaborating trade statistics while one would rather ask what fee the friend took to get through such and such a case: one might discourse on comparative religion while one would rather ask of one's hearer if so and so and his wife are still quarrelling like wild cats and if not, why not? All this is tabooed in polite company. This is one of the reasons why club-life has become somewhat dull nowadays. Members disappear into the cards room or billiard room or sit morosely reading weekly papers in a corner. There is no scope for free conversation in any club nowadays. Here and there we may see a small group talking, but there is nothing in their talk which is not found in the day's paper and known to one lakh of persons already.

It seems to me that the old town planning was based on the principle that curiosity must be kept alive. Rows and rows of houses stuck side by side, thin partition walls through which you could follow all the conversation in the next house, and narrow streets which made anyone passing thereon conspicuous, were some of the features of corporate life in our country. Every house in the street knew what was happening in every other house, what the postman had brought there, who the visitors were that came in a big car, or how much so and so had borrowed from his uncle. No one could flaunt suddenly his prosperity or suffer adversity without everyone being aware of all the reasons for it. This system has its own advantage. "Disclosure of income" is the greatest headache for the income-tax department at present. Their present difficulty is mainly due to the voluntary abstention from curiosity which has been in practice for a long time now. That the income-tax department still has faith in human nature is borne out by their latest request calling upon anyone to disclose any one else's income without any fear or reserve.

It is only through curiosity that children learn to understand the world around them, it is only through curiosity that artists and writers gather material for their work, it is only through curiosity that science has progressed. If Newton had ignored the fall of the apple as an unwanted personal question pertaining to the tree and the apple, mankind would probably never have known of gravitation.

137

The Golden Age

Historians are fond of mentioning a Golden Age in their books. It generally gives a picture of a time when a king ruled benignly, denying himself all the pleasures of life, taxing his subjects lightly, meting out justice with a blind impersonality (of course without altering the laws from time to time); the citizens displayed overwhelming affection for one another and were all engaged in pleasing and charitable activities. Our poets depict old Ayodhya as a place where there was no charity because there was no need for it, where the doors had no padlocks and the houses had no doors, and where the police were unemployed, and eventually even disbanded. Let us not ask what they did with all the disbanded policemen or how badly the padlock industry was hit or what the carpenters did for a living. Our thoughts are nowadays trained to run on lines of employment, economics, etc., which complicates our views of *Ramrajya*. It was probably very rash of them to have undertaken to shape our country into *Ramrajya* as though it could be done with a chisel and hammer: it has only made us expect too much of our rulers and offered a readymade theme for every carping journalist.

I am sure that in any Golden Age, even in the actual *Ramrajya*, people must have cherished their grouses. Life would be boring and unreal otherwise. J.B. Priestley confesses in one of his books to being a born grumbler and liking his role: this is the real privilege anyone enjoys in any corporate life. We may rest assured that on any normal working day, during any Golden Age, the citizens would have had their asides, regarding corruption in high places, the deafness of those in authority, or how the ideal king's favourite, his brother-in-law, was doing everything possible to spoil the king's judgment and ruin the country. Or the people might even have complained of the general boredom of one of those times and the hectic politics, the explosive possibilities, the newspaper screams, the radio noise, the cinema glare, and all the rugged ups-and-downs of modern life, might have appealed irresistibly to them and filled them with a longing to jump out of the Golden excellences of their own times that have made latter-day poets and historians wax so eloquent.

We experience the same difficulty in fixing the Golden Age in our personal lives too. We always think of it as something ahead or behind us. Every birthday reminds us of something achieved long ago or yet to be achieved. People have a tendency to talk of 'Good Old Days' with an undisguised sentimentality, but it never carries conviction whether it is said in the assembly of 'Old Boys' in a college or in private conversation. Actually the days of youth or boyhood, if anyone truthfully recollects, were days of travail; the constant dependence, fear of elders, varying alliances and friendships, sadistic class teachers, examination harassments, pursuit of employment, and a variety of incommunicable anxieties and gloom, made our earlier years miserable. The period between youth and middle age is considered to be good and desirable, but no one would be prepared to call it the best years of one's life. There is a widespread practice of celebrating the sixtieth birthday. "Why the sixtieth and not the fortieth?" commented a friend on receiving an invitation for a *Shashtiabda Poorthi* celebration. He suggested that they ought to find a Sanskrit equivalent for forty, as high sounding as *Shashtiabda Poorthi* and then celebrate it with the greatest vigour. "If I had the choice I would rather have a purse presented to me on attaining my fortieth year than on my sixtieth. At forty, one's responsibilities keep growing and a purse from well-wishers would come in most handy." His argument was that if one could survive the struggle for existence till sixty one needed none of the attentions of well-wishers at the end of it.

Is there anyone who can say precisely which is his Golden Age—a time when he could live without hankering after a future or regretting a vanished past, and when he could live without wasting the moment of actual existence? If this could be fixed, then it ought to be celebrated with the greatest vigour.

Rambles in a Library

A fit of spring-cleaning seized me once. I made a start with our ancient library at home. This is a respectable word for a book-museum, left over by an earlier generation. It was situated in a neutral territory of the house, in which nobody had any special interest, and persons while passing on to their rooms cast a glance at the back of the books standing there three or four deep, in shelves which were ten feet high. We were so used to this sight that we took it casually, as if these were a part of the wall. We borrowed any book we wanted from the Public Library, and never disturbed the books in these shelves. They were a respectable heirloom and nothing more. The shelves ached with their loads. Hundreds of volumes gathered for nearly half-a-century through varied means of book-acquisition: books bought, borrowed, and left behind by other book-lovers. Complete works of Milton, Tennyson, Browning and other poets, Sheridan's plays, Moliere, French Revolution, Kant's *Critique of Pure Reason*; several Sanskrit volumes whose titles we were not fit to lisp, and Tamil books. There was a whole shelf filled with the text-books that an earlier generation had read as children, youths and then as adults. Every book was there—from the colourful red-backed Nelson Primer to *Paradise Lost* and *Macbeth* in college editions with pencil notes in the margin. I felt an admiration for the preserving capacities of our forefathers. A look at them in a mass, and we understood the cultural history of our country for half-a-century or more; the root and branches of our cultural growth and the mixed sap coursing through them.

It was nearly twenty years since anyone went near those books. What was the purpose in keeping them there? I wondered. Even confirmed, accepted, junk-hoarders mention only seven years as the time-limit for an article. It must be used by that time or flung away. But these books! They collected the dust of other days, and harboured all kinds of vermin. It was a house with many mansions for any sort of insect which might care to come up and settle: wasps and silver fish, mosquitoes and bright-hued beetles had established themselves securely among these volumes.

I stayed the duster for a moment and reflected. Why let them stay here at all? But it seemed sacrilege to touch any of them. If any volume was to be removed, what was to be the basis of selection? Certainly not their innate worth, or worthlessness. This element could not weigh at all, for the bulk of them were works of the highest quality, already enthroned as classics. Who was I, a petty library worm, to sit in judgment over them? The only standard to adopt now would be to consider whether a volume looked well or ill. The dullest volume, I, decided, would be allowed to stand if it kept itself presentable. Though untouched by human beings for a long time, most of them seemed to have been well used by the book-worm, who had criss-crossed several rows of books end to end with his deep and devious tunnels.

It was evident that with the best of intentions in the world, and with every respect due to them, they could not stay. I brought in a basket, and put into it all the volumes that seemed worn out. I believe I apologized to their authors mentally promising that their works would soon be replaced in new, modern editions. There are persons to whom an edition, mellowed by time, is precious. But this luxury has to be sacrificed when classics crumple at a touch, or exude such minute dust that in turning those leaves, you tempt providence and go down with cold and cough for a week.

The basket filled up very fast. And very soon another large basket had to be called for. A Milton in microscopic type in double column, an album of European views, an obscure orator's collections, several novels of Bulwer-Lytton, and a thick book called *Indian Social Revolution,* dated 1870, challenging every kind of orthodoxy of those days.

There was some space left in the second basket. I looked about for something more that could be put in. I noticed a *Social History of India* on a top shelf, a stalwart volume over a foot-and-a-half high, and half-a-foot wide with all kinds of gilt decorations and a coat-of-arms on the binding. It had a frontispiece portrait of the author himself—a colonel of the Company days, who had evidently a lot of time to spare and a willing amanuensis at hand. I read a few pages and realized what it was: it was more a record of the gentleman's views on Indian history, geography, and sociology and anthropology or anything else that caught his fancy—written probably on the heels of Macaulay's scheme of Native Education, as a sort of supplementary study. It had in green ink the name of an Englishman's library, a second-hand bookshop's stamp and someone's inscription of presentation for someone else. Who were all these? And resting so well, disturbed neither by men nor by insects.

After the baskets filled up, I wondered what I should do with them. The only reasonable and practicable course would have been to give them away to someone, who might be willing to relieve me of them, and add a reward for his trouble. But I said to myself vaguely that I might need them again some time for urgent reference; and at the back of my mind was also a vague hope of selling them off to any fool willing to part with cash for literary dust. In this uncertainty, I brought in a ladder, put it up against a loft in another part of the house and hauled up the baskets to that region where rested a hundred oddments waiting for a second chance in life: broken locks, boxes without lids, canvas chairs minus canvas, tin boxes, and skeletons of umbrellas—it was a veritable charnel-house of all objects which should have been flung into the garbage heap long ago.

Six months later when I went up the loft again, I saw no traces of the books, nor of the basket. I noticed in their place only a great colony of white ants, moving about, looking extremely well-fed. They had consumed not only the classics without leaving a trace behind but also the baskets. Apparently they'd waited all their life for this chance. All the other objects in this place being mainly of iron and teak, they had all along been waiting for something on which they could set their teeth and they had made a thorough job of it. The only book relic on the spot was the gilt coat-of-arms of the Colonel who had written the *History of India*. This somehow seemed to have proved distasteful to the white ants, and though they had devoured the hefty volume with its binding board, they had left the coat-of-arms intact like a badge.

At An Auctioneer's

One morning, strolling along the market place, I passed by an auctioneer's shop. So far I had never stepped into an auctioneer's place, always feeling that I could never succeed in getting what I wanted there. The clamorous competitiveness of an auction crowd usually frightens me. For instance, how often have I passed a fascinating writing desk in teak in that shop but have not dared to go and ask for it because I know I shall be told, "For auction, not for sale," although I am ready to pay a fancy price to be spared the pains of bidding.

On this Sunday I stepped into the shop. "Stepping in" is not the right word, for on an auction Sunday the shop bursts its boundaries and overflows into the street, and the traffic obligingly detours on such days.

A variety of objects were dumped together. Writing desks, mirrors, bedsteads, perambulators, parts of a cycle, flower vases, a gramophone, a set of Scott's novels in an ornamental book-case, pictures, paintings, photos, and heaven knew what else.

Looking at these I wonder how they have found their way here. This seems to be a most poignant place on earth—where men are separated from their possessions. What is the story behind that double-cot? Where are its occupants now? Surely it must have gone as a gift from a father-in-law. What has happened to its owners? Have they parted in silence and tears or have they become bankrupts or have they become too prosperous to care for this cot? That single cot. Where is the man who slept on it? At this point I notice a man going round the double-cot muttering, "If I can get this! It only needs a slight retouching and polishing. My son-in-law will be asking for one, very soon, I know he won't mind a used one if it is good. In these days...." By his look I know he is going to secure it whatever happens. No man visits an auction but with an iron determination. I have imagined such a gloomy background for this cot that I send up a silent prayer for the continued happiness of the new couple who are going to acquire it. That perambulator, that high-wheeled, gawky apparatus is the only object which does not convey any unhappy impression. The very person for whom it had been bought might be auctioning it now. But who will buy it? No modern child will ever consent to be perched so high....I notice a grizzly tinsmith poking into it critically. I suspect he wants it more for its wheels, which may be put to entirely unexpected uses such as working bellows or turning a screw.

There are all kinds of pictures lumped together in a corner. Excited and exaggerated splashes in oils and watercolour, portraying waterfalls, mountains, forests, and rolling seas. What despair drives artists or art-lovers to discard masterpieces in this manner?

There are one or two large-sized group photos of very ancient times, judging by the heavy turbans of the sitters and by the side-whiskers of the European district judge or whoever he was sitting at the centre. One wonders how these pictures will interest anyone now. As I stand pondering over it I notice a person scrutinizing them. I cannot resist asking, "What use are these to you?" "Frames and glasses and the mounts! We can pay any price for them now," he says callously. What a festival they must have made of that day of photographing! This is a chamber of disillusionments. Yet the attraction of an auction is irresistible for some persons. I can speak with certainty for at least one—an opthalmic surgeon who would rather miss a patient than an auction sale. He has the instinct of a hunter in this matter. He watches the auction advertisements with a wary eye and is present at every auction in the city. He is wealthy, and his spacious bungalow chokes with unnecessary and varied furniture, radio sets, gramophones, and automobile parts. He has sometimes paid three times the ordinary price for some pieces (often duplicated). He will not miss for anything the thrill of bidding and outbidding, and he sets apart a thousand rupees a year for this joy. The members of his family naturally protest and try to hold him in check both for reasons of space and finance. But he has his own technique of dodging them just as he dodges his patients on a Sunday.

To the Englishman his home is his castle—as long as he occupies it—but on the eve of his departure it is turned into an auction chamber. The motley may walk in and out at its ease, sit on the couch, turn the gramophone handle, doubt the soundness of the springs of any mechanism, and question his taste in books. He turns over his entire possessions, from dinner table to a safety pin, for sale. No man could shed his possessions more thoroughly. Till a moment ago it looked as though he cherished these articles and would defend them with his life. But at a moment's notice he brings them under the hammer— all the knick-knacks and furniture he had gathered around him during a lifetime. There is a touch of cheerful renunciation about it.

It was in tune with this sentiment that the gramophone at the auctioneer's sang. It was tiny miserable model full of creakings and unwanted noises and the music came through a pink funnel but it made up in speed what it lacked in clarity. It stood on a rattan table with a dozen tired-looking records by its side. The table, the records, and the gramophone had come from different sources, though here, at the auctioneer's, they were united in a common purpose. Someone was grinding its handle, and someone else was putting the records on, in spite of the prolific warnings everywhere DON'T TOUCH. Through its raucous gurgle and shrill I recognized the voice of a musician who usually charged two-hundred-and-fifty rupees for a performance. He no doubt sang at top speed now, but nonetheless the song said "...All the eye-filling, eye-gladdening objects around us turn to dream and dust...Wherefore possessions?" It was a fitting song for the occasion, though difficult to discern through the babble of the crowd, and the beat of the tom-tom of the fellow sitting half on the edge of the lot.

Pride of Place

Once I met the wife of a writer, who let out a cry of
disappointment on reading the announcement of the Nobel
Prize for the year. She said, gloomily, "Once again it has
happened!"

"What?" I asked, sympathetically.

"I expected that at least this year they would give the prize to
my husband. Again he has missed it."

I made the appropriate sounds of sympathy—suppressing the
obvious remark that perhaps the judges did not share her
admiration of the man's worth. "Do you know why?" she
continued. "Because of X.Y.Z. who has a big voice in the
Committee and who is prejudiced against North Indians."

"Oh! I never thought the people of Sweden would ever notice
the difference between North and South Indians. What is the
reason for X.Y.Z.'s prejudice?"

"If you don't mind my being frank—because he has a South
Indian friend who advises him on all matters." She hinted that,
as long as X.Y.Z. had a voice in the Committee, and listened to
the advice of a Ramaswami, Subramaniam or Venkataraman,
the Nobel Prize was destined to go to Italians, Russians or the
French, rather than to a North Indian.

To counterbalance this view I have my friend, a teacher of
physics. He is up-to-date and original—I have to take his word
(or perhaps his wife's) for it, as I have no knowledge of physics
and no means of understanding his attainment. It is his constant
refrain that he should not be "rotting" in a miserable hole in
South India—("South is being neglected, I'm one more
evidence of it," he always says)—his rightful place would be the
head of one of the research institutions on a salary of Rs 2,000
or more, but he will never get there because science is a preserve
of North Indians, and no one from South can get in there even if
he holds appreciative letters, as this gentleman does from Sir or
Doctor so-and-so of Cambridge who is always urging him to get

out and do something to claim his share of recognition.

In Bombay, my friends advised me, "Why do you want to go to Calcutta? It is an awful place. They never remove dead dogs from the streets." At Calcutta, my friends said with one voice, "I can't stand Bombay. When I go there for a meeting, I take the first plane back. Bombay is colourless, sophisticated and arty-crafty." In Madras, one hears, "Delhi is all right for a trip, but I cannot understand how people can go on living there. My son is employed in Delhi, but he says the vegetables there are insipid. Poor boy was always keen on brinjals from our native village, which, even some Americans have remarked, are the best in the world. I know some people at the Secretariat. I am trying to get the boy a transfer to Madras. He is not happy in Delhi!" I have heard a Punjabi businessman say, "Engage a Madrasi! Not unless I am in a mood to commit suicide. A Madrasi will sell me under the counter if I am not watchful."

Generalization about a whole slice of the country is a common habit. "Oh, Bengalis! They are all...etc." or "Maharashtrians are as a rule...etc.," or "Madrasis, you know what they do, all are...etc." It is as if a whole population, several million men and women, were all type-designed or were pressed through a particular mould and tarred with a particular brush, like the figures turned out by the toy-makers of Kondapalli. Every person assumes the role of an expert sociologist who has made a scientific study of human behaviour and motives and could speak with authority about others, but the data gathered is mostly uncomplimentary, always underlining craftiness, stupidity, unreliability, slothfulness and so forth.

Prejudice is only the other side of the medal of pride. The mind plays tricks at all times and at no time more than when one talks boastingly of one's own ("native") place: the food, its flavour, spicing, the scenes, the roads, the flowers, and the general quality of life and cultural attainments are unmatched. This condition particularly afflicts an expatriate. He suffers doubly. He longs for a place he can't get to and hates the place where he has chosen to spend his days. The paradise one speaks of is geographically impalpable. At first, one speaks of a whole place of several thousand square miles as the paradise on earth; if you question further, it shrinks down to a part of the country one lives in, and then to a street, and a corner of the street; and all "other points of compass" are inevitably contemptible.

Even adjoining cities, such as Mysore and Bangalore, to take an immediate example, have antagonistic temperaments although they come under the same State administration and partake of the same culture, separated only by an 85-mile concrete road, which you can cover in two hours; and yet what a difference! Strangers who have passed through, inadvertently say, "I was in Mysore," when they mean Bangalore! This sort of slip distresses a true Mysorean and a Bangalorean equally. For the shades of prejudice between the two cities are not mere gradations in a chromatic scale but well-defined conflicting colours. In the shops of Mysore if any commodity is unfairly priced, and you ask for an explanation, pat comes the answer, "It is all due to Bangalore, where they have put up the prices." The Bangalorean thinks, "God, nothing will prosper in Mysore. People are too sleepy and impossible. Once, when I was in Mysore, I tried to get a plumber to fix the tap in my bathroom and for fifteen days no one turned up. In Bangalore...."

Bangalore hotels, taxis, water supply, and the colour and composition of *masala dosai* are categorically disapproved of by Mysoreans. "Mysore is dull" is balanced by "Bangalore is getting so congested that it will choke itself one of these days". If a Mysorean admits certain deficiencies in Mysore, he'll always trace them to the fact that it has no spokesmen either in Delhi or in Bangalore, most of the Ministers (at least till recently) being men of other districts, which is the reason why Mysore is without a train connection to the South through Chamarajnagar-Satyamangalam (a distance of only 45 miles through an oft-surveyed track), an airport, a broadcasting station, and a broad-gauge track. No one in authority has any feeling for Mysore. There is also a comforting view adopted sometimes that Bangalore is a sort of filter keeping out undesirable industrial elements, leaving Mysore to live in its pristine glory.

In every State, there is one particularly important town or district or city which claims for itself outstanding merits. In Madras State, this role is assumed by Tanjoreans. Every Tanjorean is convinced that there is some peculiar merit in the soil of Tanjore, in the waters of the Kaveri (blind to the fact that the Kaveri flows through several miles of other territories too) that produces geniuses in mathematics, Carnatic music, Bharata Natyam, civil service, architecture, sculpture, wit, wisdom, Sanskrit grammar, and Tamil eloquence. One wonders if anything worth a mention is left for other parts of this State since it included 24 other districts at one time. The answer is, "It is enough if others learn to appreciate our good things." The other districts don't yield the point without a fight and say, "Most of these accomplishments you catalogue are at least one century old. What have you to claim within the last two decades, please? Is your city clean, roads passable, houses modern; is there anyone in science or arts who can claim recognition within the last decade, let us say?"

"Oh, Tanjore is neglected, because the Minister in charge of development is from...district, and has starved this area. What can we do? We cannot get even ordinary water supply. All the funds are diverted elsewhere."

The "One World" idea was mooted by the late Wendell Willkie. We need not aspire for it yet. Let us make a start with the thought that we belong to one country and are not living in the midst of strangers. North, South, East, West, are relative terms. Even the Himalayas are south of some other place; and the extreme point of South India could be viewed as north by a Sinhalese.

Houses, Houses

It may be stated as a safe axiom that a house destroys human nature, tears up human relationships, and is generally responsible for much deterioration in human conduct, if it becomes a business between two persons. Under that condition they never remain just two persons but are transformed into two parties. One would never have thought that such a noble institution as a house could ever become such a disruptive force, but it is in keeping with the times when many noble objects have debased themselves in various ways. Till about 1942 we were never conscious of anything special about houses. They were just there—one went in and out of them. One shut the doors and opened the windows and did all the normal things one generally likes to do with houses. But now a house means troubles all round. If there are fifty thousand houses in a city you may be sure that there are at least fifty thousand different worries and troubles. It is all very well as long as not more than one party is involved in it. But it is like saying that cricket is a fine game and a safe one provided not more than one is involved in the playing of it. The cricket simile is not just a chance mention. There are many ways in which cricket and houses compare. In both one aims a missile at another, leaving him to guard himself with the narrowest possible shield, with every chance of being knocked out.

The contending parties may be a landlord and his tenant or a house-building enthusiast and the man who undertakes to build it for him. The trouble is that the days of perpetual landlords and perpetual tenants are gone. We have known times when a man occupied a house and paid a rent for it all his life, and nobody bothered about it. But that is all over now. Everyone knows why it is so, and it is not necessary to elaborate the point except to remind ourselves that now this relationship is being administered by the rent-controller. When a tenant finds it impossible to remain the protege of the rent-controller any longer, he moves to another house, if it is available (which remedy is in the nature of a lull in the battle and not to be mistaken for peace), or tries, if he has the hardihood and the money, to build a house of his own. This is indeed a hazardous undertaking. In fact, actually a jump from the frying pan into the fire. Later this man will have many introspective moments to decide whether he is really happier for rushing into the arms of a house-builder whose tactics seem often incalculable and baffling from those of a landlord who at least had the virtue of practising a familiar technique. The whole trend of this activity was admirably expressed in a crystallized form by a friend of mine who once said that the Final Bill (so-called,) the House-warning, and the first hearing in a court, usually coincide for most people. It is not necessary to go into details now since the causes, symptoms, and the course of this disease, are well-known. Heart-burns, disillusionments, shocks, cold despair, nervous tremors, impossible rage, and an unshakable conviction that one is being let down and persecuted, are some of the observable signs in a man stricken with the building disease. Everyone knows about it and has heard about it. All that we must ponder over is if there is any record in human history of the same pair, namely the house-dreamer and the house-builder, coming together again for a second transaction.

Even when all things are nicely settled, I don't think a house leaves one in peace. We have complicated our lives. It was enough in other days for men to have a little privacy, a little shelter, and a few comforts, and a few ornamentations; men did not demand too much of their houses. But now we seek too many facilities in a house. The first thing seems to be to keep up a general pretence that one got up from bed radiant, dressed, groomed, and was in every way fit at the breakfast table. It is a noble attempt, no doubt, but involves architectural modifications. It means that each bedroom should have a bathroom. This sounds simple enough, but the man who seeks to accomplish it will really find himself engaged in strange quests. It is understandable when we remember that nowadays a man's good sense, taste, and capacity are indicated not so much by what he does with his front hall as by what he has done in the bathrooms. In spite of all expense and trouble he may still find himself far away from perfection. In these matters opinions are widely varying. I have heard people remark with a shudder, after inspecting a house, "Did you notice that towel-rail! ..."

Electricity is another headache. It is not enough that a bulb hangs down and sheds its light. There are a dozen fine points to be observed: the wiring must not be seen, the bulb must not be seen, and the light itself must not be seen. They call everything "concealed this" or "concealed that" where electricity is concerned; (which object, if logically followed, is best achieved by short-circuiting the entire system), and everything that is sought to be concealed costs four times the one left open. A lamp-shade has not only to obstruct the diffusing light rays but has also to proclaim the house-owner to be a man of sound taste and finances. But it can at best be only an attempt. Approbation of our fellow-men is not so easily obtained—whatever may be the expense one has put oneself to for its sake. Unless it is a saint who has been taken round to see a new house, most normal men think that many items in the new house seem unnecessary, extravagant, garish, and in bad taste, which they neither feel nor say. If a man says what he feels, he will probably be thrown out; if he doesn't,it puts an undue strain on his conscience. Anyway, it doesn't appear to be a healthy state of affairs. I never fail to sigh whenever I see one of the good old houses, the type we see in what is sneeringly called "Moffusil Places'. It is the house with a few walls and a single roof sloping down and covering the entire structure. Here is an example of a house built without undue worry or fuss, something that grew out of bricks, apparently without the aid of an engineer or architect. Traditionally speaking I don't think there has been much distinction between a builder and an architect in our country. I wonder if more than five per cent of the public are aware of the functions of an architect. Most people are likely to confuse him with the contractor or with the engineer—neither of which a true architect is likely to appreciate. It is as if you did not see the difference between the sonnet-writer and the compositor who put it into type. An architect is in the category of an artist rather than an artisan. He dreams and theorizes and calculates: this is why a house-owner feels less perturbed when dealing with the contractor who is plainly mercenary, than with the architect whose idioms are strange, complex, abstract, and concrete, at the same time. The architect constantly says, "I will have this" or "I will not have that", "Your house must have horizontal lines", "Your house must have vertical lines." He may declare that the house must merge with the landscape or that it must stand out in contrast. He may love symmetry or he may adore a deliberate asymmetry; he may want all corridors to diverge or he may demand that they run parallel, he may declare the rectangular outlook a curse on buildings, he may champion all hexagons and what not. The result may terrify the prospective house-owner, especially when he finds that the architect has a clear-cut definite outlook in these matters. He may accommodate the novice's notions ultimately but only with contempt and resignation. Here again is a possibly explosive situation, where the human relationship is likely to strain and snap.

A house in construction is a meeting-point of many minds and faculties: engineer, labourer, financier, architect, etc., etc., and eventually perhaps a doctor, preferably a nerve-specialist who can put the house-owner back into shape at the end of it all. But there is this satisfaction for any man who undertakes the task: even a mighty institution like the Central Government fares no better when it tries to build houses. We have more than a hint of it in the news-item. 'The Government of India considered that it would not be in the public interest to disclose the findings and the recommendations on the working of the "pre-fab" housing factory in Delhi,' said the Health Minister in Parliament today ...'

A Picture of Years

He is past eighty. In his own home there are a great many corners, which he has not visited for years and years now. It is seventeen years since he climbed the staircase. He has lost all recollection of what the upstair rooms look like. They are all being occupied by his sons, grand-sons and grand-nephews. They seem to be stamping their feet there all the time, the din they make all through the day! It keeps his nerves on edge, as he dwells in his corner down below. He has a long cane-chair placed in a corner of the hall passage, with a window behind him through which he can see the street, but that is a minor consideration; he likes to be here because he can watch the movements of the entire household without moving himself. He watches; that is the only activity which his condition permits him now. He watches the young children going off to school early in the morning, he watches his grand-daughters dressing and decorating themselves, and the other women-folk running the household. He sees his eldest son rushing up and down at office time, and the stream of visitors who pour in to consult him professionally. He finds he has a word to say to everyone that passes near him but only they do not stop to hear him out fully. Half-finished sentences throughout. He has so many unfinished sentences, trailing one into another that he feels perplexed and worried. He often wonders "Why can't they settle down and and listen to what I have to say? Where is everybody hurrying away? In those days—" Those days! How long back? It seems like five hundred years ago. They were more restful in those days. They stopped and listened while one spoke; phrases issued from one's lips, fuller and slower; one sat down for food and went through it with a zestful calm. Not that there were no offices or law courts to attend then. He did stand before a mirror and wind a turban round his head, every day after breakfast, and then climb into his bullock-cart and was off to the Court. The pace of life was more in harmony with human capacities. One went to the Court rather leisurely, perhaps, but the Judge would never be there earlier. But it made no difference. One returned home laden with money. If necessary, one continued one's work while eating, washing, or undressing: the clients followed about everywhere, talking and talking: the office table was not the only place where business was done; and one even slept off in the middle of a talk and it did no one any harm. With all his there was no lack of earning, no lack of health and industry. Clients held on for a lifetime, he built this huge house and a dozen others, and he reared and brought up nearly a hundred souls. Looking at him now they perhaps think that he has always been like this, not worth a moment's pause. The entire family, quite a population of all ages and both sexes, flourished under his care and guidance in those days. The education of some young men here, suitable match for a maiden there, extricating someone from a financial or legal entanglement, and so on: every question ultimately drifted down to him for handling. His wisdom. His wisdom, instinct, and judgement, served for the entire family, and they were none the worse for it. But nowadays one notices everywhere an aggressive notion of independence. The youngest boy of the house, seven years old, to the eldermost member of the family, his own son bordering on sixty, everybody thinks he is qualified to judge and act for himself. You may tell the youngster every day not to carry his fountain pen to school, but only slate and pencil, but he persists and loses one pen every week. Why does his father indulge all his fancies! In those days, even if they studied in M.A., they never possessed fountain pens. He himself would not have had one, but for the fact that his father-in-law bought him one for Deepavali. That was as it should be. Fountain pens, watches, and rings were not playthings but precious gifts given or received on rare occasions. But now, the youngest fellow has a watch on his wrist. It is all foolish luxury. They do not know how to bring up children.

He thinks that he used to be very strict in his days, but it is only a trick of memory. The person against whom he complains now, the present head of the house, used to receive ten rupees every time his father went out of station. The old gentleman does not remember now how he once prolonged his stay in another town because he heard that a pedlar would be arriving next day with a wooden horse on wheels, the sort of thing the youngster had been demanding so long. He has no recollection of it now. The only person who could bring it back to his mind is his wife, but she is not here. That good soul left the earth a dozen years ago, a piece of memory which hurts even at this distance. This is the worst of living to an advanced age. One sees the fingers of death too often, plucking up a life here and a life there. He has lost count of all the bereavements he has suffered in life: friends, nephews, children, and elders.

At this point, however, he feels less bewildered by death than by life. As years advance gradually, unnoticed, the swing of existence narrows down: the orbit of movement shrinks visibly. Till sixty he walked six miles for recreation, went round the tank, and visited the market once a week. Next the excursion was confined to a visit to the third street, and then up to the bungalow gate, and now he never steps beyond the verandah. He feels dazzled even at twilight, under an open sky. His boundary is the bench on the verandah, an ancient twelve-legged piece of furniture which he acquired in his younger days. No one goes near it, but it is his favourite piece of furniture. All through the day he is in eager expectation of moving on to it in the evening. At four he seizes his staff and moves on to the bench. He sits there watching the street. He stops almost every hawker who cries his ware in the street and calls him in; he has a feeling that he is helping the household with its supplies. Very rarely does he find himself in agreement with the price quoted; he finds the prices at least ten times over what he used to pay in his days. Or if, by rare chance, the price is acceptable, he finds it again a great source of worry; he has to undertake an excursion back to his room, get through the maze of old furniture there, and open the drawer in which he keeps his cash. This activity cuts badly into his evening.

His great joy is when a neighbour, an old friend, occasionally drops in for a chat. This man is very vivacious, and much stronger, though of the same age. He visits all parts of the town and acts as a sort of compendium of information of persons and places. The gentleman sees the world through him. On the days he arrives, the old gentleman prolongs his stay in the verandah by half an hour. Otherwise, normally before the twilight is gone, he gets up and hobbles back to his room. In a few minutes, he sits in a corner of the hall with his eyes shut in prayer, his fingers turning the rosary. He does not open his eyes for nearly half-an-hour, although the children return home from play, shout and create a din over their books, and their home tutor comes and drowns their voices. At his dinner time he goes in, calling everyone to join him. But no one heeds his invitation and he eats alone. He has had a lonely dinner for years now.

After he has been in bed, and slept and dreamed for hours, he opens his eyes and still hears voices in the house. He picks himself up with difficulty, goes to his threshold and cries, "Why are the lights still burning? Such noise even at midnight!"

"It is not midnight, it is only 8-30 now, grandfather," corrects the youngest child, and he goes back to his bed. He is up before 3.00 a.m., and wonders why everyone is still asleep. "Something wrong with all their time", he mutters to himself, resigning himself to staying in bed for an hour more.

LATER ESSAYS

Sorry, No Room

At the portals of Heaven, he stood forlorn. The guard would not let him in. When the man identified himself, the guard scrutinized a long scroll, and shook his head, 'Your are perhaps ahead of your time... The chart relating to you has not come; nearer the time of your scheduled departure from the earth they'll send it. You are far, far ahead of your time. Why are you here?'

'Because I'm, dead, I suppose, that's all....' The angel became thoughtful... 'I've no power to admit you immaturely. What happened? You are not expected to be dead yet.'

The man began to explain: 'For years I was unaware of my body or its functioning, but you know there is a dreadful habit among mortals of making a fuss over each other's birthdays. My children bestirred themselves on my sixtieth birthday. In spite of my protests, they combined to organize elaborate rituals, ceremonies, *pujas* and feasting on the day I reached sixty. My wife and I were garlanded and made to pose for photographs like newly-weds. During the rituals, they emptied on our heads gallons of holy waters collected from all the rivers, crowded round us suffocatingly, and deafened us with chants, greetings, chatter and loud music. Further, they planned to bundle us off on a second honeymoon. But this part of the programme had to be dropped, all that dousing of holy water brought on cough, cold and fever; we were bed-ridden after the festivities. My wife, being younger, recovered and was on her feet again in a couple of weeks, but I became an invalid. Our doctor had to examine me daily, and later, four different specialists at different parts of the day I had no interests other than anticipating the doctors' arrival. Each doctor ordered a particular test on me to be carried out, only by his favourite pathologist, and my waking hours thereafter were spent in going round proffering samples of my excreta and blood and what not to the analysts. In a short while, a nice portfolio had developed detailing every inch of my inner mechanism and chemistry.

"Avoid sugar," said one doctor. "Avoid salt," said another. "Avoid hot water," "Avoid cold water," "Drink plenty of water," "Avoid smoking," "Smoke in moderation," "Avoid alcohol," "Drink in moderation because sudden change of habit may produce symptoms of withdrawal," were some of the expert suggestions; also observations such as "Overweight," "Underweight," "Eat less," "Eat heartily." I got rather muddled and my normal routine of life was soon gone. I fell into complete disarray as I tried to respect and fit in all the advice and suggestions into logical pattern. I had no time for anything but attending to the repairs and patchwork of my dilapidated system, in addition to a weekly check-up to certify, it seemed to me, that I was a living creature.

'The accumulation of vials, injection tubes, and tablet cases, grew into a little hillock at a corner, as the portfolio of my health reports swelled to the size of an abridged edition of the *Mahabharata*. At the stated hours my doctors came in one by one, and briskly turned the covers of the portfolio, pored over the papers and left, without so much as a glance in my direction, muttering, "Nothing serious, but be careful and relaxed." An impossible combination.

'At last I found a physician who said, "Nothing wrong with you. It's all purely psychological. Throw away all the medicines. Say to yourself constantly, 'Day by day in every way I'm getting better and better', and then leave it to Nature."

'Nature? "No, Sir, Nature has no use for the likes of me. She would sooner see me in my grave," I said, quoting a classical hypochondriac. However, I gave Nature a trial, and here I am as a result.'

The angel said, 'I'm definite I cannot let you in. Try the other gate.'

The lost soul hesitated at the other gate as it led to Hell, but feeling that that would be preferable to drifting in mid-air like a fluff of cotton wool, he presented himself at the portal, which was guarded by an angel with slightly forbidding aspect, who barred his way once again for the same reason as before, there being no notice of his arrival. When he explained his predicament, the dark angel took out the records, double-checked them, and shook his head, 'Impossible. Admission here is more difficult than at the other place. The standards here are much stricter, being reserved for VIPs from the world of politics, diplomacy, and business (while the commoners are sorted out and sent elsewhere). Here we have to be careful with the VIPs. They hate to be crowded or inconvenienced in any way.'

'Being used to comforts at all times, how do they manage here?'

'That's no problem. They have a knack of having their own way everywhere, and live quite comfortably here.'

'But the chastisement and chastening processes which are reputedly the purpose of this region?'

'That's only a formality here. Not for them the rigours. Although they are put through all that in a routine manner, the purging of sins is gradual and in agreeable doses. We apply a system called "Tempered Torment," "Cold Branding," and "Cushioned Flogging"—but all that is a formal procedure once a day. On the whole they are at peace with themselves and do not want a change.'

'Let me in,' pleaded the lost soul.

The angel considered his appeal and said, 'I could at best put you on the waiting list. Sometimes a vacancy occurs through a freak cancellation or absence and if you are around we can fix something. Till then go back to Earth, to your familiar haunts.'

'No, no, there they will think I am a ghost and chase me off.'

'In that case why don't you float around the galaxies or better still get on to one of those satellites and you'll be near enough earth too, and maybe you could also communicate with your kith and kin.'

God and the Atheist

At the round table the talk was all about atheism and faith. The dialectician was in his element. If anyone in the company sounded religious, he at once championed the atheist and vice-versa. And finally we arrived at a stage where the antagonists were brought together face to face.

The atheist stood in the presence of God who was enthroned and radiant. He turned to his visitor questioningly. The atheist said, 'If you are omniscient, as your followers claim, you should know what I am. It is a test. I do not know how to address you, Sir; should I say "Your Almighty"?'

'Oh, no. The second person pronoun will be adequate.'

'I do not remember my grammar. What is second person pronoun?'

'Y-O-U, I cannot afford to forget my grammar. I do not have the freedom an atheist enjoys.'

'Oh, you know me, though I have not announced myself!'

'I don't have to be told. I hope I have passed the test.'

'Let us now go on, with your permission, in the manner of a press interview.'

'Excellent idea. Only you cannot have my photograph. I am not opaque nor photogenic.'

'It does not matter, we have enough portrayals for your worshippers. Now, first of all, I want to know if you have really created the entire Universe.'

'How does it seem to you?'

'Rationally viewing it, the Universe and all that it contains seems to be self-created through various evolutionary processes and molecular actions. Where is the need for a Maker, like a potter, to give shape and colour to things?'

'The potter at least can smash up his handiwork if he is not satisfied. But I cannot do it.'

'Oh, come on, what about catastrophies, calamities and holocausts one sees all around?'

'Most of it is man-made, and the others are caused by —, we need not go into all that now. Normally the Universe is stable, Stars run their course without bumping into each other, you can calculate with precision, as your almanacs prove, the movements and career of planets. Only human beings are unpredictable. They are ready to pounce on and exterminate each other individually or as groups, communities or armies. In all creation, human beings alone display so much ego, aggression, and greed. On the other hand, animals, birds and other creatures naturally practise a philosophy of "live and let live." Even beasts which kill for food attack only when they are hungry. But man will attack, pillage and grab and jealously hold on to it, whether it be food, money or territory.'

'Why is it so? You are the creator and you should know.'

'Creatures which follow their instincts do less damage than man, who exercises intelligence.'

'Why did you endow man with intelligence?'

'As I told you it is all built-in, to use your popular phrase. I have no control over the mind of a human being, which he is free to exercise for any purpose; and that is the trouble. I sometimes feel, watching human antics, that I am like an author whose characters have jumped off the page and are running wild. But I do not have the freedom enjoyed by your author who can tear up the page and dismiss the characters.'

'God, your flights into the philosophy are unconvincing. I would prefer a down-to-earth talk.'

'Down-to-earth? Very well. On Earth you create a lot of commotion in my name. There can be nothing more absurd than the bloody feuds over nomenclature and over the label to hang around my neck, each asserting that such and such alone is my name. Champions of God have perpetrated unspeakable cruelties on anyone suspected of heresy which is a convenient term applied against anyone voicing an unorthodox view. At one time in your history, scientists and thinkers have been tortured for the sin of declaring that the Earth is round and revolves round the Sun—this was considered an ungodly statement. Save me from my champions, I say, but to whom am I to appeal to, considering the evil generated by my followers who have provoked holy wars and perfected instruments of persecution? I feel atheists have done less harm, although fanatical in their own way.'

'Thank you, God, for your down-to-earth talk.'

'Only remember that the planet you live in with its problems is just a speck compared to the rest of the Universe I have to mind. Good bye. Are you now convinced of my existence?'

'Not yet. How am I to be sure that our talk is real and not just a piece of self-deception?'

'What does it matter, what difference could it make?'

On Funny Encounters

Literally a nodding acquaintance I come across on his motor-cycle when I go out for a walk. I do not know his full name, nor have any idea of his features since his helmet covers his brow, but we never fail to greet each other although he generally flashes past at thirty kilometres.

Today, he suddenly applied the brake, pushed his vehicle along to a side of the road and waited for me. In Mysore, as was in ancient Greece, many worthwhile, encounters take place when people meet at a street-crossing. We don't mind stopping to exchange the news of the day, and discuss and deplore the state of affairs in general. I am quite used to this practice and appreciate its value—saves a lot of mutual visiting and all the labour involved. Nowadays such encounters have become more frequent for me—especially after Doordarshan exposed me in their "Newsline" programme. People stop by to say, "I saw you on TV," and then ask for details of the modalities of a TV production.

During the week after the Presidential announcement of the nominations to the Rajya Sabha, people stopped to cry, "Congratulations! Great honour to us!" and after I mumbled a thanks, a question as to when I'm "joining". I always say something and continue my journey.

But today, the motor-cyclist stood beside his vehicle after hoisting it on its stand, and seemed determined to congratulate me rather elaborately. So I slackened my steps. After so much preparation on his part it did not seem fair to pass him by.

"Congratulations!" he cried, and held out his hand.

"Thanks," I said, responding with a warm grip. First time I was getting a close view of his personality, although the goggles he wore covered half his face.

"When are you reporting for duty?" he asked.

I did not know the answer myself.

"You should do it immediately," he said. "From the moment

it is announced you become an MP and entitled to free calls on the telephone. Otherwise you will be paying fifty paise a call unncessarily."

"I don't mind it," I said.

"Why not?" he argued. "Why should you not enjoy all the benefits? Will you be given a house?"

"I have no idea," I said.

"I'm sure you will be given a house," he said, apparently more informed than I was in such matters. He looked triumphant at the fact that he could tell me one or two things.

He paused, and said suddenly, "Could you refuse this nomination?"

"What a question! Why?"

"When I heard the announcement, I got a funny feeling," he said.

"Perhaps you thought the Government was out to amuse you?"

He ignored my quip, but went on with his own thoughts. "How can you live in Delhi, bundling up everything here, and living all alone in Delhi?"

He looked quite panic-stricken on my account. It was as if I were being banished to the heart of the Sahara. I was touched by his solicitude (though it was unwarranted). I said placatingly, "I'm used to it, often visit Delhi on some committee business...."

"What committee?"

I explained the nature of the committee I served on.

He clicked his tongue and made a sound which can only be indicated by the letters "Pshaw". He added, "Committees! Committees! Don't I know about them—you nibble glucose biscuits sitting around an oval table, sip tea and collect your air fare....."

"Are you a member of committee by any chance?", I asked, feeling it was time I put in a question from my side.

"I have a boss who goes to Delhi five times in a month and I know what he and others do...."

I felt relieved that he was straying away from the Rajya Sabha nominations. Perhaps he also realised it and returned immediately to the subject.

"I can't imagine you living in Delhi. I get a funny feeling when I think of it." Once again this man was using the word 'funny' and I resisted the impulse to ask him to define 'fun' and 'funny'. But I left it at that.

He suddenly said, "If you have decided to go, be sure that you are not cheated—you will be entitled to a house, free travel, etc., and other amenities, make sure you get them all. After all, we tax-payers support you, and I'm keen...."

I asked, "When I secure them all—will you cease to feel funny?"

"No," he added, "I'm not sure, after all, this is not your line...."

"What do you suppose is my line?" I asked.

"You are after all a journalist and story-writer, and you must stick to your job."

"Do you know of any of my books?"

"I'm busy from late morning till night and have no time to read. But my wife reads a lot of novels and such things and tells me about them. I'm interested in you as a neighbour and I want you to progress...."

At this point I felt outraged at this man's patronising talk. I said, "Perhaps you were going on some business. I shouldn't stop you."

"You are not stopping me. I stopped myself because ever since I heard the announcement I have had a funny feeling....."

Once again that "funny feeling"!

"May I know what your policies and plans are going to be? As a tax-payer I'm entitled to know. Will you do anything useful such as getting us broad-gauge, airport, railway connection from Chamarajanagar to Satyamangalam—problems plaguing us for fifty years? Will you do anything about it?"

"I'll bear it in mind," I said loftily.

"Yes, you'll promise, of course, now, but will do nothing about it once you step in there. Don't know our MPs!"

At this point I cautioned him, "Are you aware that if you comment recklessly abut MPs you are likely to be hauled up for contempt and may face a jail sentence? Now kick your starter and be off before you do yourself any damage."

The Testament of a Walker

There are persons who have no ear for music, being tone-deaf; others who have no eye for art, who may in a sense be called 'colour blind'. In a similar category, I am impervious to the subtler values in a car. To me an automobile is only the means to an end; I am satisfied if I am provided a seat and four wheels that can roll, and I am blind to all other points in a car. In spite of this constitutional defect, by a quirk of fate I came to own an 'imported' car, flashy and full of sophistication, which caused ecstacy in every auto-pundit who saw it. 'Ah'! Recessed handle!' would cry one. 'Look at this steering, maneuverable with a flick of the finger! Pushbutton glass-raiser! Floating seats! Multi-coloured speedometer! Ah, controlled-air-conditioner! Tape-recorder-digital alarm with calculator!' They would examine my dash-board panel admiringly, although I never understood at any time the purpose of most of the buttons, switches, and gadgets, and found it safer to leave them alone. The air-conditioner which was supposed to make one's journey free from dust, and heat, and noise, was switched on, during the ten years I used the car, for a total period of thirty minutes, which worked out to less than three minutes a year. Whenever the air-conditioner was on, the windows were to be closed; which inhibited my driver, whose habit was to show right or left turn by thrusting his arm out, who, when the glass was raised, constantly hit it with his fist. He was also in the habit of gesticulating at erring pedestrians and addressing them volubly in passing, now he felt constricted, encapsulated, and tongue-tied, and drove morosely. Also, I think, he was conditioned to driving to the tune of the rattle and roar of other vehicles beside, behind, and ahead, and without such accompaniments he could not proceed with any confidence.

I lack automobile sensibility and do not regret it. I have a strong belief that man's ultimate destiny lies in walking, that is why he is endowed with a pair of legs, which can operate without petrol or gears. It is this philosophy that leaves me indifferent at the mention of any petrol 'hike' (a hybrid term, which seems to flourish in oil). I know that the hiking will culminate where it can't 'hike' any further (that will be at a stage where it may cost a thousand rupees to travel one kilometre), and man will rediscover the use of his feet; when that happens oil wells will over-flow into storm drains or stagnate for want of takers, and petro-civilization will have become defunct. The most ambitious work I have been planning for years is to be called 'Testament of a Walker'. The title has been ready for decades although the book may never be written, considering its boundless scope and ramification. Whether written or unwritten, the philosophy is deep-rooted in me. Time was when I walked ten miles a day morning and evening (Mysore being ideal for such an occupation) and even now, I continue the habit on a lesser scale, wherever I may be, and in any season. If I am compelled to stay indoors through bad weather I can still get the mileage out in my verandah, though I may be presenting an odd spectacle pacing up and down like a bear in his cage. For a fanatic of this sort the possession of a car is an anachronism: and especially the acquisition of a sophisticated, imported-make, an irrelevancy and a nuisance.

Among the things I value are privacy and anonymity—both are lost when I allow myself to be carried about in a gaudy car. It is like sitting in a *howdah* on elephant-back and hoping not to be noticed.

In a compact city like Mysore (where everyone can met everyone else at will), my movements became known to the whole town and someone or other would remark 'Ah, you were at the store this morning' or 'I saw you going down the Market Road.' No harm, normally speaking, in such observation or enquiry; but in my case it leads to complications, and embarrassment, since I generally avoid all public engagements and invitations with the excuse that I will be away at Bangalore (100 miles) or Madras (300 miles) or Delhi (1,000 miles) depending upon the persistence of the man asking me. Apart from all this, I was in constant dread lest my driver should feel inspired to test my car's special virtue of being able to attain a speed of one-hundred-and-sixty kilometres from zero, within two minutes. At the workshop I could not help noticing the

171

battered remains of many cars which had tried this facility on our roads. Our mechanic blithely explained, 'No problem. We can always bring them back to shape. Part of our job. Nothing is impossible. Insurance will take care of our bills even if we have to charge thirty or forty thousand for repairs. So why worry?'

Since my car was of a special pedigree, it was inadvisable to allow any ordinary workshop to open the bonnet. The accredited workshop with mechanics, wielding special tools, was a hundred miles away at Bangalore. For any attention I had to drive a hundred miles every time.

At Bangalore a team of experts would stand around and pronounce their verdict. 'Engine mountings need replacement, if you want to get rid of the "dug dug" sound which is bothering you; one of the front shock-absorbers must be replaced, better while you do it replace the pair so that your tyre were will be uniform, otherwise your steering system will be damaged'. After their diagnosis, they would direct me to the one and only establishment, this side of the Vindhyas, which stocked imported spares, an exclusive shop catering only to the elite. They could toss across the counter anything you wanted from a little screw to a whole engine, at a price fit, indeed, for royalty still on their thrones. A customer entering this shop was expected to be loftyminded and discreet enough not to question the price but part with his cash with an air of amused nonchalance and even benevolence.

I began to fear that at this rate (I was obliged to visit the workshop every other week to shed my savings), I should soon reach the brink of bankruptcy effortlessly. I seemed to have let myself into a strange world peopled by a class of high-priests and voodoo-men, the workings of whose minds I could never fathom, but still, who held sway over me.

Two cyclists collided and fell on my car parked in front of the hospital, and smashed the parking light on the left side. It could not ordinarily be replaced in this country. The elite shop could produce one if I was prepared to pay two thousand for the piece. My mechanic suggested why not I visit New York and pick it up there. I had to remind him as gently as I could that he was talking nonsense. Then he examined the damage closely and declared: 'Oh, yes,—only the glass is broken—we will fabricate a cover in plastic—though it may be difficult to get the curvature of the original—I will try—'. Briskly, he unscrewed the whole assembly and left. He was away from the workshop for ten weeks on sick leave. When I met him again and enquired about the parking light, he looked puzzled and said, 'I remember I gave it to you. I needed only the measurement of the socket. Please check if it is at home in Mysore...As a rule I do not like to keep such things with me.' No further reference was made to the subject. It was impossible that both of us could be right. One of us must surely have suffered from hallucination; either myself seeing a vision of his taking out the light with the words, 'Let me keep it for safety—otherwise the boys in this workshop may steal it—' or he had an illusion of handing it over to me with appropriate words.

That settled it. I was appalled at the thought of all the travail I had undergone and the expense, and considering that actually I had no use for a car, having no office or outside engagements, and using it only to catch it at the end of a long walk—it seemed to me the most thoughtless thing I had done in my life to have acquired this car. I decided to be rid of it, lock it up in the shed as soon as possible to turn my energies again to writing stories.

I am not the sort of person who would enjoy getting under the car on a Sunday, as is the case with a friend of mine, who generally spends his leisure hours under his imported car, having no trust in any mechanic or workshop in our motherland. All his time is spent in collecting spare parts from far and near; he has succeeded in piling up enough stock to assemble a couple of new cars if he so desires. Whenever it becomes necessary, he strips his car bare, cuts away a diseased part, and grafts a new one. At such moments he speaks like a surgeon specialized in heart bypass and kidney transplants. I admire his competence, though I cannot accept his advice, which generally runs on the following lines, 'Don't give up your car—the thing to do is to be on the look out for a similar model, buy it at any price and then you could transfer all the necessary parts from one car to another. It will work out cheaper that way. Ultimately you can sell away the shell of the remaining car to any fellow who is planning to set up a wayside tea-stall, or you could convert it into a little garden house in your own compound.'

Love and Lovers

When I feel the need for an academic discussion, I walk across to the professor's study and wait for him to open a subject. Normally a monologist, today he was in a cross-examining mood. After a few perfunctory observations on the weather and corruption in public life, he suddenly shot out an angry question, 'Is literature dying in our country?'

'Not seen its obituary yet,' I replied, in keeping with his mood of enquiry.

'Where is Tolstoy or 'Dostoyevsky?' he asked with passion.

'Rather hard to say, but definitely not in this world, not been around for a long time now.'

'You don't have to tell me that, I am asking where is our Tolstoy or Dostoyevsky? Why has our country not produced a Tolstoy or Dostoyevsky?"

'For the same reason it hasn't produced a Grand Canyon or Aurora Borealis. Certain things in this world, including men of genius, are gifts from a mysterious source, and cannot be made to order, or duplicated internationally like cosmetics or drugs. As for me, I am content to read Tolstoy or anyone in translation, without sighing that we do not have a replica in our country.'

'Which shows you have no national pride or aspiration. No wonder you are not taken seriously. Have you ever tried to place your finger on the pulse of our nation or made any attempt to echo our national aspirations?'

'No, because I am interested only in the individual, and I am extremely suspicious of the phrase "national aspiration". It is pretentious and phoney. Each person has a private universe and lives many lives. You will be nearer the mark if you speak of the problems, hopes, and aspirations of a person: say a doctor's hope to see more sick people coming in; the sick man hoping that his doctor is a minor god capable of holding him back from the grave; the politician's jugglery to win votes; the voter's fleeting euphoria of being a king-maker; the boy's hope that his school roof would have collapsed at week-end; the policeman's dream that the thief would walk in with the stolen property and save him all the trouble; the cobbler at the street-corner watching passing feet for worn-out soles; the householder's concern to keep his budget and family in proper shape; the snake charmer with his assets curled up in the bamboo basket; the peripatetic knife-grinder's cry down the street on a hot afternoon, an infinite variety of lives overlapping and complementing one another. I am moved by such patterns of life, and not by your "national aspiration". What is it really? Do you visualize six hundred million to look skyward on a given day and shout their aspiration in a single voice?'

'Now let us dismiss this aspect, as you implicitly admit your failure as a national interpreter. You probably assume and want me to accept you as an expert on the individual. May we examine your writing from his point of view? Are you going to tell me that you portray the individual in his fulness? There are areas you have neglected. For example, do you deal with man-woman relationship with any seriousess? Aren't you prudish when it comes to sex?'

'Not exactly prudish, only I take the hint. When a couple, even if they happen to be characters in my own novel, want privacy, I leave the room; surely you wouldn't expect one, at such moments, to sit on the edge of their bed and take notes?'

'Why not? Just what would be expected of a novelist concerned with realism. I have closely studied your handling of this particular aspect, and found you wanting. Take your earliest *Dark Room* where the head of an office seduces his pretty trainee. Your latest *'Painter of Signs'* where Daisy and Raman are thrown physically together for days on end, and then of course your *Guide,* that masterpiece of glorified adultery, in all these and others, while one expects a great deal from your pen as a realist, you dismiss the time hastily; the utmost you afford the reader is a quick eavesdropper's or keyhole-viewer's report, slurring over the dynamism of love.'

'Is there any need for elaboration? I find that the very mention of a darkened room with whispers coming through the bolted door, stirs your imagination to such an extent that you ask for more. I am confident that at a certain point I can safely leave it all to the reader's imagination without fettering it with

175

wordy descriptions. Particularly after D.H. Lawrence, no writer can have anything original or fresh to say about lovers. However, to please you, I am prepared to add a footnote at appropriate places in my novels: "For further details look up *Lady Chatterly's Lover."* Even the authors of American best-sellers, which provide its readers bed scenes at regular intervals, say once every five thousand words, exhibit nervousness while seeking new phrases for an old experience, and often let their narrative degenerate into a sort of popular treatise on anatomy.'

'How can any honest writer avoid sex where it serves an artistic purpose?'

'Could you please define the phrase "artistic purpose"? Once I served on a censorship enquiry committee. Every film-producer who appeared before us pleaded for a liberal interpretation of the code where sex and nudity served an artistic purpose; it turned out on scrutiny that they only wanted freedom to copy the new-wave Swedish or French films, in which the costume-departments have obviously been abolished, and the camera does not move beyond a double-bed all through the story.'

'You are putting it crudely...but you have no right to skip any fundamental human experience...'

'Experience is vast and one is forced to be selective. If every bodily function and physical and mental activity is to be recorded without any omission, not all the world's paper supply will suffice even for a single novel. Anyway I now have an ideal of what you are looking for. Why don't you go and contemplate the sculptural masterpieces at Khajuraho to start with? There you will find an exuberance, beside which Swedish films will look like the work of starched Puritans.'

'I have never visited Khajuraho,' he said with a sigh.

'Nor I, like a million others in our country, I have only seen them in colour slides projected at the homes of some friends in America. Why don't you visit our famous temples?'

'Oh, I don't believe in idol worship...'

'Makes no difference. You may avoid the *sanctum sanctorum,* where the sculptor has probably shaped God's image with restraints and reverence—but after finishing the main image he appears to have gone wild when carving the pillars and cornices. Words cannot match the sculptor's art in directness, although a finicky person is likely to find it embarrassing.' The professor became pensive for a moment as he remarked. 'Oh, how little we know of our own treasures! We have to discover them only through foreigners!'

'Ancient sculptors seemed to have anticipated the philosophy of tourism and did their bit to attract visitors from beyond the "seven seas".'

'Yes, yes, quite a plausible hypothesis. Travel is important, Sir. *Bharat Darshan* should find a place in every educational programme, I shall promote the idea at all conferences, hereafter.'

A Matter of Statues

Although the motive for installing a statue is a solemn one, I find statues in general rather comical. There is something ludicrous in stationing a figure permanently in the open, in sun or rain, night and day, in a frozen attitude of benevolence, heroism, or contemplation.

I never look at a statue without thinking, here is a perfect instance of human miscalculation, the crown of the would-be immortal serving only as a bird-perch if not something worse. Within a couple of years of unveiling, people cease to notice the statue, and never look up. Time and usage having successfully rubbed off all significance the statue might as well be a mound of rubble or a rusty tar-drum abandoned on the roadside.

Laxman once suggested in a cartoon detachable heads for all statues. The idea seemed to be that when an old hero yields place to a new one, on account of change of values or a dimming of public memory, you will only be investing in a new head with a device to screw it on, after unscrewing the other one, which could be stowed away in a museum vault or in a time-capsule, for future reference or even a possible restoration if the old head should regain public esteem. This will mean a great saving of national resources, through a sort of recycling of the existing pedestal and torso, which form the major part of any statue. The main concern at this stage should be to fit the head on a relevant torso, keeping in mind the broad distinction between a civilian and a soldier in their respective dress and deportments. However, it will only be a matter of detail, easily adjusted, with a certain amount of planning and forethought. Thus we may also save the labour of moving a whole statue, when necessity arises

Now and then certain historical causes may create a sudden uproar against a long-standing statue, with demands to move or remove it. I remember the Neil Statue Satyagraha in Madras, about 50 years ago. Colonel (?) Neil stood at an important

178

crossing on Mount Road, surveying superciliously the native population flowing past. That was the heyday of imperial rule. In the wake of our national struggle, there was an outcry against the Colonel followed by *jathas* and *satyagraha*, and not all the police *lathis* and arrests could stem the forces out to topple this tyrant, who 'dressed in brief authority' had left a hideous record of oppression. British rulers had installed the statue with a dual purpose: to immortalize their hero and also remind Indians to behave themselves.

Finally the public did succeed in dislodging the statue and putting it away in a cell in the museum. But not every statue is likely to end that way. Most statues, as I have already mentioned, are ignored and thus survive according to a natural law which says that a statue less noticed has a greater chance of survival. Along the same Mount Road at the northern end looms over the landcape a figure astride a horse. The details on the top portion are obscured by the height. Normally one noticed only the pedestal which rose to over fifty feet above sea level, and beyond it the figure of a flamboyant equestrian probably flourishing a lance or sword, I am not sure. It was so high that kites and vultures normally circling in high heavens glided down to rest on the shoulder of this gentleman.

Just known as Munroe Statue, no one bothered about its history, or could stop at that point in Mount Road to gaze upward. However once it attracted much notice, when a canard was started that an eagle had dropped a necklace of gold sovereigns over its head. Enormous crowds gathered around the statue, and naturally the police also had to be there to prevent possible attempts to climb the statue. People stood about shading their eyes and looking up for hours.

If any statue could be imagined to nurse within its stony heart a craving to be stared at, here it was fulfilled. But a reaction set in, presently official moves were afoot to eliminate the statue, as a traffic hazard though not for political reasons. The corporation invited contractors to demolish it, and found it would cost over a lakh of rupees to demolish the pedestal alone, and then there was the question of how to dispose of the statue once it was taken down. It was rumoured that even Whitehall was consulted whether they would be interested in acquiring it for the British Museum. Finally the corporators decided to leave it alone, and made a virtue of necessity by cultivating a lawn and flower-beds around it.

Sometimes the identity of a statue becomes a matter of controversy, mostly due to indifferent workmanship. While statue-making is an arduous and difficult undertaking, it is also the most hazardous one. Often the statue-maker has to build up from a photograph and oral descriptions of one who may not be in our midst; a living person normally would not think of his own statue. I say 'normally', since I remember an exception, a chief minister who supposedly spends a part of his day helping his statue-maker shape him in marble; obviously he does not wish to risk being ignored or forgotten when his term of office is over. ('It is not for myself, but I want my philosophy and the principles for which I have fought remembered,' he is quoted). He is a busy man but never too busy to keep an eye on his statue-maker. Whether he has also chosen a site for it and intends to preside over its unveiling are 'classified material', and hence my information is limited.

I think it is better to have a self-approved statue in any place than a controversial one. In Mysore we have a certain marble statue installed about ten or twenty years ago to honour the memory of a pioneer journalist, complete with his long coat, turban, and upper cloth, but passers-by, particularly the younger generation, do not recognize him as such but think the statue represents a composer, who lived till recently and was a familiar figure in our city. Having had occasions to see them both, I cannot blame anyone for taking one for the other, mainly due to the height of the statue. The veteran journalist possessed a tall, imposing figure as I remember; but the composer was short and stocky, and the statue is made to the latter specification.

Height must be a grave problem for any statue-maker; while features could be studied in a photo, the exact figure of a person can only be guessed. I remember another case where a deadlock arose between the promoters of a statue and the sculptor over the question of the height of the subject; the sculptor was charged with making the worthy gentleman look absurdly short and stooping. It ended in a protracted litigation, with the statue lying prone in the sculptor's backyard, all parties involved in the affair being gone.

Portraits are simpler. The subject sits before the painter and can express an opinion, which may not be accepted. Once a portrait painter asked me to sit for him. When he finished his work, I did not think the portrait looked like me; but the artist brushed aside my objections with, 'You would not know, but that is how you really look, it may not be what your mirror shows; but I see your soul and portray it.'

I suppose the painter was right; few of us can have a correct impression of our own personalities; the only exception I can think of was a friend of mine, a vice-chancellor, who asked me to tea one evening. After tea he took me along to his library, switched on the light and said 'See there—' pointing at a large, gorgeous, colourful portrait of himself on the wall in a red academic gown, one hand resting on a tall flower stand, and the other clutching a scroll. He had lit up the frame brightly though not tastefully. As he stood there entranced and bewitched by his own portrait, I did not know what to say and so remarked: 'I suppose you will present it to the University?' 'Oh no, why should I?' he said, 'I have paid for it hard cash. It is mine, and it goes where I go, that is all', with an air of finality. When I subsequently learnt of his retirement and death a few months later, my first reaction was to speculate on the fate of that portrait.

History is a Delicate Subject

The only Latin I know, *De mortuis nil nisi bonum*, meaning. "Of the dead, nothing but good", has always seemed to me an unsound philosophy although implying tolerance and forgiveness, and based on the hypothesis "Death sanctifies and canonizes". I am not able to accept this notion, which seems to be the result of sentimentality and confused reactions in the face of death. An honest obituary should be possible. One must not hesitate to say: "Sorry to report of so-and so's death: he had some good points and several unholy traits too. We need not go into details now, but suffice it to say that the cooperative institution to which he had stuck all his life by hook or by crook may function hereafter in a better way and benefit the public" or "Very sorry. He was after all a harmless crack-pot and would not have hurt anyone even if he had continued to live...."

"Of the living too, nothing but good" is a corollary if the man is powerful and can afford to engage the services of a first-rate P.R.O.

The ancient rulers employed court chroniclers whose sole business was to record unceasingly their master's virtues and valour. Much of ancient history, I suspect, is derived from such sources.

I have myself observed in the days of Palace Durbars, when His Highness stepped down from the throne to move to his chambers, he was escorted by uniformed attendants crying, what they called parak—"Glory and victory to this Emperor of the World, the unvanquished, undefeatable one etc etc..." It was a formal cry, of course, and I don't think that any Maharaja in his right mind ever believed a word of it. But its significance is there, and its origin is in history. Every ruler, according to the court chronicler, became the supreme lord of the earth, having vanquished other rulers, whose chroniclers also made a similar claim. If there were three neighbouring kingdoms, each claimed that he became supreme after defeating the other two. As a

182

result, all history became just a record of bloody encounters and extravagant heroic claims.

I am happy that someone is taking a second look at all history. But I feel uneasy that this Committee is prescribing how to write the new history which, I fear, is likely to produce history made to order again: a true historian must have the hardihood to call a spade a spade and present it instead of wrapping it up in gold foil.

I love to study history, but with a lot of distrust. In our college days we read British historians. We found the postage-stamp size portraits of kings and governors dotting the pages of our text-book charming, and the writing itself competent and readable. One did not doubt the veracity of their statements and conclusions at any stage, until a young professor, in an aside, announced one day. "There was neither Black, nor Hole, nor Calcutta". referring to Siraj-ud-Dowlah, the ruler of Bengal who was supposed to have packed in a jam his prisoners of war, leaving them to suffocate in a small room. The same professor also disproved that certain Muslim rulers who were supposed to have demolished temples and proselytized with fire and sword, were actually tolerant and endowed temples. And thugs and bandits actually were freedom-fighters—guerrilla fighters of those days.

Ancient history was also part of our study. The Vedic and Indo-Aryan period was taught by a specialist who entered the classroom in flowing academic robes, carrying a load of source material in his arms. While we sat up expectantly, he turned the leaves of heavy tomes and read out, "In those days men rode on horses and women ground corn and sometimes wove mats", in a tone of profound discovery. "They do it even today, what is historical in it?" one felt tempted to ask. He then continued, turning the leaves of another tome. "Here we have evidence that all those ancient cities had a wonderful drainage system...." "Where is that skill gone?" one felt like asking, while the Professor went on to announce from yet another voluminous document, "They buried the dead, and sometimes cremated them too". One began to suspect that the historian was desperately trying to squeeze information out of obvious and puerile data and from broken pottery, and thus made ancient history a vulnerable subject.

I found it all bewildering. One did not know what to believe.

History is a delicate subject, the slightest falsehood could poison the whole body, like the invasion of bacteria in the human system. There are many sources of confusion for the historian, and many misleading paths open to him.

While we felt that British historians were unreliable. I heard the remark from a British scholar, 'Indians have no sense of history, no scientific attitude.' Store for me when he explained tritely, 'One must learn to view history as a continuum, a resultant of an endless process of Challenge and Response,' which probably conveyed some esoteric message only to other historians.

A future historian will have more headaches than any of his predecessors. The plethora of memorials and statues and newsreports, often contradictory, will bewilder him. The cartoonist's version of a Minister's manner of speech and form and intentions, and the portrait of the same man by his P.R.O. are likely to be conflicting, and succeed in paralysing the historian's judgement. He may also conclude that the country had more Ministers than ordinary citizens, similar to a certain Lichchavi Republic of ancient days which is said to have had nine-hundred-and-ninety-nine kings—perhaps for a population of one. He may state from a study of photographs that Ministers stationed themselves before microphones all the time expect when they went up in helicopters to survey disasters when they wore looks of profound sympathy.

The future historian's greatest headache, however, will be reports of celebrations of death anniversaries. He won't be able to make out how the twenty-fifth Memorial Day of a particular person could be followed, shortly, by and birth anniversaries the 105th Birthday of the same person. The future historian will probably say, "Normally, a person can either be living or dead, but not both; we can only assume that in the later 20th century, somehow they had perfected the art of resurrecting certain very important persons, so that they continued to exist without any time limit, and the days of their death would be mourned publicly, without in any way lessening the joyful celebrations of their birthdays."

Junk

Of late more and more of my time is taken up, not in reading, writing or contemplation but in searching for something desperately: could be a life-saving tax-receipt, diary, or a key-bunch. Whatever it may be, at the moment of your need it seems to be irrevocably lost, to be followed by a prolonged mood of frustration and hopelessness. After repeatedly experiencing this unproductive, pathological state, I have come to the conclusion that it is all due to one's tendency to accumulate irrelevant odds and ends, which are not necessary either for one's welfare or wise living.

A rough listing of my treasure, I decided, would be the first step in any campaign to tidy up my surroudings. Four tape-recorders in different states of disrepair, a movie camera not taken out of its leather case for ten years or more, and all kinds of accessories, spools, and reels, a handful of nickel-cadmium cells guaranteed for ten years but dead in the first week itself, battery-chargers (only in theory), assorted ballpoint pens, transistor radios under a vow of silence, calculators which defeat all my calculations, and so on. The list is extensive. One picks up thoughtlessly all sorts of things at an airport duty-free shop or a discount store during one's travels, stands sheepishly and sleepily at the customs at an unearthly hour of arrival, and brings them home. Ultimately when their novelty has worn off all that stuff is entombed in a large cupboard.

The Oxford English Dictionary defines 'junk' as 'worthless stuff, rubbish'. I would extend the definition to cover all possessions that have lain in a cupboard untouched for any length of time. The need of the hour seems to me a new phrase "de-junk", and a revolutionary programme arising thereof. For a start I ought to empty my large cupboard without compunction; but one takes time to ripen to this philosophy. "Ultimately of course," I say to myself. "But immediately let us make a beginning with lesser stuff".

And so a whole afternoon I devoted to this task. Carrying around a large basket, I visited every nook and corner of our ancient house. Under the staircase, I discovered an armful of bathroom fittings left by a plumber a year ago with the verdict, "Completely worn out, throw them away." Still preserved out of a mad belief that they could be reconditioned. A less frequented corner of the terrace yielded broken light switches, holders, bits of electric wires, and several unidentified porcelain and bakelite objects. From the garage I collected bushes, brushes, points, cylinder-kits and brake-kits and fanbelt and hose-pipe and whatnot, dismantled from my car and replaced with new parts from time to time.

I filled up my basket with all the junk I could gather that afternoon, and tipped it over the compound wall on the northern side, beyond which lies a sort of no-man's-land. Once over the wall, I didn't care what happened to it. It might be picked up by others or sink underground after the rains, sink deeper and deeper into the bowels of the earth until dug up by a future archeologist who may plan to reconstruct a picture of our civilization from a study of the oddments.

After the hardware comes the software junk. Extreme sophistication in packaging techniques has brought about a condition in which a container or a wrapping appears more attractive than the content. Long after the perfume is gone, you keep the bottle for its peculiar shape and the golden top, as also all kinds of little tubes with screwlids, aluminium containers with air-tight covers and cartons. Day by day such a collection is bound to grow in both volume and kind. If one does not wake up in time one is likely to be crowded out of one's home, a situation similar to the one visualized by Bernard Shaw when he said that the Dead would crowd the Living out of this earth some day if the custom of burial continued indefinitely.

My greatest burden, however, is paper. Every other day three waste-baskets under my table get filled up. A variety of gratuitous information from foreign missions, advertisements, appeals and announcements that don't concern me, seminar papers, and thundering manifestos, and above all cyclostyled letters which begin "Dear Friend" and end with a facsimile signature. I consider cyclostyled letters an abomination and will not look at one even if it's from the noblest Akademi in the country.

I have said nothing about the literary litter which is special to my profession. Before a piece of writing is ready for the printer it has to pass through phases of 'growing pains': a page of printed matter may leave behind four 'unprintable' ones. I am not one of those gifted men who generally claim, "Once I finish a piece of writing, I never have to look at it again, not a syllable to be touched." This is the writer who perhaps could straightaway dictate his magnum opus to the linotype operator without its having to go through the intermediary stages of paper-work. But an ordinary writer not so endowed has to write, rewrite, correct, tear up and begin all over again and write on the margin and in between lines before he can present the composition to his editor. After the final copy is mailed, whether of a long work or a short one, the residue in the shape of manuscript, typescript, galleys, and final proofs, clutter the desk until they are pushed away to yield place to fresh litter.

Side by side with the proliferation of junk I notice nowadays a hopeful development. A young fellow with a sack over his shoulder, slowly, watchfully perambulates along the edge of our street picking up litter and stuffing them into the sack. I view him as my saviour, often invite him in, and empty my baskets directly into his sack.

Of Age and Birthdays

As though one grew up every day attached to a mercury column indicating the day, hour, and minute, of one's age, a gentleman keeps asking whenever I have the ill-luck to run into him during the evening walk (his good point being that he is also a fervent walker), "If I am not inquisitive, what's your age?"

"Always on the wrong side," I say.

"Are you older than me? How is it you are going about without a stick as I do?"

"Perhaps I don't have one," I say, and he walks away greatly puzzled. A few days later he crosses my path again—this time in a park on a narrow path without any scope for a detour and escape. He greets me and begins, "If I am not inquisitive etc. ...." and I have to say, "You are definitely inquisitive—I told you last week my age and I couldn't have grown very much older within a week....."

"But you didn't tell me your exact age...."

"Oh, add one week to the 'wrong side' which is my age, and you will have the latest figure.' He looks crestfallen and passes on. I notice him farther off the path stopping another acquaintance of his—perhaps again to say, "If I am not inquisitive...."

I do not bother about my years, but a lot of others seem to be worried about it. I have no idea what I look like, how I appear to others, my use of a mirror being confined and limited to a few minutes while shaving in the morning. It seems to me from the questions asked of me that I look decrepit and pitiful, stooping and ambling and shuffling along somehow, leaving others to marvel at the feat. I have continuously to dodge enquiries after my health. Formerly if someone wanted to open a conversation, "What are you doing now?" or "How is the family?" would be the line of enquiry. But nowadays even the most sensible person begins with, "How is your health?" and is satisfied with any answer I may give. The question is so casual and habitual that it need not be answered in any detail. You are not obliged to explain, "My blood-pressure this week is—, sugar percentage in blood and urine is—, my weight has gone up but I assure you I am taking necessary steps....."

"How is your health?" is in the same category as the "How do you do?" you hear when an introduction is taking place. Only a naive simpleton would aswer "How do you do?" with, say, "Alas! I have not brought my bio-data and health certificate— May I run up and fetch it?" while shaking hands.

Health is a preoccupation nowadays—even when there is no need for concern. It cannot be otherwise. We are being continuously bombarded with information regarding all sorts of disasters and diseases, accidents and warnings. Sub-consciously everyone is keyed up and apprehensive and naturally view those advanced in years as freaks of nature if they are seen moving about freely.

*

Birthdays should be forgotten, except of children. What is the point in reminding or being reminded that one is past the age of innocence or has attained maturity or middle age or is on the verge of decline or has achieved decrepitude and must be ready to meet his Maker?

While I recommend that birthdays of the living be over-looked, I would suggest the total abolition of the birthdays of those who are no longer with us. The two-hundredth birth anniversary of someone who died a hundred years ago is an impossible concept. One is either living or dead, can't be both. It is illogical to perform a Memorial Service to someone and follow it later with a birthday celebration of the same person.

*

The dialectician in our company objected to the saying, "God helps those who help themselves."

He explained? "It is no credit to the Almighty that He should commit an act of redundancy by going out to help one who is competent to help himself: On the contrary, God's help may be needed for one who is such a blunderer or idiot that he cannot direct a spoon to his mouth. It is only this type that needs a constant pilot at his elbow to direct his spoon, so to speak.

"Or is God like the banker who is prepared to give you a loan if you give him twenty-five per cent of what you need, which seems to be based on the philosophy that one may attain wealth

189

if one is rich enough! Or does the saying mean that God will watch the self-helper to gauge how far he can struggle to achieve something, and at some point take charge like a manager, and leave the man to sit back and grow lazy and fat? I wonder where this God-helps-those etc. idea originated! The more I think on this, the more I am confused."

Pickpockets

During a train journey recently (where else could it be?) I came across an original thinker sitting next to me. After half-an-hour of silence, he suddenly asked, 'Have you ever had your pocket picked?' I cast my mind back and said: 'Yes, years ago. I was strap-hanging in a bus going from the market to Laxmipuram in Mysore when I suddenly realized that I had lost my Parker Pen with its glittering gold-cap and I couldn't imagine what I could ever do without it, as it had been with me for nearly two decades. Of course I looked about and must have seemed so stricken that a man standing next to me asked: "Lost something?" When I explained, he just lifted his left foot slightly and produced, like a conjuror, my pen from under his toes; and jumped off the bus before it approached the police station at the next stop.' 'Wise fellow!' commented my train companion. 'He knew when he should make himself scarce—in all my experience this is the first time I hear of a pickpocket restoring an article. He was a noble soul—so are most of them. I have made a special study of pickpockets—one thing I admire about them is that they are gentle and nonviolent; in their profession they have to practise untouchability—that means, in substance, non-violence—although we hear instances of a knife being flourished when a pickpocket is cornered. By and large they are harmless, and they rob you only when you invite them by flaunting your purse or a pen over your breast pocket, especially in these days of "bush-coats", the invention of which has encouraged this particular social malaise. What prevents you from having button-up flaps for your pocket or as in earlier days keep your things in an inner pocket. Nowadays it's a piece of vanity to display a glittering pen clip or a leather purse over your pocket, or parade a bulging hip-pocket over a T-shirt. If your tailor can redesign your dress, particularly the pocket, the pickpocket will automatically cease to be and you may rest assured that no World Federation of Pickpockets will ever protest. However my mission in life is not to encourage but to rehabilitate the pickpocket. For it must be agreed on all counts that a pickpocket exercises a delicate skill. You cannot deny that his sensitive fingers could be put to better use—such as thrumming musical strings, working delicate embroidery or knitting, and even minor surgery, with proper education and training. His genius for painless extraction must be utilized, his presence or pressure is no more than that of a butterfly flitting past. I have appealed to the Government to permit me to meet pickpockets serving their term in prisons, talk to them, and conduct classes for them regularly. I hope to educate and rededicate this class for constructive work. But before I start on this mission I'd urge pickpockets to observe certain restraints and codes. First and foremost, every member of their Society must take an oath to observe a strict holiday on the first of a month, when most people get their salaries. It is heart-rending to watch a family man discover the absence of his purse just when he is about to pay the bill at the provision store after parcels are made up. "God, how am I to manage this month-food, rent, childrens' school fees, electricity bill to be paid on the 5th, insurance premium to avoid penalty—and scores of other commitments!" This painful situation must be avoided. I hope to achieve results in that direction. I shall also urge the LIC to devise some kind of insurance against pocket losses for the citizen. Next a pickpocket should also vow never to use a razor blade to slash pockets. It's unsportive; in the category of using folidol to hunt a tiger. A pickpocket should at least return important documents and papers found in a wallet. I learn that in New York, pickpockets generally drop passports, social security cards, insurance certificates etc., into the nearest mailbox; and this admirable practice must be followed in our country also.'

When his station arrived, the monologist hurriedly got up, held to me his card, saying casually, 'Any donation, whatever the amount, will be welcome at this address to promote our cause,' and left. Later I patted my pockets to make sure that this reformer was not an adept himself. The contents of my pocket were intact. I realized he was only a zealot or Messiah looking for a cause to champion.

Monkeys

I have a partiality for the monkey. My earliest associate was one Rama (as I have described in *My Days*), a slender yellowish creature with the face of an angel, with whom I was on talking terms. He was my only companion in childhood, in my grandmother's home at Number One, Vellala Street, Purasawalkam (now the building is gone, to make way for a modern 'complex'. Fortunately, the massive, brass-studded, street door which must have been pushed and pulled a million times during its century-old existence, alone was saved, and acquired as a memento by a friend.)

To go back to Rama, he lived in a cabin in the garden at the end of a long chain with a leather-band around his waist. As soon as I came home from school, I released him from bondage and kept his company, taking care not to let go his waist-band. He nestled close to me as we sat on the threshold and watched the traffic in the street.

We quietly commented on the scene passing before us: "See those sweets—why don't you hop across and snatch the red coloured *mittai*—one for you and one for me.....?", I suggested once. "Done," he replied, "If only you will let go your hold." On one occasion when I acted on his advice, he not only sprang away and toppled the tray of the vendor, after gobbling up the sweets, but roamed the neighbourhood, creating quite a stir, till he was caught two days later—but that is another story. The point I am trying to make is that the monkey was an ideal companion, an agreeable conversationalist, and listened to my remarks and narrations (mostly about my class teachers at the Lutheran Mission) with grave attention. He was capable of speech at a wave-length which I alone could catch.

Now, after countless decades, I have retained my faith and interest in the monkey. When I notice on my walks along a trunk road, a family on treetops, chattering and hopping about, I wish I had not lost, through inevitable adulthood, the receptivity I used to possess in childhood. Now I can only speculate on what they are saying. When I watch a big group in their hierarchy of male and female and juniors perched in their proper ranks, while the leader goes through the agenda for the day, with an attendant picking off fleas and ticks from his coat, I can almost hear him say:

"It's a pity we do not have an all-India identity. We still think of Mysore Monkey and Madras Monkey, Tirupati Monkey or Benares Monkey, and never of a moment talk of the Indian Monkey. We must strive for an all-India federation from which we should, naturally, exclude chimps, gorillas and orangutans, none of which possess a recognizable tail; being almost human in gestures, postures and movement, they are actually bipeds. We must be positive and make it universally understood that they are not our class—let them learn human speech and get merged in their society. As far as we are concerned, we will state our own hopes and demands as follows:

"First, we must thank human beings for becoming aware, after all, of the importance of trees. We welcome their Grow More Trees ideals, and support them heartily unlike the short-sighted cattle and goat (and their human keepers) which display irresponsibility and won't allow a sapling to grow in peace. Humans should, in addition to growing more trees, also pay attention to the kind of tree planted. They must be discouraged from planting conifers, eucalyptus and even casuarina trees which provide neither shade nor accommodation, nor nourishing fruits. We must urge upon the authorities the importance of cultivating fruit-bearing trees which grow to a desirable height with spreading branches. Orchards must, of course, be encouraged and mango, guava, jambu and berries of many kinds must be cultivated. Human beings must be made to realize that God created fruits exclusively for our benefit and not for their consumption; they should be satisfied with corns, cereals and such stuff which they cultivate for their nourishment. Man has made fruit-cultivation a commercial activity, which must be condemned. They guard their orchards fiercely; there are instances where they have shot our kinsmen with double-barrelled guns and have caused indescribable tragedy and hardship in some families which happened to camp in certain orchards. One way in which a recurrence of such tragedy could be prevented is to make the humans realize that

194

we are the descendants of the great God Hanuman whom humans worship with fear and faith. As a protective measure let us adopt the emblem of Maruti although there are partisans among us who revere Vali and Sugreeva. I cannot welcome such mischievous attitudes. After all, Vali and Sugreeva are controversial characters in the Ramayana. Vali was guilty of appropriating his brother Sugreeva's wife and driving him out of the kingdom, for which he was punished by Sri Rama, and Sugreeva himself has displayed certain weak points, but we need not go into all that now. Hanuman alone stands, pure and serene like the Ganga at Gangotri, and we shall adopt him as our protector from gunmen. Until humans firmly realize, without any doubt, that fruit is god-given food meant for us, we should keep away from orchards and content ourselves with food from roadside figs and berries.

"We on our part should also observe certain disciplines and restraints so that humans may get confidence in us and feel that we could co-exist with them. We must not invite trouble by slipping in through any open window and creating panic in a household. We must not frighten school children, even for a joke, and above all, our compatriots who dwell in temples like Tirupati or Benares must not take undue advantage of the sanctuary by snatching away fruits and offerings from unwary pilgrims. The kind of warning posted on temple pillars, "Guard your Bags and Spectacles" should be viewed as a discredit to our tribe. At our next meeting we shall formulate a precise code after consulting our cousins dwelling on other trees."

A Literary Alchemy

What is so special about *The Golden Gate*?

—It is a novel in verse form, three hundred and odd pages, written by a young Indian, and it seems to me no small achievement.

—Poetry? I don't read poetry. I had enough of it in the classroom long ago. I'm not prepared to struggle anymore to squeeze any sense out of a stanza, with notes and annotation and explanation. I have had enough of it. Today, I'm impervious to poetry. Even "Baa Baa Black Sheep" would need an annotator for me today.

—Nonsense, I won't believe you. It's a pose many persons adopt to show how mature they are. Of course, memories of one's experience in a classroom could produced a trauma, in which state all poetry and prose might sound dreadful. However, I do not doubt that you secretly dip into *Palgrave's Golden Treasury* from time to time.

—How do you know?

—I noticed a copy on your table this morning, and it looks well thumbed.

—You are right. I enjoy going over lines such as, "The curfew tolls the knell of parting day" or "Awake! for Morning in the Bowl of Night/has flung the Stone that puts the Stars to flight:/And lo! the Hunter of the East has caught/The Sultan's Turret in a noose of Light."

—I like particularly Shakespeare's sonnet. "When to the sessions of sweet silent thought/I summon up remembrance of things past,/I sigh the lack of many a thing I sought....." It is good to start the day with a few lines of the *Golden Treasury* in addition to any religious hymn or prayer one may be accustomed to.

—You were talking about The Golden Gate.

—Yes. Coming back to it—an extraordinary work. I've never come across any other modern writer who has ventured almost recklessly to narrate a story in verse. The book was recommended to me at a dinner party by a lady in such ecstatic terms that it produced a contrary effect as it always happens when someone recommends anything too obviously. I resist it. Now *The Golden Gate* seemed to be the in thing, like the American fashion to display the Book of the Month choice on the hall table. Whether it is read or not is another matter.

—You started with *The Golden Gate* but are straying from the subject.

—Yes. When the lady recommended it at the dinner, my host dashed out, went down to the book stall and brought me a copy. Next day, I opened the first page, glanced through a few lines; the lady's overzealous recommendation still rankling in my mind, I put away the book. Weeks later, the author, Vikram Seth, appeared in a TV interview and I realized, here was a genuine writer with the right values, gift and outlook, not writing in order to blow off steam or to reform society but a genuine artist who takes pleasure in writing. Here I found rhyme, reason and humour, and above all sensed a rhythm which "vibrates in the memory" even after the book is shut and put away. Vikram Seth shows absolute mastery of the English language, and has created a unique literary alchemy. Yes, this is a book fit to be kept beside *Palgrave's Golden Treasury* for frequent literary refreshment.

*

Passing from literature to language, "Indian English" is often mentioned with some amount of contempt and patronage, but is a legitimate development and needs no apology. We have fostered the language for over a century and we are entitled to bring it in line with our own habits of thought and idiom. Americans have adapted the English language to suit their native mood and speech without feeling apologetic, and have achieved directness and unambiguity in expression.

I noticed in *The Hindu* 'Know Your English' column, Professor Subrahmanian referring to the expression 'needful' as being permissible. I was relieved to note it since I have always felt 'Do the Needful' as being a practical, compact, and comprehensive tabloid expression. In our college days, Prof. J.C. Rollo, who was a purist, would spend the first quarter of an hour to denounce Indianisms. 'Needful' was one such. He said, "Avoid like the plague the expression 'Needful.' Never say, 'Do the Needful' under any circumstance." He was also opposed to the expression 'And oblige.' "You may say, 'I will be obliged if you etc..' but never, 'and oblige' at the end of a letter. It's hideous."

I have always rebelled against Prof. Rollo's decrees, feeling that 'Please do the needful' 'And oblige' are a brilliant combination which conveys all the meaning, command and request in a couple of phrases. 'Do the needful and oblige' is a masterpiece of economy and contribution to the English language.

The Writerly Life

'Are you still writing?' I am sometimes questioned. It may be
no more than an attempt on the part of a visitor to make polite
conversation, but, alas, I do not like it. The question seems to
be in the category of 'Have you stopped beating your wife?'
which cannot be answered with a simple 'yes' or 'no'. The
questioner has come prepared for a long afternoon's chit-chat,
and his question may be only an opening gambit. Assuming it
might be so I generally respond to his query with vague sounds
at the throat or mumble about the weather, and then if
necessary proceed to familiar topics such as corruption, bribery
and nepotism, and their subtleties and variations noticeable in
public life, the inside story of some corporate take-over
scandal, and so on, practically a resume of the newspaper
headlines of the morning. Most times I succeed in warding off
the questioner. All the same, the question itself causes
uneasiness, particularly the *still* in the query. Probably, the
questioner sees me differently from the image I am accustomed
to in the mirror during the morning shave, when I do not pause
to note the pouches and webs under the eye, the sagging jowl,
and other marks of years. Or perhaps this man is in possession
of some scientific information to prove that prolonged gripping
of pen between the thumb and forefinger results in deadly
symptoms, proved by experiments with strait-jacketed monkeys
trained to drive the quill non-stop. To please the visitor if he
persists with his question I may say, 'Oh no, how can I? One
must retire at the right time. Our *Shastras* have decreed
Vanaprastha at some point in one's life. Even governments
have fixed fifty-five or fifty-eight years (depending upon the
mood of the Chief Minister of the hour) for the retirement of
government officials. One must make way for the younger
generation, you know.' This sentiment, I hope, sounds noble
enough for the man to leave me alone. But he may suddenly
turn round and declare, 'Impossible, sir, impossible. How can

there be retirement for a writer! You must go on giving pleasure to the public', as if I were a performing artiste. It is at this point that I decide to get the ultimate weapon out to quell the questioner. 'Did you like the ending of my *Man-Eater of Malgudi,* where the evil man hits his skull with his own fist and collapses?' He looks perplexed and says, 'Tell me, what's the story about?'

'It has taken me nearly eighty-thousand words to tell that story. If you haven't read it don't worry about it.'

'That particular book I have not been able to get. Where is it sold, what is its price?'

I go on to the next question. 'Can you tell me if Raju the *Guide* dies at the end of the story, and whether it rained, after all?'

'Is that also a novel? I only saw the film, but not fully. I had to go away somewhere'.

'Perhaps', I added, 'the electricity also failed. Quite a possibility, you know, with the services being what they are.' I could put in a fresh question every two minutes like the *Yaksha* in the *Mahabharata*. But I desist, saying to myself that no man is under any compulsion to read my books even if he likes to talk about them. And then, I am in complete agreement with him when he says, 'In these days what with the office work and the hunt for kerosene and gas all the time, so little time is left'. 'Truer words were never uttered,' I say. Feeling encouraged, he ventures to explain, 'My little daughter has one of your stories about a dog in her school book, she is a bright girl and speaks to me about you, you know'.

I really do not mind daughter-guided innocent enthusiasts of this type, but the man who really puts me off is the academician who cannot read a book for the pleasure (if any) or the pain (in which case he is free to throw it out of the window.) But this man will not read a book without an air of biting into it. I prefer a reader who picks up a book casually. I write a story or a sketch primarily because it is my habit and profession and I enjoy doing it. I'm not out to enlighten the world or improve it. But the academic man views a book only as raw material for a thesis or seminar paper, hunts for hidden meanings, social implications, 'commitments' and 'concerns', or the 'Nation's ethos.' When he finds a novel yielding none of these results he will busy himself over the work in other ways. A certain English

professor has managed to draw an intricate map of Malgudi
with its landmarks laboriously culled out of the pages of all my
novels. To see an imaginary place so solidly presented with its
streets and rivers and temples, did not appeal to me; it seemed
to me rather a petrification or fossilzation of light wish-like
things floating across one's vision while one is writing.

Another scholar sought the following clarification: 'In one of
your novels you mention that the distance between Trichy and
Malgudi is 150 miles but you have placed Malgudi midway
between Trichy and Madras while Trichy is only a night's
journey from Madras. Also in a certain novel you have put the
distance from Malgudi railway station to Albert Mission as
three miles while in another...' He was offended when I replied,
'If you are obliged to calculate such distances you should
employ not an ordinary measuring tape but a special one made
of India rubber, since distances in fiction are likely to be
according to Einstein's theory.'

The man who really charmed me was a slightly drunken
stranger who was introduced to me as one of my admirers at a
friend's house. The man looked me up and down sceptically and
said, 'You are the novelist? No you can't be.'

'Why not?' I asked.

'All the time I had pictured in my mind the author of my
favourite novels such as the *Guide* etc., so differently. Now you
look like this. You must be an impostor'.

'Absolutely right,' I cried, 'You are the first sane person I
have come across. So difficult to convince others that I'm not
myself.'

The Nobel Prize and All That

These days everyone feels the right to comment on any subject not necessarily concerning them. The flood of printed material available to an individual for browsing at the news-stand, the circulating library around the corner, the free reading room or on an obliging neighbour's book-shelf, not to speak of the radio and TV, fills the eyes and ears, and (one hopes) also the mind to overflowing with information, facts, and fancies, so that everyone feels convinced that he knows everything and comments freely on every subject.

Five years ago no one would bother about the Nobel Prize, as to who got it or missed it. One would glance at the announcement without any reaction and pass on to the next item in the newspaper.

Now the month of October has become a season of general speculation about the Nobel winners, especially for Peace and Literature. The awards for Science and Medicine sound too technical and beyond the understanding of the average citizen, who accepts those announcements without a murmur, feeling: "Lucky fellows, let them flourish, God knows what they have achieved. However not our business...."

The awards for Peace and Literature, on the other hand, provoke universal comment on the following lines "Oh! this is sheer politics and nothing less. So and so is a war-monger, racketeer in arms, smuggler, CIA agent and to say he has striven for world peace, preposterous!" If the recipient's name is unfamiliar, the comment would be "Who is this character? Which corner of the globe does he inhabit? No one has heard of this man or his country! And to say that he was dedicated to the cause of world peace, too ridiculous for words!"

The prize for Literature when announced causes the utmost flutter among the speculators. The proliferation of lotteries, with the promise of a Bumper Prize of crores on the following morning, has created a chronic gambler's temperament in everyone. The speculator even if he is beyond the pale of the ever-hopeful literary fraternity, would like to back up a favourite every year just to enjoy a vicarious thrill if his candidate wins, and then reacts bitterly when the announcement actually comes. "Never heard of this poet, where was he hidden all these centuries? Who is he? What on earth is his language? The Nobel committee has a genius for ferreting out obscure languages and writers."

Another might say, "If you were a Russian citizen at one time and expelled or likely to be expelled from your native land and then wrote poems and novels, you have a ninety per cent chance of becoming a Nobel Laureate."

"Statistics prove that the Third World writers, with occasional exceptions, are normally ignored." William Golding, the British Nobel winner, is reported to have stated that it was time that Asian writers were given their share of recognition by the Nobel Committee, as if one were talking of an equitable distribution of cabbage soup in a relief camp.

Geographical, topographical, hemispherical, or ethnic considerations are irrelevant in literature. One cannot, for instance, compel a selection committee to turn its attention to Antarctica since the claims of that part of the world have been consistently overlooked. On the other hand it must also be said that if the soil (or rather the snow) of Antarctica produces a literary masterpiece it is bound to emerge like a shining star in the firmament even if the Nobel Committee remains ignorant of its existence. A classic does not have to wait for the Nobel stamp of approval. World masterpieces, plays of Shakespeare, Dante's Divine Comedy, and the Ramayana, were known before Alfred Nobel lighted the first fuse.

However, the Nobel-Award-watchers seem to be self-appointed busybodies. Alfred Nobel the dynamitician might not have possessed deep or wide conceptions of science or literature or other subjects, but created an endowment because he liked to do so.

Alfred Nobel might not have been aware of the subtler aspects of language or literature, but seems to have just specified, rather naively, that a work should promote "idealism". If his condition is strictly followed, the only literature qualifying for the Nobel Prize would have been *Self-Help* by Samuel Smiles or *How to Win Friends and Influence People*; or

Baby Care by Dr. Spock. But judges have stretched the notion of 'idealism' so that Hemingway and Neruda, Patrick White, Canetti, and another could be chosen for the award.

That the award is practically confined to the West is a general complaint but seems inevitable. European languages are the only ones known to the judges. Alfred Nobel could well have thought that all the non-European continents were areas of darkness, populated by human beings who had not yet evolved an alphabet. Even if he had mentioned the word 'global" anywhere, he could have only meant the Western world. At some point, the Nobel Committee might legitimately turn round and say: "It is none of your business to criticize us. We are the executors of a certain individual's will and testament. Nobody can question our authority or judgement."

"Accepted, but here are a few suggestions to enhance your efficiency. Beyond sixty if an author is already established, your recognition will not be of any real value; at that stage he cannot become more famous or richer by your recognition; as GBS has said, 'Your money is a life-belt thrown to a swimmer who has already reached the shore in safety.' So you must set an age-limit for the recipient in literature. Secondly, they recipient should be of an age when he can travel comfortably to Stockholm, to receive the honour without a physician in attendance."

Kawabata, though he was comparatively junior to most awardees, said: "I had to travel to Stockholm all the way, and felt exhausted. It took a long time to recoup my strength."

"What did you do with the money?"

"Nothing much. Only thing I could think of buying was a wooden chair in Denmark or Sweden, I forget; it is for guests like you who cannot sit down on the floor comfortably. There you see it on the verandah."

A few weeks later he ended his life leaving a note that he had nothing more to live for and saw no reason to continue to exist, although he had disapproved of the idea of suicide when we discussed the subject earlier.

I heard that John Steinbeck had to flee to an unknown destination to escape the mail mounting up in sacks in his parlour, when he became a Nobel Laureate. Shaw mentions that the volume of correspondence following the Nobel Award (though he declined it) was unmanageable, leaving him no time to write his plays; he was forced to cry out: "I can forgive Alfred Nobel for having invented dynamite. But only a fiend in human form could have invented the Nobel Prize."

Misguided 'Guide'

The letter came by airmail from Los Angeles. 'I am a producer and actor from Bombay,' it read. 'I don't know if my name is familiar to you.'

He was too modest. Millions of young men copied his screen image, walking as he did, slinging a folded coat over the shoulder carelessly, buffing up a lock of hair over the right temple, and assuming that the total effect would make the girls sigh with hopeless longing. My young nephews at home were thrilled at the sight of the handwriting of Dev Anand.

The Letter went on to say, 'I was in London and came across your novel *The Guide*. I am anxious to make it into a film. I can promise you that I will keep to the spirit and quality of your writing. My plans are to make both a Hindi and an English film of this story.' He explained how he had arranged with an American film producer for collaboration. He also described how he had flown from London to New York in search of me, since someone had told him I lived there, and then across the whole continent before he could discover my address. He was ready to come to Mysore if I should indicate the slightest willingness to consider his proposal.

I cabled him an invitiation, already catching the fever of hurry characteristic of the film world. He flew from Los Angeles to Bombay to Bangalore, and motored down a hundred miles without losing a moment.

A small crowd of autograph-hunters had gathered at the gate of my house in Yadava Giri. He expertly eluded the inquisitive crowd, and we were soon closeted in the dining room, breakfasting on *idli*, *dosai*, and other South Indian delicacies, my nephews attending on the star in a state of elation. The talk was all about *The Guide* and its cinematic merits. Within an hour we had become so friendly that he could ask without embarrassment, 'What price will you demand for your story?' The checkbook was out and the pen poised over it. I had the impression that if I had suggested that the entire face of the check be covered with closely knit figures, he would have obliged me. But I hemmed and hawed, suggested a slight advance, and told him to go ahead. I was sure that if the picture turned out to be a success he would share with me the glory and the profits. "Oh, certainly," he affirmed, "if the picture, by God's grace, turns out to be a success, we will be on top of the world, and the sky will be the limit!"

The following months were filled with a sense of importance: Long Distance Calls, Urgent Telegrams, Express Letters, sudden arrivals and departures by plane and car. I received constant summonses to be present here or there. "PLEASE COME TO DELHI. SUIT RESERVED AT IMPERIALL HOTEL. URGENTLY NEED YOUR PRESENCE."

Locking away my novel-in-progress, I fly to Delhi. There is the press conference, with introductions, speeches and over-flowing conviviality. The American director explains the unique nature of their present effort: for the first time in the history of Indian movie-making, they are going to bring out a hundred-percent-Indian story, with a hundred-percent-Indian cast, and a hundred-percent-Indian setting, for an international audience. And mark this: actually in colour-and-wide-screen-first-time-in-the-history-of-this-country.

A distinguished group of Americans, headed by the Nobel Prize winner Pearl Buck, would produce the film. Again and again I heard the phrase: "Sky is the limit", and the repeated assurances: "We will make the picture just as Narayan has written it, with his co-operation at every stage." Reporters pressed me for a statement. It was impossible to say anything but the pleasantest things in such an atmosphere of overwhelming optimism and good fellowship.

Soon we were assembled in Mysore. They wanted to see the exact spots which had inspired me to write *The Guide*. Could I show them the locations? A photographer, and some others whose business with us I never quite understood, were in the party. We started out in two cars. The American director, Tad Danielewski, explained that he would direct the English version first. He kept discussing with me the finer points of my novel. "I guess your hero is a man of impulsive plans? Self-made, given to daydreaming?" he would ask, and add, before I could muster an answer, "Am I not right?" Of course he had to be right. Once or twice when I attempted to mitigate his impressions, he brushed aside my comments and went on with his own explanation as to what I must have had in mind when I created such-and-such a character.

I began to realize that monologue is the privilege of the film maker, and that it was futile to try butting in with my own observations. But for some obscure reason, they seemed to need my presence, though not my voice. I must be seen and not heard.

We drove about 300 miles that day, during the course of which I showed them the river steps and a little shrine overshadowed by a banyan on the banks of Kaveri, which was the actual spot around which I wrote *The Guide*. As I had recalled, nothing more needed to be done than put the actors there and start the camera. They uttered little cries of joy at finding a "set" so readily available. In the summer, when the river dried up, they could shoot the drought scenes with equal ease. Then I took them to the tiny town of Nanjangud, with its little streets, its shops selling sweets and toys and ribbons, and a pilgrim crowd bathing in the holy waters of the Kabini, which flowed through the town. The crowd was colourful and lively around the temple, and in a few weeks it would increase a hundredfold when people from the surrounding villages arrived to participate in the annual festival—the sort of crowd described in the last pages of my novel. If the film makers made a note of the date and sent down a cameraman at that time, they could secure the last scene of my novel in an authentic manner and absolutely free of cost.

The producer at once passed an order to his assistant to arrange for an outdoor unit to arrive here at the right time. Then we all posed at the portals of the ancient temple, with arms encircling each other's necks and smiling. This was but the first of innumerable similar scenes in which I found myself posing with the starry folk, crushed in the friendliest embrace.

From Nanjangud we dove up mountains and the forests and photographed our radiant smiles against every possible background. It was a fatiguing business on the whole, but the American director claimed that it was nothing to what he was used to. He generally went 5,000 miles in search of locations, exposing hundreds of rolls of film on the way.

After inspecting jungles, mountains, village streets, hamlets and huts, we reached the base of Gopalaswami Hill in the afternoon, and drove up the five-mile mud track; the cars had to be pushed up the steep hill after encroaching vegetation had been cleared from the path. This was a part of the forest country where at any bend of the road one could anticipate a tiger or a herd of elephants; but, luckily for us, they were out of view today.

At the summit I showed them the original of the "Peak House" in my novel, a bungalow built 50 years ago, with glassed in verandas affording a view of wildlife at night, and a 2,000-foot drop to a valley beyond. A hundred yards off, a foot-track wound through the undergrowth, leading on to an ancient temple whose walls were crumbling and whose immense timber doors moved on rusty hinges with a groan. Once again I felt that here everything was ready-made for the film. They could shoot in the bright sunlight, and for the indoor scenes they assured me that it would be a simple matter to haul up a generator and lights.

Sitting under a banyan tree and consuming sandwiches and lemonade, we discussed and settled the practical aspects of the expedition: where to locate the base camp and where the advance units consisting of engineers, mechanics, and truck drivers, in charge of the generator and lights. All through the journey back the talk involved schedules and arrangements for shooting the scenes in this part of the country. I was impressed with the ease they displayed in accepting such mighty logistical tasks. Film executives, it seemed to me, could solve mankind's problems on a global scale with the casual confidence of demigods, if only they could take time off their illusory pursuits and notice the serious aspects of existence.

Then came total silence, for many weeks. Finally I discovered that they were busy searching for their locations in Northern India.

This was a shock. I had never visualized my story in that part of India, where costumes, human types and details of daily life are different. They had settled upon Jaipur and Udaipur in Rajaputana, a thousand miles away from my location for the story.

Our next meeting was in Bombay, and I wasted no time in speaking of this problem. "My story takes place in south India, in Malgudi, an imaginary town known to thousands of my readers all over the world", I explained. "It is South India in costume, tone and contents. Although the whole country is one, there are diversities, and one has to be faithful in delineating them. You have to stick to my geography and sociology. Although it is a world of fiction there are certain inner veracities."

One of them replied: "We feel it a privilege to be doing your story." This sounded irrelevant as an answer to my statement.

We were sitting under a gaudy umbrella beside a blue swimming pool on Juhu Beach, where the American party was housed in princely suites in a modern hotel. It was hard to believe that we were in India. Most of our discussions took place somewhat amphibiously, on the edge of the swimming pool, in which the director spent a great deal of his time.

This particular discussion was interrupted as a bulky European tourist in swimming briefs fell off the diving plank, hit the bottom and had to be hauled out and rendered first aid. After the atmosphere had cleared, I resumed my speech. They listened with a mixture of respect and condescension, evidently willing to make allowances for an author's whims.

"Please remember", one of them tried to explain, "that we are shooting, for the first time in India, in wide screen and Eastman Colour, and we must shoot where there is spectacle. Hence Jaipur."

"In that case", I had to ask, "Why all that strenuous motoring near my home? Why my story at all, if what you need is a picturesque spectacle?"

I was taken aback when their reply came! "How do you know that Malgudi is where you think it is?"

Somewhat bewildered, I said, with what I hoped was proper humility, "I suppose I know because I have imagined it, created it and have been writing novel after novel set in the area for the last 30 years."

"We are out to expand the notion of Malgudi", one of them explained. "Malgudi will be where we place it, in Kashmir, Rajasthan, Bombay, Delhi, even Ceylon."

I could not share the flexibility of their outlook or the expanse of their vision. It seemed to me that for their purpose a focal point was unnecessary. They appeared to be striving to achieve mere optical effects.

I recalled a talk with Satyajit Ray, the great director, some years earlier, when I met him in Calcutta. He expressed his admiration for *The Guide* but also his doubts as to whether he could ever capture the tone and atmosphere of its background. He had said, "Its roots are so deep in the soil of your part of our country that I doubt if I could do justice to your book, being unfamiliar with its milieu..." Such misgivings did not bother the American director. I noticed that though he was visiting India for the first time, he never paused to ask what was what in this bewildering country.

Finally he solved the whole problem by declaring, "Why should we mention where the story takes place? We will aovid the name 'Malgudi.'" Thereafter the director not only avoided the word Malgudi but fell foul of anyone who uttered that sound.

My brother, an artist who has illustrated my stories for 25 years, tried to expound his view. At a dinner in his home in Bombay, he mentioned the forbidden word to the director. Malgudi, he explained, meant a little town, not so picturesque as Jaipur, of a neutral shade, with characters wearing dhoti and jibba when they were not barebodied. The Guide himself was a man of charm, creating history and archaeology out of thin air for his clients, and to provide him with solid, concrete monuments to talk about would go against the grain of the tale. The director listened and firmly said, "There is no Malgudi, and that is all there is to it."

But my brother persisted. I became concerned that the controversy threatened to spoil our dinner. The director replied, in a sad tone, that they could as well have planned a picture for black and white and narrow screen if all one wanted was what he contemptuously termed a "Festival Film", while he was planning a million-dollar spectacle to open simultaneously in 2,000 theaters in America. I was getting used to arguments everyday over details. My story is about a dancer in a small town, an exponent of the strictly classical tradition of South Indian *Bharat Natyam*. The film makers felt this was inadequate. They therefore engaged an expensive, popular dance director with a troupe of a hundred or more dancers, and converted my heroine's performances into an extravaganza in delirious, fruity colours and costumes. Their dancer was constantly traveling hither and thither in an Air India Boeing no matter how short the distance to be covered. The moviegoer, too, I began to realize, would be whisked all over India.

Although he would see none of the countryside in which the novel was set, he would see the latest U.S. Embassy building in New Delhi, Parliament House, the Ashoka Hotel, the Lake Palace, Elephanta Caves and whatnot. Unity of place seemed an unknown concept for a film maker. (Later Mrs Indira Gandhi, whom I met after she had seen a special showing of the film, asked, "Why should they have dragged the story all over as if it were a travelogue, instead of confining themselves to the simple background of your book?" She added as an after-thought, and in what seemed to me an understatement: "Perhaps they have other considerations.")

The co-operation of many persons was needed in the course of the film making, and anyone whose help was requested had to be given a copy of *The Guide*. Thus there occurred a shortage, and an inevitable black market, in copies of the book. A production executive searched the bookshops in Bombay, and cornered all the available copies at any price. He could usually be seen going about like a scholar with a bundle of books under his arm. I was also intrigued by the intense study and pencil-marking that the director was making on his copy of the book; it was as if he were studying it for a doctoral thesis. Not until I had a chance to read his "treatment" did I understand what all his penciling meant: he had been marking off passages and portions that were to be avoided in the film.

When the script came, I read through it with mixed feelings. The director answered my complaints with "I have only exteriorized what you have expressed. It is all in your book."

'In which part of my book' I would ask without any hope of an answer.

Or he would say, "I could give you two hundred reasons why this change should be so." I did not feel up to hearing them all. If I still proved truculent he would explain away "This is only a first draft. We could make any change you want in the final screenplay."

The screenplay was finally presented to me with a great flourish and expressions of fraternal sentiments at a hotel in Bangalore. But I learned at this time that they had already started shooting and had even completed a number of scenes. Whenever expressed my views, the answer would be either, "Oh, it will all be rectified in the editing", or, "We will deal with it when we decide about the retakes. But please wait until we have a chance to see the rushes". By now a bewildering number of hands were behind the scenes, at laboratories, workshops, carpentries, editing rooms and so forth. It was impossible to keep track of what was going on, or get hold of anyone with a final say. Soon I trained myself to give up all attempts to connect the film with the book of which I happened to be the author.

But I was not sufficiently braced for the shock that came the day when the director insisted upon the production of two tigers to fight and destroy each other over a spotted deer. He wished to establish the destructive animality of two men clashing over one woman: my heroine's husband and lover fighting over her. The director intended a tiger fight to portray depths of symbolism. It struck me as obvious. Moreover it was not in the story. But he asserted that it was; evidently I had intended the scene without realizing it.

The Indian producer, who was financing the project, groaned at the thought of the tigers. He begged me privately, "Please do something about it. We have no time for tigers; and it will cost hell of a lot to hire them, just for a passing fancy." I spoke to the director again, but he was insistent. No tiger, no film, and two tigers or none.

Scouts were sent out through the length and breadth of India to explore the tiger possibilities. They returned to report that only one tiger was available. It belonged to a circus and the circus owner would under no circumstance consent to have the tiger injured or killed. The director decreed, "I want the beast to die, otherwise the scene will have no meaning." They finally found a man in Madras, living in the heart of the city with a full-grown Bengal tiger which he occasionally lent for jungle pictures, after sewing its lips and pulling out its claws.

The director examined a photograph of the tiger, in order to satisfy himself that they were not trying to palm off a pi-dog in tiger clothing, and signed it up. Since a second tiger was not available, he had to settle for its fighting a leopard. It was an easier matter to find a deer for the sacrifice. What they termed a "second unit" was dispatched to Madras to shoot the sequence. Ten days later the unit returned, looking forlorn.

The tiger had shrunk at the sight of the leopard, and the leopard had shown no inclination to maul the deer, whose cries of fright had been so heart-rending that they had paralyzed the technicians. By prodding, kicking and irritating the animals, they had succeeded in producing a spectacle gory enough to make them retch. "The deer was actually lifted and fed into the jaws of the other two", said an assistant cameraman. (This shot passes on the screen, in the finished film, in the winking of an eye as a bloody smudge, to the accompaniment of a lot of wild uproar.)

Presently another crisis developed. The director wanted the hero to kiss the heroine, who of course rejected the suggestion as unbecoming an Indian woman. The director was distraught. The hero, for his part, was willing to obey the director, but he was helpless, since kissing is a co-operative effort. The Amercian director realized that it is against Indian custom to kiss in public; but he insisted that the public in his country would boo if they missed the kiss. I am told that the heroine replied: "There is enough kissing in your country at all times and places, off and on the screen, and your public, I am sure, will flock to a picture where, for a change, no kissing is shown." She stood firm. Finally, the required situation was apparently faked by tricky editing.

Next: trouble at the governmental level. A representation was made to the Ministry dealing with films, by an influential group, that *The Guide* glorified adultery, and hence was not fit to be presented as a film, since it might degrade Indian womanhood. The dancer in my story, to hear their arguments, has no justification for preferring Raju the Guide to her legally wedded husband. The Ministry summoned the movie principals to Delhi and asked them to explain how they proposed to meet the situation. They promised to revise the film script to the Ministry's satisfaction.

In my story the dancer's husband is a preoccupied archaeologist who has no time or inclination for marital life and is not interested in her artistic aspirations. Raju the Guide exploits the situation and weans her away from her husband. That is all there is to it—in my story. But now a justification had to be found for adultery.

So the archaeological husband was converted into a drunkard and womanizer who kicks out his wife when he discovers that another man has watched her dance in her room and has spoken encouragingly to her. I knew nothing about this drastic change of my characters until I saw the 'rushes' some months later. This was the point at which I lamented most over my naivete: the contract that I had signed in blind faith, in the intoxication of cheques bonhomie, and backslapping, empowered them to do whatever they pleased with my story, and I had no recourse.

Near the end of the project I made another discovery: the extent to which movie producers will go to publicize a film. The excessive affability to pressmen, the entertaining of V.I.P.s, the button-holding of ministers and officials in authority, the extravagant advertising campaigns, seem to me to drain off money, energy and ingenuity that might be reserved for the creation of an honest and sensible product.

On one occasion Lord Mountbatten was passing through India,and someone was seized with the sudden idea that he could help make a success of the picture. A banquet was held at Raj Bhavan in his honor, and the Governor of Bombay, Mrs. Vijayalaxmi Pandit, was kind enough to invite us to it. I was home in Mysore as Operation Mountbatten was launched, so telegrams and long-distance telephone calls poured in on me to urge me to come to Bombay at once. I flew in just in time to dress and reach Raj Bhavan. It was red-carpeted, crowded and gorgeous. When dinner was over, leaving the guests aside, our hostess managed to isolate his Lordship and the 'Guide'-makers on a side veranda of this noble building. His Lordship sat on a sofa surrounded by us; close to him sat Pearl Buck, who was one of the producers and who, by virtue of her seniority and standing, was to speak for us. As she opened the theme with a brief explanation of the epoch-making effort that was being made in India, in colour and wide-screen, with a hundred-percent-Indian cast, story and background, his Lordship displayed no special emotion. Then came the practical demand: in order that this grand, stupendous achievement might bear fruit, would Lord Mountbatten influence Queen Elizabeth to preside at the world premiere of the film in London in due course?

Lord Mountbatten responded promptly, "I don't think it is possible. Anyway what is the story?"

There was dead silence for a moment, as each looked at the other wondering who was to begin. I was fully aware that they ruled me out; they feared that I might take 80,000 words to narrate the story, as I had in the book. The obvious alternative was Pearl Buck, who was supposed to have written the screenplay.

Time was running out and his Lordship had others to talk to. Pearl Buck began.

"It is the story of a man called Raju. He was a tourist guide...."

"Where does it take place?"

I wanted to shout, "Malgudi, of course." But they were explaining, "We have taken the story through many interesting locations—Jaipur, Udaipur."

"Let me hear the story."

"Raju was a guide", began Pearl Buck again.

"In Jaipur?" asked his Lordship.

"Well, no. Anyway he did not remain a guide because when Rosie came..."

"Who is Rosie"

"A dancer...but she changed her name when she became a...a...dancer...."

"But the guide? What happened to him?"

"I am coming to it. Rosie's husband..."

"Rosie is the dancer?"

'Yes, of course...' Pearl Buck struggled on, but I was in no mood to extricate her.

Within several minutes Lord Mountbatten said, "Most interesting." His deep bass voice was a delight to the ear, but it also had a ring of finality and discouraged further talk. "Elizabeth's appointments are complicated these days. Anyway her private secretary Lord—must know more about it than I do. I am rather out of touch now. Anyway, perhaps I could ask Philip." He summoned an aide and said, "William, please remind me when we get to London...." Our Producers went home feeling that a definite step had been taken to establish the film in proper quarters. As for myself, I was not so sure.

Elaborate efforts were made to shoot the last scene of the story, in which the saint fasts on the dry river's edge, in hopes of bringing rain, and a huge crowd turns up to witness the spectacle. For this scene the director selected a site at a village called Okla, outside Delhi on the bank of the Jamuna river, which was dry and provided enormous stretches of sand. He had, of course, ruled out the spot we had visited near Mysore, explaining that two coconut trees were visible a mile away on the horizon and might spoil the appearance of unrelieved desert which he wanted. Thirty truckloads of property, carpenters, lumber, painters, artisans and art department personnel arrived at Okla to erect a two-dimensional temple beside a dry river, at a cost of 80,000 rupees. As the director kept demanding, "I must have 100,000 people for a helicopter shot", I thought of the cost: five rupees per head for extras, while both the festival crowd at Nanjangud and the little temple on the river would cost nothing.

The crowd had been mobilized, the sets readied and lights mounted, and all other preparations completed for shooting the scene next morning when, at midnight, news was brought to the chiefs relaxing at the Ashoka Hotel that the Jamuna was rising dangerously as a result of unexpected rains in Simla. All hands were mobilized and they rushed desperately to the location to save the equipment. Wading in knee-deep water, they salvaged a few things. But I believe the two-dimensional temple was carried off in the floods.

Like a colony of ants laboriously building up again, the carpenters and artisans rebuilt, this time at a place in Western India called Limdi, which was reputed to have an annual rainfall of a few droplets. Within one week the last scene was completed, the hero collapsing in harrowing fashion as a result of his penance. The director and technicians paid off the huge crowd and packed up their cameras and sound equipment, and were just leaving the scene when a storm broke—an unknown phenomenon in that part of the country—uprooting and tearing off everything that stood. Those who had lingered had to make their exit with dispatch.

This seemed to me an appropriate conclusion for my story, which, after all, was concerned with the subject of rain, and in which Nature, rather than film makers, acted in consonance with the subject. I remembered that years ago when I was in New York City on my way to sign the contract, before writing *The Guide*, a sudden downpour caught me on Madison Avenue and I entered the Viking Press offices dripping wet. I still treasure a letter from Keith Jennison, who was then my editor. "Somehow I will always, from now on", he wrote, "associate the rainiest days in New York with you. The afternoon we officially became your publishers was wet enough to have made me feel like a fish ever since."

Indira Gandhi

I NOTICED a brief entry in my diary dated, 10th March, 1984: "Promised P.M. a set of my books autographed, Heinemann Collected Edition." Mrs. Gandhi had remarked during our meeting that day, "People take away books from my library and never return them. I don't have any of your books now." I used to send her hardcover editions of my books for her library, which was stocked with a wide range of literature both in English and French. She was in the habit of reading far into the night, as I learnt, even when she carried files home.

Now to my profound regret, I realized that I had failed to keep my promise, not out of forgetfulness but through a habit of postponing things. I had hoped that I could take the books personally on my next visit. My next visit happened to be in May, but without the promised books in hand, and that turned out to be my last interview with Indira Gandhi.

Normally, once a quarter, some committee meeting or other would give me an excuse to visit Delhi. I can't really pretend that we achieved much at those meetings in Shastri Bhavan or any other Bhavan. We assembled around an oval table and carried on discussions, nibbling biscuits and sipping tea or (impossible) coffee, while also gently working our way through an agenda. At the end we dispersed amidst a general babble of How-Do-You-do, Must Get-Together-sometime, How-Long-in-Delhi, and so forth. Apart from the committee business, the trip itself had a value: I enjoyed the scene and air of Delhi, above all meeting people. Sometimes, during one of those visits, I could also call on Mrs. Gandhi. If my friend Sharada Prasad mentioned to her that I was in town, she would always find a little time for me even if only a half hour, at her office in the Parliament House or in the South Block. She suggested once, "Why don't you come home? You have not seen my grandchildren."

She was a dedicated grandparent, and anticipated with a

quiet joy rejoining the family at the end of the day. Once she remarked, "I don't really mind the long hours at the office but the worst of it is that some days the children are asleep when I go home." I met her in the March of this year at her residence, when she was about to leave for her office and she suggested that I go along with her. From the car she called Sanjay's child to come up for a ride with her, and explained, "I don't have enough time for this child. He has temperature. I don't know why." She kept feeling his brow all the time. In the brief journey between her residence and office, she somehow managed to keep up her conversation with me and also with the child, pointing to him the trees in bloom and birds along the way. After reaching the office she sent the child back home with many words of caution and also told him pointing to me, "You know this uncle writes very interesting stories."

She was generally calm, gentle, and cheerful, and never displayed any sign of strain or irritation. Only once did I notice that she was agitated and upset. Three or four years ago at about eight in the evening she noticed a long window in the drawing room open, which gave on the fateful lawn bordered with dark shrubs and a wicket-gate beyond. She almost shouted at an attendant, -"Who opened this window? Shut it immediately." She calmed down presently and remarked, "Sometimes they are very careless."

I really had no definite purpose in seeing her, I had no requests, or comments to offer, or political interests. We discussed mostly books and the environment, and problems of urban development. She admired Mysore for its natural charms, and was concerned how long the special quality of life and atmosphere there would last with the industrial developments around.

She was highly critical of the film version of my novel "The Guide" and never ceased to wonder why I had permitted all that distortion. She was critical of my version of the Ramayana too, "Your Ramayana is very readable, of course, but one misses in it details and the poetic grandeur of the epic."

Some years ago, during a visit to the South, she had gone to see the Kamakoti Acharya. Later, when I referred to her darshan, she explained, "Some of my friends in Madras persuaded me to call on the Swami. They took me somewhere and made me sit on a bench in a narrow passage, and wait for a

219

long time, with a well in front of me. It was uncomfortable, sitting on that bench. Eventually the Swami appeared on the other side of the well. We remained in silence looking at each other across the well. My friends whispered that I should seek his guidance for any problem I might have. I really had no questions but they pressed me. So I put to him a very long question in English. I spoke to him of the travails, sufferings, and hardship of our countrymen since the beginning of history, and asked why it was so and what would help. He listened attentively but gave no reply since he was under a vow of silence but I felt I had an answer. There were no words of course but it did not mean there was no communication."

Our first meeting was in 1961 when I was taken by my friend Natwar Singh to Teen Murti in order to call on Jawaharlal Nehru after I had received the Sahitya Academy Award on the previous evening. Nehru came downstairs and received the book I had for him, talked casually for a few minutes and left, saying, "I am sorry I have to go, but....," he hailed across the hall, "Indira, here is Narayan. Look after him. Give him coffee and breakfast and talk to him." She took charge of me, led me to a table and organized an exquisite breakfast of fruits and toast and porridge and above all very good coffee. She put me at my ease in a few minutes and soon we were discussing a wide range of subjects. She was gracious and informal, and continued to be so, unvaryingly, all through the years I have known her.

In the May of this year she gave me an appointment at her office, but the security proceedings seemed to be unusually elaborate. Finally, after a series of checks, I was taken to the waiting hall adjoining the P.M.'s room, which was crowded. I despaired how long I might have to wait to get my turn. But presently an officer came in looking for me and said, "Please follow me."

Indira Gandhi left her office table and moved to the sofas in a corner, and showed me a seat. "More comfortable here," she said. "Quite a crowd is waiting in the other room, some of them look like Ministers," I told her. "Actually, they may be Ministers," she said laughing, "and may be full of problems too. I have to give them a lot of time....sometimes all I can do is to give them a hearing....Anyway, let that not bother you, they will wait." She was more leisurely today than ever before and was lively in her talk.

I said, noting mentally how frail she was looking, "The Punjab situation must be a big strain." She remained in thought for a moment and said, "Yes, undoubtedly it is." And changing the subject asked, "Is any other novel of yours being made into a film?"

I mentioned "The Financial Expert" which was recently produced in Kannada. She said, "I want to see it, Doordarshan should be able to present it sub-titled. I hope it's better than "The Guide."

Apropos nothing she suddenly announced, "When I retire, I really do not know where I will live. I don't own a house anywhere..." When I took leave of her, she said with a laugh "Your brother is hard on some of us, you know!" referring to Laxman's political cartoons. "Oh, he is made that way, he could be equally hard on himself and on all of us too," was all I could say.

When India was a Colony

A sudden outbreak of Anglo-India has occurred in the cinema world, involving million-dollar budgets and movement of actors and equipment on a global scale—a minor, modern version of such historic globe-trotters as Hannibal, Alexander, Napoleon and heaven knows who else, who moved their hordes and elaborate engines of destruction across continents. Their Indian-oriented counterpart today carries an elaborate load of equipment of a different type—to set up his camp in a strange land, to create illusions of his own choice.

Sir Richard Attenborough's South Africa (of "Gandhi") was in Poona, David Lean's Chandrapore (of "A Passage to India," which has recently completed filming) was located in Bangalore, Ootacamund and in Kashmir. First "Gandhi," now "A Passage to India," and, in between, "The Far Pavilions," "Heat and Dust," "Kim" and whatnot. It's a trend and a phenomenon.

Anglo-India apparently has a market, while a purely Indian subject has none, perhaps too drab for a commercial film maker. India is interesting only in relation to the "Anglo" part of it, although that relevance lasted less than 200 years in the timeless history of India.

I suspect that a film maker values, rather childishly, the glamour of the feudal trappings of the British raj, with Indians in the background as liveried menials or for comic relief. In Attenborough's "Gandhi," Indians are usually shown in a mass, while the few Europeans—viceroys, governors and generals—are clear-cut individuals, in full regalia wherever it is warranted. Indian personalities, such as Prime Minister Nehru, the Congress Party leader Vallabhbhai Patel and Maulana Azad, the Moslem nationalist, lack substance; even Mohammad Ali Jinnah, the founder of Pakistan, is presented slightly, and not as a dynamic man. Other Indian leaders who were associates of Gandhi and who suffered and sacrificed along with him and were responsible for major decisions are left out.

This inadequacy must be a result of bewilderment, to put it mildly. The Indian character was puzzling and the Englishman suppressed his curiosity as bad manners. Incidentally, he was unlike the American who came later under different circumstances but chose to live like Indians, tasted Indian food, wore Indian dress and tried to understand everything about Indian life.

The Englishman preferred to leave the Indian alone, carrying his home on his back like a snail. He was content to isolate himself as, a ruler, keeper of law and order and collector of revenue, leaving Indians alone to their religion and ancient activities. He maintained his distance from the native all through. Indeed, the theme of E.M. Forster's "A Passage to India" was that an unbridgeable racial chasm existed between colonial India and imperial England.

I had a few occasions to meet Forster whenever I visited London. I enjoyed those visits to Cambridge. We would spend about an hour talking of books, Indian writing and Indian affairs in general. His interest in India was deep and abiding. My second novel, "The Bachelor of Arts," was launched some years before with his blessing, and owed its survival to his brief comment printed on the jacket. Since then, he had kept in touch with my writing. He would always ask: "What next?" Once, when I mentioned my next one, a book of mythology, "Gods, Demons and Others," he paused for a moment and genially asked, "Who is left out?"

Forster would offer me tea in his room and escort me halfway down to the station. When he visited London, he would send me a note and spend a little time with me before catching his train at King's Cross. When he inscribed a copy of "A Passage of India," he was apologetic that he could lay hand only on a paperback, at a second hand bookshop, and gave it with the remark, "You will find it amusing, but don't read too much into it..."

I had heard a rumour in New York that David Selznick or someone had offered $250,000 for a movie option on "A Passage to India," but that Forster had rejected it. When I asked him about it, he just said, "I am not interested." When I questioned him further, he said, rather petulantly, "No more of it. Let us talk of other things." He was, however, happy with the stage adaptation of his novel by Santha Rama Rau, who had worked in close consultation with him all through.

How did a little island so far away maintain its authority over another country many times its size? It used to be said by political orators of those days that the British Isles could be drowned out of sight if every Indian spat simultaneously in that direction. It was a David-Goliath ratio, and Britain maintained its authority for nearly two centuries. How was the feat achieved? Through a masterly organization, which utilized Indians themselves to run the bureaucratic and military machinery. Very much like the *Kheddah* operations in Mysore forests, where wild elephants are hemmed in and driven into stockades by trained ones, and then pushed and pummeled until they realize the advantages of remaining loyal and useful, in order to earn their ration of sugarcane and rice. Take this as a symbol of the British rule in India.

The Indian branch of the army was well trained and disciplined, and could be trusted to carry out imperial orders. So was the civil service. Instead of taking the trouble to understand India and deal directly with the public, Britain transmuted Indians themselves into Brown Sahibs. After a period of training at Oxford and Cambridge, first-class men were recruited for the Indian Civil Service. They turned out to be excellent administrators. They were also educated to carry about them an air of superiority at all times and were expected to keep other Indians at a distance.

I had a close relative in the I.C.S. who could not be seen or spoken to even by members of his family living under the same roof, except by appointment. He had organized his life in a perfect colonial pattern, with a turbaned butler knocking on his door with tea in the morning; black tie and dinner jacket while dining with other I.C.S. men, even if the table were laid in a desert; dropping of visiting cards in "Not at Home" boxes brought by servants when they formally called on each other. At home, when he joined the family gathering, he occupied a chair like a president, laughed and joked in a measured way; the utmost familiarity he could display was to correct other people's English pronunciation in an effort to promote Oxford style.

The I.C.S. manual was his Bible that warned him against being too familiar with anyone. He was advised how many mangoes he could accept out of a basket that a favour-seeker proffered; how far away he should hold himself when a garland was brought to be slipped over his neck. It was a matter of propriety for an average visitor to leave his vehicle at the gate and walk down the drive; only men of certain status could come in their cars and alight at the portico.

The I.C.S. was made up of well-paid men, above corruption, efficient and proud to maintain the traditions of the service, but it dehumanized the man, especially during the national struggle for independence. These men proved ruthless in dealing with agitators, and may well be said to have out-Heroded Herod. Under such circumstances, they were viewed as a monstrous creation of the British. An elder statesman once defined the I.C.S. as being neither Indian nor civil nor service. When Nehru became the Prime Minister, he weeded out many of them.

Nomination to high offices, conferment of the King's or Queen's birthday honours in which titles were announced from knighthood to rai sahib (the lowest in the list) that could be prefixed to names; such men also enjoyed privileges and precedence in the seating arrangements during public functions and official parties. This system brought into existence a large body of Indians who avidly pursued titles and exhibited loyalty to the Government, ever hoping to be promoted to the next grade in the coming year.

There were also instances of rejection of titles as a patrotic gesture. The Bengali poet Rabindranath Tagore returned the knighthood after the 1919 Jallianwalla Bagh massacre (General Dyer ordered troops to fire on a crowd of Indians assembled for a political meeting in a narrow, enclosed space, expertly presented in Attenborough's "Gandhi").

The British managed to create a solid core of Anglophiles who were so brainwashed that they would harangue and argue that India would be in chaos if the British left, and called Mahatma Gandhi a demagogue and mischief maker, and would congratulate Churchill on his calling Mahatma Gandhi "half-naked fakir" (although Gandhi himself commented, "I am glad my friend Churchill recognizes my nakedness, but I feel I am not naked enough").

The map of India was multicoloured; red patches for British India and the yellow ones were independent states under the rule of maharajahs and nawabs. At the head of a British province was a governor, a chosen man from Britain, one who was not expected to display any special brilliance, but possessed enough wit to keep his territory in peace, get on with the local population in general, report to the viceroy in Delhi and carry out his orders. He in turn took his orders from London. The secretary of state for India was at the apex, with the British Parliament at his back.

The governor of a province lived like a sultan with undreamt-of luxury. He was loaded with the trappings of authority and housed in a mansion set in a vast parkland. During summer, he moved with his entire retinue and the secretariat to a hill station and there lived in a style so well described by Kipling. His Excellency generally divided his time between horse racing and polo, golf and swimming. He presided over elegant public functions, such as flower shows and school-prize distribution.

The governor (and, of course, his family) lived a life of quiet splendour and came in contact with only the upper classes of society and never noticed poverty or squalor. His geographical outlook was limited to government-house vistas, parade routes, and whatever he could glimpse of the landscape from his saloon while travelling in a special train. Most of the governors were generally kept above want and were believed to be incorrupti-ble, although a couple of names were associated with dark tales of expecting, under the roses in a garland, gold sovereigns or currency notes; of engaging themselves in titillating encounters with society butterflies and so forth, all unverifiable, of course, but whispered about in the bazaar.

A province was divided into districts. At the head of a district was a collector (until the late 1930's, always a British I.C.S. man) and under him the Indian subcollector in the subdivisions, who would be responsible for the collection of revenue in the villages.

The native states, more that 500 in number, existed earlier as so many principalities ruled by hereditary princes, all indepen-dent of each other at one time. Through intricate historical processes, wars and mutual rivalries that offered ready opportu-nities for the British to intervene, they were brought, in course of time, under the sovereignty of Delhi, and had to pay subsidies. As long as the subsidy was regularly paid and subversive activities were suppressed, the ruler of a state was left alone to pursue his life of pleasure and court intrigue. In order to keep an eye on the maharajah, there was a resident representing the crown, living in the cantonment area (also known as civil lines, as in "A Passage to India").

Every capital had a cantonment, which was better town-planned and more comfortable that the downtown districts sprawling around the maharajah's palace. A cantonment had barracks with soldiers under a commandant to help the Government in any possible emergency. The resident was a puppeteer behind the throne. He and his European community formed a special class living in the cantonment and enjoying exclusive privileges. It would be the maharajah's duty to guarantee from time to time enough tigers and wildlife for his white masters when they desired to hunt. Especially when the viceroy visited the state, His Highness must make sure that the honoured guest could pose for photographs with at least one tiger stretched under his feet.

Before this point could be reached, preparations would be made weeks ahead—spotting the quarry, building platforms on trees for the huntsmen to remain in safety while aiming at the tiger, which would follow the scent of a bleating goat tethered near a waterhole. After a ride on an elephant through the jungle, His Excellency would sit up on a *machan* with his party, with their guns at the ready. It was a foregone conclusion that the viceroy could never miss. However, in the darkness one can never say whose shot kills. But the credit always goes to the honoured guest, although back at home he might not hurt a fly. It would be whispered sometimes that a captive tiger driven crazy by beaters' drums and torches, and famished, and half-dead, already might well have collapsed at the very sound of a rifle shot; thereupon news would be relayed that the V.I.P. had bagged one or more tigers that were terrorizing the countryside.

The banquet that concluded the visit of the viceroy lent a touch of comic opera—the solemnity, the stiff formality and the steel-frame gradation in the seating plan were inflexible. When pudding was to be served, the band in attendance should always strike up "Roast Beef of Old England."

I live in Mysore, once a native state, where the annual nine-day celebration called *Navaratri* was a season of festivity in the palace. At this time, the maharajah sat in the evenings on his ancient throne in the durbar hall. Invitees would sit cross-legged and barefoot in the gallery, go up one by one, bow to the maharajah on the throne and resume their seats. On a certain day, a European reception would be held, when the resident would arrive in state with several European guests. The timing of the resident's arrival was fixed with precision to a split second, so that he would enter the hall neither before nor after the maharajah, but at the same time with him, when the guns fired the salute.

On this occasion, the throne would quietly have been moved out of sight as it was too sacred and no one could go before it with shoes on. But Europeans could not be told to remove their shoes and so a silver chair would be substituted for the maharajah with a footstool, and a parallel silver chair provided at its side for the resident, also with footstool, whose imperial status would thus be preserved and protected. In that situation, when the European guests bowed before the maharajah, it was shared by the resident.

It was of the utmost importance to preserve British superiority under any circumstance. In the railways, they had reserved carriages for "Europeans Only," in which no Indian would dare to step. Certain shops in the cantonment catered exclusively to Europeans; memsahibs could buy groceries without feeling contaminated by the stares of Indians. Theatre entrances and seats were marked "Europeans Only." Exclusiveness was important and inevitable. One noticed it even in hospitals, where European wards and Indian wards were segregated.

In 1924, there was a public outcry against this system. A young student needed urgent medical help and would not be admitted to the General Hospital, Madras, because there was a vacancy only in the European ward and none in the Indian ward. The young man died. Following this, there was a furor in the Madras Legislative Assembly. Satyamurthy, one of the boldest among Indian patriots, whose forthright comments and questions confounded the British rulers and their Indian friends, said:

"Then, sir, the last sentence is: 'On the day in question, there were five vacant Indian beds and seven cases were admitted.' Now, we are all told that we ought not to be racial in this country: We ought to rise above racial prejudice and that we

228

ought to be cosmopolitan. I try my best to be like that, but my best at times fails when I am reminded that in my own country, in our own Indian hospitals maintained by the Indian taxpayer's money and run, above all, by an Indian minister, there should be beds which should be called 'non-Indian' beds. Why, in the name of common sense, why?

"Have you ever heard, Mr. President, of any country in the world except ours where beds are being maintained for patients on racial considerations? Do you find in England beds for Indians in those English hospitals specially maintained at the expense of the taxpayer? Do you know what it means, Mr. President? You may go in mortal illness to the General Hospital—I trust you will not—" laughter—"but if you had to go, although all the available European beds be vacant, you will not be taken in because you are an Indian, whereas a fifth-rate European without a name can be admitted and given a European bed because he has the European blood. Can flesh and blood stand this? Is it right?

"I should like to know from the honorable minister," continued Satyamurthy, "Why he maintains in this country at the expense of the taxpayer this racial distinction in hospitals? It seems to me that the time has arrived when we must speak up against this..."

There used to be heard a traditional rumour that in the days of the East India Company the thumbs of weavers of Dacca muslin (the finest fabric in the world) were cut off in order to prevent competition with textiles from Manchester and Lancashire. This may sound bizarre but the story has persisted for decades. The British were essentially merchants and India was primarily a market. The British temperament seemed to have been market-oriented—even in the 1930's and 1940's. An adviser and secretary to the maharajah whom I shall name Sir Charles Blimp (with apologies to the cartoonist David Low) promptly sabotaged a proposal for starting an automobile factory in Bangalore when land, machinery, capital and management were ready. He "strongly" advised the young maharajah not to approve the proposal and said, "Indians lack experience and cannot run an automobile factory successfully."

All the while, he looked benignly on the maharajah's monthly import of a new Daimler, Austin or Rolls Royce, with special fittings for his garage, which was already crowded with cars, like the showroom of an automobile dealer. This "adviser" to the young maharajah was a beefy, red-faced giant before whom any Indian looked puny and felt overwhelmed when he raised his arm as if to strike and issued commands. The man believed that that would be the only practical way to handle Indians. He drove his staff of "writers" (clerical staff) to slave for him round the clock, cooped them up in a shed under a hot tin roof at the farthest end of his spacious compound, summoned them through a buzzer every 10 minutes to the main building where he was settled under a fan with, perhaps, Lady Blimp "doing fruits." They never swerved even by a second from their ritual eating, while his clerks found it difficult to break off for lunch, as he would invariably growl, "Why are you fellows always hungry?" Poverty and want were normally unnoticed by this gentleman.

Poverty, however, was in the province of the missionary who lived among the lowliest and the lost. Although conversion was his main aim, he established hospitals and schools and in many ways raised the standard of living and outlook of the poorer classes. Before reaching that stage, the missionary went through much travail. He viewed Indians as heathens to be saved by loud preaching.

The street-corner assembly was a routine entertainment for us in our boyhood at Madras. A preacher would arrive with harmonium and drum and, facing heavy odds and violent opposition, begin a tirade against Indian gods. A crowd would gather around and gradually music and speech would be drowned in catcalls, howls and yelling, and the audience would not rest till the preacher was chased off. It was a sort of martyrdom and he could have saved his skin and got a hearing but for a naive notion that he should denigrate our gods as a preparation for proposing the glory of Jesus.

Even in the classroom, this was a routine procedure. I studied in a mission school and the daily Scripture class proved a torment. Our Scripture master, though a native, was so devout a convert that he would spend the first 10 minutes calling Krishna a lecher and thief full of devilry. How could one ever pray to him while Jesus was waiting there to save us? His voice quavered at the thought of his God. Once, incensed by his remarks, I put the question, "If Jesus were a real God, why did he not kill the bad men?" which made the teacher so angry that he screamed, "Stand up on the bench, you idiot."

The school textbooks were all British manufactured at one time, compiled by Englishmen, published by British firms and shipped to India on P. and O. steamers. From a child's primer with "A was an apple" or "Baa, Baa, Black Sheep" to college physics by Dexter and Garlick, algebra by Ross and logarithm tables compiled by Clark, not a single Indian name was on any book either as author or publisher. Indian history was written by British historians—extremely well documented and researched, but not always impartial. History had to serve its purpose: Everything was made subservient to the glory of the Union Jack. Latter-day Indian scholars presented a contrary picture. The Black Hole of Calcutta never existed. Various Moslem rulers who invaded and proselytized with fire and sword were proved to have protected and endowed Hindu temples. When I mentioned this aspect to a distinguished British historian some years ago in London, he brushed aside my observation with: "I'm sorry, Indians are without a sense of history. Indians are temperamentally nonhistorical."

We had professors from English universities to teach literature, which I always feel was a blessing. But the professor's contact was strictly limited to the classroom. When he left the class, he rushed back to his citadel of professors' quarters and the English club where no Indian was admitted except a bearer to serve drinks. Our British principal never encouraged political activities or strikes, which were a regular feature in our days, whenever Gandhi or Nehru gave the call or were arrested.

The hardiest among the British settlers was the planter who, born and bred in his little village in England, was somehow attracted to India, not to a city and its comforts but to a deserted virgin soil on a remote mountain tract where he struggled and built up, little by little, a plantation and raised coffee, tea and cardamom, which remain our national assets even today. He was firmly settled on his land, loved his work, now and then visiting a neighbour 50 miles away or a country club 100 miles off. He loved his isolation, he loved the hill folk working on his plantation, learned their language and their habits and became a native in all but name.

He sailed home once in two years, but always chose to come back, and ultimately planned to die in India. There were hundreds like him scattered all over India wherever there was an elevation and the possibility of cultivation. Some of them left their fortunes to Indian beneficiaries, institutionally or individually. One might hope that when the glamour of the royal trappings of the British raj is past, some film maker will see the value of the subject of an early British planter who alone could be called a pioneer and a true colonial hero.

India and America

The silent movies of the Twenties were the main source of our knowledge of America when I was growing up in Madras. We had a theatre called the Roxy in our neighbourhood. For an outlay of two annas (about two cents) one could sit on a long teakwood bench, with a lot of others, facing the screen. When the hall darkened, there came before us our idols and heroes—hard-hitting valorous men such as Eddie Polo and Elmo Lincoln, whose arms whirled around and smashed up the evil-minded gang, no matter how many came on at a time, retrieved the treasure plan and saved the heroine while on the verge of losing her life or chastity. The entire saga as a serial would be covered in twenty-four instalments at a rate of six a week, with new episodes presented every Saturday. When Eddie Polo went out of vogue, we were shown wild men of the Wild West, cowboys in broad-brimmed hats and cartridge-studded belts, walking arsenals who lived on horseback forever chasing, lassoing and shooting. We watched this daredevilry enthralled, but now and then questioned, when and where do Americans sit down to eat or sleep? Do they never have walls and doors and roofs under which to live? In essence the question amounted to, "After Columbus, what?"

In the Thirties, as Hollywood progressed, we were presented with more plausible types on the screen. Greta Garbo and Bette Davis and who else? Ramon Novarro, John Gilbert and other pensive, poignant or turbulent romantics acting against the more versatile backdrops of Arabian deserts, European mansions and glamorous drawing rooms.

Our knowledge of America was still undergoing an evolutionary process. It took time, but ultimately one was bound to hear of Lincoln, Emerson, Mark Twain and Thoreau. The British connection had been firmly established. The British way of life and culture were the only other ones we Indians knew. All books, periodicals and educational material were British. These said very little about America, except for Dickens or Chesterton, who had travelled and lectured in America and had written humorously of American scenes and character—after accepting a great deal of hospitality, and dollars of course. This seemed to us a peculiar trait of Americans—why should they invest so heavily in foreign authors only to be presented as oddities at the end?

After World War II, the Indian media focused attention on American affairs and personalities and we became familiar with such esoteric terms as the Point-Four Plan, Public Law 480, and grants and fellowships, which in practical terms meant technical training and cultural exchanges. In the postwar period, more and more Americans were to be seen in India while more and more Indians went to America. Americans came to India as consultants, technicians and engineers and to participate in the vast projects of our Five Year Plan. We noticed that Coca-Cola and Virginia tobacco and chewing gum were soon making their appearance in shop windows, and American bestsellers in the bookstores. For their part, Americans displayed on their mantelpieces Indian bric-a-brac of ivory, sandalwood and bronze. Academicians from America came to India to study its culture and social organizations, as did political scientists (unsuspected of having CIA connections), and returned home to establish departments of South Asian studies in such universities as Chicago, Pennsylvania, Columbia and the University of California at Berkeley. Some American scholars of Sanskrit, Hindi or Tamil are unquestioned authorities, and a match for the orthodox pundits in India.

Americans working in India adapted themselves to Indian style with ease—visited Indian homes, sat down to eat with their fingers, savoured Indian curry, wore *kurta* and *pajamas*, enjoyed Indian music. Some even mastered Indian music well enough to be able to give public concerts at a professional level before Indian audiences. Such colleges as Wesleyan and Colgate started regular departments of Indian music. Young Indians began applying for admission to American institutions for higher studies or training.

My first chance to visit America came when I was offered a Rockefeller grant, which enabled me to see a great deal of the country—perhaps more than any American could. By train from New York to the Midwest and the West Coast, down

234

south to Santa Fe, then through Texas to Nashville and Washington and back to New York, where I spent a couple of months. The more cities I saw, the more I was convinced that all America was contained in New York. For more than two decades I have been visiting New York off and on and never tire of it. I could not send down roots anywhere in America outside of New York. An exception was Berkeley, where I stayed, in a hotel room, long enough to write a novel. From my window I could watch young men and women hurrying along to their classes or hanging around the cafe or bookstore across the street. I divided my time between writing and window shopping along Telegraph Avenue or strolling along the mountain paths.

When the time came for me to leave Berkeley, I felt depressed. I could not imagine how I was to survive without all those echantments I had got used to. The day's routine in my hotel on the fringe of the campus, the familiar shops, the Campanile, which I could see from my hotel window if the Bay smog was not too dense and by whose chime I regulated my daily activities (I had sworn to live through the American trip without a watch), and the walk along picturesque highways and byways with such sonorous names as Sonoma, Pomona and Venice. Even the voice of the ice cream vendor who parked his cart at Sather Gate and sounded a bell crying, "Crunchymunchies, them's good for you," was part of the charm.

On the whole my memories of America are happy ones. I enjoy them in retrospect. If I were to maintain a single outstanding experience, it would be my visit to the Grand Canyon. To call it a visit is not right; a better word is "*pilgrimage*"—I understood why certain areas of the canyon's outcrops have been named after the temples of Brahma, Shiva and Zoroaster. I spent a day at the canyon. At dawn or a little before, I left my room at El Tovaro before other guests woke up, then took myself to a seat on the brink of the canyon. It was still dark under a starry sky. At that hour the whole scene acquired a different dimension and a strange, indescribable quality. Far down below, the Colorado River wound its course, muffled and softened. The wind roared in the valley; as the stars gradually vanished a faint light appeared on the horizon. At first there was absolute, enveloping darkness. But If you kept looking on, contours gently emerged, little by little, as if at the beginning of creation itself. The Grand Canyon seemed to

235

me not a geological object, but some cosmic creature spanning the horizons. I felt a thrill more mystic than physical, and that sensation has unfadingly remained with me all through the years. At any moment I can relive that ecstasy. For me the word "immortal" has a meaning now.

The variety of college campuses is an impressive feature of American life. One can lead a life of complete satisfaction at any campus, whether Berkeley or Michigan State or tiny Sewanee in Nashville. Any university campus is a self-contained world, with its avenues and lawns, libraries, student union, tuck-shops, campus stores and restaurants. I spent a term or two as lecturer or Distinguished Visiting Professor or Very Distinguished Visiting Professor in various universities. Whatever my designation, it seemed more an opportunity to enjoy the facilities of a campus in comfortable surroundings, among agreeable and intelligent people. The duties I was expected to perfom were light–give a couple of lectures and be accessible to students or faculty members when they desired to meet me. I have found campus life enjoyable in all seasons—when the lakes froze in Wisconsin or the snows piled up ten feet high in Michigan; during the ever-moderate climate of Berkeley or springtime at Columbia.

If I were asked where I would rather not live, I would say, "No American suburban life for me, please." It is boring. The sameness of houses, gardens, lawns and dogs and two automobiles parked at every door, with not a soul in sight nor a shop except in a one-block stretch containing a post office, firehouse and bank, similar to a hundred other places in the country. Interesting at first, but monotonous in the long run. I have lived for weeks at a stretch in Briarcliff Manor, an hour's run from Grand Central Station. I could survive it because of the lovely home of my hosts and their family, but outside their home the only relief was when I could escape to Manhattan. The surroundings of Briarcliff were perfect and charming, but life there was like existing amidst painted cardboard scenes. I never felt this kind of desolation in New York at any time, although I have stayed there for months at a time, usually at the Hotel Chelsea.

New York takes you out of yourself. A walk along Fifth Avenue or Madison or even 14th Street, with its dazzling variety of merchandise displayed on the pavement, can be a completely satisfying experience. You can visit a new ethnic quarter every day—German, Italian, Spanish, even Arab and Chinese; or choose an entertainment or concert or show from the newspaper, from page after page of listings. If you prefer to stay awake all night and jostle with a crowd, you can always go to Washington Square or Times Square, especially on a weekend.

At the American consulate the visa section is kept busy nowadays as more and more young men from India seek the green card or profess to enter on a limited visa, then try to extend their stay once they get in. The official has a difficult task filtering out the "permanent", letting in only the "transients". The average American is liberal-minded and isn't bothered that more and more Indian engineers and doctors are snapping up the opportunities available in the U.S., possibly to the disadvantage of an American. I discussed the subject with Professor Ainslie T. Embree, chairman of Columbia University's history department, who has had a long association with Indian affairs and culture. His reply was noteworthy. "Why not Indians as well? In the course of time they will be Americans. The American citizen of today was once an expatriate, a foreigner who had come out of a European or African country. Why not Indians too? We certainly love to have Indians in the country."

The young man who goes to the States for higher training or studies declares when leaving home, "I will come back as soon as I complete my course, maybe two years or more, but I'll surely come and work for our country—of course, also to help the family." Excellent intentions, but it will not work out that way. Later, when he returns home full of dreams, plans and projects, he finds only hurdles wherever he tries to get a job or to start an enterprise of his own. Form-filling, bureaucracy, caste and other restrictions, and a generally feudal style of functioning waste a lot of time for the young aspirant. He frets and fumes as he spends his days running about presenting or collecting papers at various places, achieving nothing. He is not used to this sort of treatment in America, where, he claims, he can walk into the office of the top man anywhere, address him by his first name and explain his purpose. When he attempts to visit a man of similar rank in India to discuss his plans, he finds he has no access to him, but is forced to meet only subordinates in a hierarchical system. Some years ago a biochemist returning from America with a lot of experience and bursting with proposals was curtly told off when he pushed open the door of a big executive, and stepped in innocently. "You should not come to me directly. Send your papers through proper channels." Thereafter the young Indian biochemist left India once and for all, having kept his retreat open with the help of a sympathetic professor at the American end.

In this respect American democratic habits have rather spoiled our young men. They have no patience with our Indian tempo, whereas the non-Americanized Indian accepts the hurdles as inevitable karma. An Indian who returns from America expects special treatment, forgetting the fact that the chancellors of Indian universities will see only other chancellors, and top executives will see only other top executives, and no one of lesser position under any circumstances. Our administrative machinery is slow, tedious and feudal in its operation.

Another reason for a young man's final retreat from India could be a lack of jobs for one with his particular training and qualifications. A young engineer qualified in robotics spent hours explaining the value of his speciality to prospective sponsors, until eventually he realized that there could be no place for robots in an overcrowded country.

The Indian in America is a rather lonely being, having lost his roots in one place and not grown them in the other. Few Indians in America make any attempt to integrate into American culture or social life. Few visit a American home or a theatre or an opera, or try to understand the American psyche. An Indian's contact with Americans is confined to working with his colleagues and to official luncheons. He may mutter a "Hi" across the hedge to an American neighbour while mowing the lawn.

After he has equipped his new home with the latest dishwasher and video and his garage with two cars, once he has acquired all that the others have, he sits back with his family and counts his blessings. Outwardly happy, he is secretly gnawed at by some vague discontent and aware of some inner turbulence or vacuum he cannot define. All the comfort is physically satisfying, he has immense "job satisfaction" and that is about all. On weekends he drives his family fifty miles or more to visit another Indian family to eat an Indian dinner, discuss Indian politics or tax problems (for doctors, who are in the highest income bracket, this is a constant topic of conversation).

There is monotony in this pattern of life, so mechanical and standardized. India may have lost an intellectual or an expert, but it must not be forgotton that he has lost India too—and that is a more serious loss in the final reckoning. The quality of life in India is different. Despite all the deficiencies, irritations, lack of material comforts and amenities, and general confusions, Indian life builds inner strength. It is through subtle, inexplicable influences, through religion, family ties and human relationships in general—let us call them psychological "inputs", to use a modern term—which cumulatively sustain and lend variety and richness to existence. Building imposing Indian temples in America, installing our gods therein and importing Indian priests to perform the *pooja* ritual and preside at festivals are only imitating Indian existence and could have only a limited value. Social and religious assemblies at the temples in America might mitigate boredom, but only temporarily. I have lived as a guest in many Indian homes in America for extended periods, and have noticed the ennui that descends on a family when they are stuck at home.

Indian children growing up in America present a special problem. Without the gentleness and courtesy and respect for parents that—unlike the American upbringing, whereby a child is left alone to discover for himself the right code of conduct—is the basic training for a child in India, Indian children have to develop themselves on a shallow foundation without a cultural basis either Indian or American. They are ignorant of Indian life; aware of this, the Indian parent tries to cram into his children's little heads every possible bit of cultural information during a rushed trip to the mother country.

Ultimately, America and India are profoundly different in attitude and philosophy, though it would be wonderful if they could complement each other's values. Indian philosophy stresses austerity and unencumbered, uncomplicated day-to-day living. America's emphasis, on the other hand, is on material acquisition and the limitless pursuit of prosperity. From childhood an Indian is brought up on the notion that austerity and a contented life are good; a certain otherworldliness is inculcated through a grandmother's tales, the discourses at the temple hall, and moral books. The American temperament, on the contrary, is pragmatic. The American has a robust indifference to eternity. "Attend church on Sunday and listen to the sermon, but don't bother about the future," he seems to say. Also, he seems to echo Omar Khayyam's philosophy: "Dead yesterday and unborn tomorrow, why fret about them if today be sweet?" He works hard and earnestly, acquires wealth and enjoys life. He has no time to worry about the afterlife, only taking care to draw up a proper will and trusting the funeral home to take care of the rest. The Indian in America who is not able to live wholeheartedly on this basis finds himself in a halfway house; he is unable to overcome his conflicts while physically flourishing on American soil. One may hope that the next generation of Indians (American-grown) will do better by accepting the American climate spontaneously; or, alternatively, return to India to live a different life.